Embrace

Cherie Colyer

OMNIFIC PUBLISHING

DALLAS

Omnific Publishing
10000 North Central Expressway, Dallas, TX 75231
www.omnificpublishing.com

First Omnific eBook edition, December 2011
First Omnific trade paperback edition, December 2011
Revised Cover, June 2013

The characters and events in this book are fictitious.
Any similarity to real persons, living or dead,
is coincidental and not intended by the author.

Library of Congress Cataloguing-in-Publication Data

Colyer, Cherie.
    Embrace / Cherie Colyer – 1st ed.
    ISBN: 978-1-623420-96-4
    1. Witchcraft — Fiction. 2. Paranormal — Fiction.
    3. Romance — Fiction. 4. Magic — Fiction. I. Title

10 9 8 7 6 5 4 3 2 1

Cover Design by Micha Stone and Amy Brokaw
Interior Book Design by Coreen Montagna

Printed in the United States of America

*To Dad and Mom -
Thanks for encouraging me to dream.*

Chapter 1

The Party

I should have cared what I wore, but I couldn't quite get there. I didn't see any point in dressing up just to get knocked down. Now, if my best friend had said, *Epic party and we're going,* I would have rushed upstairs and changed out of the cream tank top I'd rescued from the hamper that morning, and I would have put on my new jeans, the ones with the rhinestones on the pockets. But that's not what Kaylee said.

"Your life's about to change, and there's nothing you can do about it."

That's what she'd blurted into the phone just after she had told me she'd be by in fifteen minutes to pick me up for the party at Wingaersheek Beach. She hadn't said, *I have a great surprise for you,* or, *You'll never believe how happy you're going to be.* She hadn't said anything to hint this change was good, and that bothered me.

For me, change meant major adjustments in my life. It meant learning to live without people I loved. Taking on responsibilities I wasn't ready for. It meant even a tub of chocolate and peanut butter ice cream and all the lattes in the world wouldn't make things better.

I called her back several times. She wasn't answering. Whatever she had to tell me, it had to be bad or she would have told me over the phone.

Several years ago, just after my tenth birthday, my mom had said, "Our lives are going to change." And then the bell on the toaster had rung and two pieces of toast popped up as if excited to hear the news.

I remember every detail about that conversation. Mom had been at the stove, scrambling eggs, ham, and cheddar cheese together to make my favorite breakfast. Her hazel eyes had this happy twinkle to them, and her cheeks almost glowed. I'd been wearing my birthday gift — Ugg boots I had begged and begged for — with my pastel blue pajamas. Her excitement had been contagious. It had made me giddy.

"I'm pregnant," she'd gushed. "You're going to be a big sister!"

Don't get me wrong, my little brother is great — a pain in the butt, but a pretty cool kid nonetheless. Yet his birth had marked the first time I had to learn the meaning of change.

The clock on my nightstand announced twelve minutes had passed since Kaylee had called. With cell phone in hand, I hurried downstairs, stuffed my feet into my pink plaid canvas sneakers, and raced out the front door. A cool breeze circled past, reminding me that it would be even colder near the water. I reached inside the door and grabbed my white hoodie from the banister.

Outside, there was no sign of Kaylee.

"Argh," I grunted. The sound of dishes being loaded in the dishwasher drifted out of the open windows, making me feel a little guilty that I wasn't helping my dad clean up dinner.

I flipped my cell phone open. Fifteen minutes and still no Kaylee. I took a seat on the stoop, with elbows on my knees and chin cradled in my hands, and blew out a breath that sent my bangs flying upward.

Finally, Kaylee's faded green MINI Cooper rounded the corner at the end of the block. I jogged down the walk and had the car door open before she came to a full stop. My nerves untangled themselves when I saw she hadn't picked up lattes and didn't have a half-gallon of ice cream waiting for me.

"You're late." I slid into the passenger seat.

"Two minutes." She wore a white top, jeans, and sneakers. Her bangs had grown out to her chin and curved perfectly to frame her heart-shaped face. I couldn't have managed that with an entire bottle of hair spray and a flat iron.

"So, what's going to change my life?" I asked as soon as I was buckled in.

She looked me right in the eyes. "You'll see."

Then she drove off as if she didn't know the anticipation was killing me.

"Oh come on! You have to tell me," I begged.

"I signed us up for the Harvest Committee at school," she said. She took a right at the end of the block.

"That's not what you called about. Please tell me it's not."

It didn't surprise me that Kaylee volunteered to help with the festival. She loves fall and everything that comes with it, but being part of a committee doesn't exactly change your life, and she knows that.

Kaylee giggled. "Of course not. And I'm not going to tell you, so stop asking."

I crossed my arms over my chest and gave her a sidelong look, hoping if I pouted she'd break and spill the news.

She shook her head and said with a smile, "Still not saying."

I dropped my head back against the headrest in frustration. "You can be completely impossible when you want to be. You know that?"

She burst into laughter. "Trust me, will you?"

"Fine." It wasn't like I had much choice. "But this change better be good."

We drove with the windows down, letting the wind comb through our hair. The smell of burning wood from fire pits filled the crisp fall air. Cornstalks and pumpkins decorated porches, and the sound of children's squeals echoed up and down the street.

"I haven't heard from Kevin this month. I was going to give him a call over the weekend," I said.

Kaylee glanced at me, her expression serious. "Madison, I think it's great that you and Kevin are keeping in touch, I really do, but don't you think it's about time you moved on? I mean, he did break up with you."

"Because he moved to Minnesota."

"Exactly. What's it been? Four, five months now?"

Kevin and I had dated close to two years, ever since the beginning of our freshman year. We could finish each other's sentences and always knew what the other was feeling without having to say a word. We fit together like two pieces of a puzzle. He was familiar, and our relationship had been comfortable. It was hard to just forget about him. "What's wrong with us keeping in touch?"

"Nothing." Kaylee sighed. She stopped at a red light and looked at me. "Just promise me if you meet someone else, you'll give that person a chance."

"Whatever." It wasn't like I was avoiding other guys. Much.

Ten minutes later, we reached the trees near the shore. Kaylee pulled in and parked between two SUVs.

"It's been too long since we've been to a party," Kaylee said as she dropped her keys into her purse and grabbed her cell phone.

We walked toward the beach. I could see out of the corner of my eye Kaylee's fingers flying over the small keypad on her phone. The chime signaling she'd received a text played a few seconds later.

"Josh's waiting for us near the water." She dropped her phone back into her bag.

I nodded my reply.

There must have been forty or fifty people at the party. Ben Taylor had pulled his pickup truck close to the water and was blasting music from two large speakers in the bed. We weaved our way past the various groups of people dancing and talking.

"The committee meets next Wednesday to discuss what we want to have at the festival this year."

"Can't wait," I replied with as much enthusiasm as I could muster. The festival wasn't what I couldn't stop thinking about. I stepped in front of her. "I can't take it any longer. What's going to change my life?"

"I thought you were going to trust me?" She started walking again.

"I do," I moaned, following her. "But I really, really want to know. What if I guess? Is something going to happen at school?"

"Nothing you don't already know about."

"Will it affect my wardrobe?"

"Nope, but there is a sale going on at that little shop you love."

We passed a group of girls who were tossing logs onto one of the two bonfires.

I glanced toward the ocean, looking for Josh. The last of the evening light spilled over the water, making it look like a sea of lava. "Your dad upped your allowance and lattes are on you for the rest of the year? Oh! You're getting a new car and you're going to give me the MINI!"

"Ah, no and no."

I pursed my lips as I thought. "You're not an alien or anything like that."

"Totally. Just don't tell Josh. He's not into the whole interspecies scene." Kaylee shook her head as she nudged me with her shoulder. "You still love me, right?"

"Definitely."

"There they are." She grabbed my wrist and steered me to the right.

"They?"

Josh was talking to someone I'd never seen before. This new guy was almost as tall as Josh (which was saying a lot since Josh was six-foot-two), only he had broader shoulders and wore his brown hair spiked, as opposed to Josh, who was lanky and had black hair that fell in masses around his face.

"Who's that with Josh?" I asked as we walked closer to them.

"New neighbor, I think," she said, but her smirk told me she knew for sure.

As if he had heard us, the new guy glanced around, his gaze stopping on me. We were still too far to see the color of his eyes, but they were dark, and his skin had a hint of a tan that had faded with the warm weather. I couldn't look away from him. I don't know exactly how to explain what I felt, but it was almost as if he was the sweet nectar of a honeysuckle and I was the bee.

A smile stretched across Josh's face when he saw Kaylee. "There's my girl."

Kaylee stood on her tiptoes as she wrapped her arms around his neck and gave him a quick kiss hello. Josh's friend glanced away from them, first looking at the rocks and shells that littered the long stretch of beach, then back up at me.

Josh draped an arm over Kaylee's shoulders and said hello to me.

"Is this new?" Kaylee touched the dark metal cross around Josh's neck.

I stopped listening to them and instead turned my attention to Josh's friend. I brushed my dark brown bangs away from my eyes and said, "Hi, I'm Madison."

He smiled. "Isaac."

"Sorry," Josh said, as if just realizing we didn't know his friend. "Isaac's parents bought the house across the street from me. Isaac, this is Kaylee and Madison."

Isaac said hello to both of us, but his eyes locked on mine. I returned his smile with a shy one of my own.

"Where did you move from?" I asked.

"Amesbury, about forty miles north of here."

Josh picked Kaylee up, tossing her over his shoulder like a sack of potatoes. "Come on. Let's move our party down the beach."

Kaylee giggled and then screamed as Josh jogged toward one of the bonfires.

"Shall we?" Isaac held his hand in front of him, indicating the direction Josh and Kaylee had gone.

We followed Kaylee's laughter. A hundred butterflies fluttered around inside my stomach, making me all too aware of Isaac's eyes on me. When I glanced up at him, I was met with a smile.

"Have you started school yet?" I was pretty sure news of a hot new guy would have been the talk of the lunchroom.

He shook his head. "I start Monday."

"Are you nervous? I mean, I know I'd be, if I had to switch schools mid-semester."

"Not too much." He picked up a piece of driftwood. "I'll know Josh and you and Kaylee. It won't be too bad."

"Are you a junior?" We might have had a couple of classes together if he was.

"Senior."

"That sucks." As soon as the words were out of my mouth, I wanted to shove them back in. "Not that you're a senior. That you had to move with only — " I quickly did the math in my head " — seven months left of high school."

"It's okay." He passed the piece of driftwood from one hand to the other and back again. "The move puts my dad closer to work."

I nodded. "Where's he work?"

"Rowley."

I bit down on my lips to keep from pointing out that Rowley was smack dab in the middle of Gloucester and Amesbury.

Josh and Kaylee were already sitting down when we reached the bonfire. I stepped over a long log and took a seat next to Kaylee. Isaac sat on my other side. The salt from the sea had turned several of the flames blue and violet. Kaylee and Josh were having an argument with someone near them about the effects of the moon on the tide.

"Are you all moved in?" I asked Isaac.

"For the most part." Isaac spun the driftwood in his hand, end over end. "We still have a few things at our old place."

"Are you in the mocha house directly across from Josh or the white one a few doors down?"

"The mocha one." He tossed the driftwood into the fire, causing a spray of sparks to shoot upward into the air. "We almost didn't get it, though."

"Were your parents bidding against someone else?"

"No. My mom found out the previous owner was, well…" He paused as if searching for the right word. "Eccentric."

I knew he meant crazy. People liked to joke that Mrs. Lawson was a few brain cells short of sane, but in reality she was a nice old lady who grew her own herbs and made her own soap.

"She's sweet," I said, thinking about all the times I'd seen her outside tending to her flower gardens. "Why'd your parents care?"

"It was more my mom." Isaac leaned toward me as if he was about to tell me a family secret. "She believes that every house takes on the personality of its owner. When Mom found out the previous owner was…different, she had my dad find out everything he could about the place before she'd agree to move there."

"And?" I inched closer to him, suddenly curious about the history of that house.

Isaac looked to his left then his right before he whispered, "About thirty years ago, an entire family was murdered there: the dad, the mom, two kids, even Spot the dog."

I gasped. Before I could say something stupid, he nudged my shoulder with his.

"I'm only kidding about the murders. He did find out that the house was built in the late 1800s. It's been passed down from one generation to the next. There has been a Lawson living there for over a hundred years. Mrs. Lawson was the last in her family, though. She didn't have anyone to leave it to, and she needed the money for her new place. She had to sell."

"Our house is pretty old too." Although, I didn't know when it was built or how many families had lived there before my parents had bought it. I doubted they knew, and if the house did have a personality, I didn't know if it would be a mix of all the families that had lived there or just my family's.

"Have you always lived in Gloucester?" Isaac asked.

"Yeah." I played with my leather bracelets as I talked. "My parents moved here when Mom was pregnant with me. How about you? How many places have you lived?"

"Three, but the first two were within a few miles of each other." Isaac went on to talk about the last house he'd lived in. I nodded and added a few comments, but mostly I listened. It gave me time to memorize the curve of his jaw and the shape of his nose. His voice had a silken undertone, and his words, which seemed to be chosen carefully, flowed from his lips to my ears like a band's music to its dancers, captivating me.

After a while, Josh and Kaylee joined Isaac's and my conversation. It was just before eleven when the breeze picked up. It cut across the water, carrying the spray to us like unmerciful shards of glass. I turned slightly so the mist wouldn't hit my face and wrapped my arms around myself trying to keep warm. Isaac took off his jacket and draped it over my shoulders, touching my neck in the process and sending a jolt — like static electricity — through me.

I winced from the unexpected shock of it. "Did you feel that?"

"Yeah." The word dragged on. He stared at me with wide eyes, probably thinking that getting shocked on the beach was just as weird as I thought it was. "Are you—"

"Fine." I said, interrupting him. "I'm fine. It just surprised me, that's all." I slipped my arms though the sleeves of his jacket. "Thanks."

Kaylee checked her cell phone. "We better go before my dad sends out a search party."

Josh and Isaac stood when we did. Josh said, "We'll walk you to your car."

Isaac left a couple of feet between us as we walked toward the trees. I wanted to close the gap to test how he'd react. I moved closer to him as I stepped around a natural pothole, and like we were two negative magnets forced in opposite directions, he swayed away from me, giving me the impression that I liked him more than he liked me.

Before I could register the disappointment of that, Kaylee's shriek stopped me in my tracks. I turned to look at her. She buried her face in Josh's chest. He had an arm around her back as he used the toe of his gym shoe to nudge a large brown lump on the ground in front of them.

"What is it?" Curiosity got the better of me. I stepped closer, and immediately regretted that I had. I could see red glistening off brown fur and what looked like intestines pooling in a puddle of blood. I covered my mouth with my hand as my dinner threatened to come back up.

Isaac crouched down for a closer look. "It was a rabbit. Hind feet are missing."

"Seriously?" Josh craned his neck, trying to get a better view without letting go of Kaylee.

I wished we'd start walking already.

"What's so interesting?" Paige Osborne pushed by me and looked over Isaac's shoulder. Her recently dyed dark red hair brushed the side of his face. "Oh! That's—" she tilted her head to the side "—beyond disgusting."

Her friend Emma stopped next to me, arms folded over her chest. "Paige, come on. I want to find Mark before he leaves."

Paige and Isaac stood. Their arms touched for a brief moment before they took a step away from each other.

"Can we go?" Emma asked impatiently. She had this whole chic-in-jeans-and-a-T-shirt thing going on that sort of fit her blond and black pixie haircut. Not that I would have told her that. Emma and Paige barely acknowledged Kaylee's or my existence those days.

Paige ignored Emma. She looked at Isaac as if she were a hawk ready to pounce on a mouse. "You're new here, aren't you?"

"Yeah." Isaac shoved his hands into the front pockets of his jeans.

Paige dug around in her purse. A moment later, she pulled out a black eyeliner pencil. She grabbed Isaac's arm, turning his palm upward. "Call me if you want to hang out."

I couldn't believe she was giving Isaac her phone number. I mean, I knew I'd just met him, but she had no way of knowing that. As far as she was concerned, we were on a double date with Josh and Kaylee.

Paige bounced past me before I could say anything. Emma followed her. I watched them get swallowed by the darkness.

"Jealousy doesn't suit you," Isaac whispered into my ear.

He was right behind me. His breath moved a few strands of my hair and tickled my neck.

"I'm not jealous." The words came out with a sharp bite I hadn't intended to use, and I was sure I hadn't fooled him. I wanted to spit in his hand and smear Paige's number so that he couldn't read it.

Isaac smirked. He rested a hand on the small of my back. "Let's get out of here."

Josh and Kaylee were a few steps ahead of us. We walked in silence until we could see Kaylee's car.

Kaylee was the first to say something. "Josh and I are going to the movies tomorrow. You guys want to come?"

"Sure," I said at the same time Isaac said, "I can't."

I bit down on my bottom lip as my heart came to a sudden stop. He didn't like me. He was going to call Paige. My eyes met Kaylee's. She looked almost as dejected as I felt.

"I promised my parents I'd help them paint the house," Isaac added, watching me closely. "Maybe next time?"

Kaylee winked at me. I hoped Isaac hadn't noticed.

"Unless you like painting?" He looked at me with an expression I couldn't quite read. Joking. Maybe hopeful. I wanted it to be the latter.

"I can't paint for anything," Kaylee quickly replied. "But Madison's pretty good at it."

She jammed her elbow into Josh's ribcage when he started to laugh. If there was one thing I'd learned from the few times I had helped my dad paint houses for his handyman business, it was that I hadn't inherited his steady hand. I had to tell myself to keep walking or risk Isaac seeing my feeble attempt to rearrange my expression to be anything but shock over Kaylee's outright lie. She nudged me with her arm and looked meaningfully at Isaac.

We reached the car. I was all too aware of Isaac's gaze on me, and I wanted to see him again. I quickly weighed my options: a day of painting with Isaac, intruding on Kaylee and Josh's day together, or sitting home with Dad and my little brother.

Painting was sounding better and better. When you think about it, slapping paint on a flat surface should be easy. I hoped Isaac's expression was sincere as I tucked one side of my hair behind my ear.

"I wouldn't mind helping," I said. Isaac's smile let me know he was glad I volunteered.

"Great," he replied. "I'll have Josh tell me how to get to your house. Ten o'clock okay?"

"Sure." I would have woken up at dawn if he wanted me to.

I said bye to the guys and got into the MINI Cooper. I tried to be completely casual as the guys watched Kaylee turn the car around and drive off.

Kaylee's lips curled upward into a knowing smile. "I think Isaac likes you," she teased in a singsong voice. "And I think you like him."

I couldn't help but grin. A big silly grin from ear to ear. Kaylee knew me well enough to know that was a yes.

Chapter 2

We All Fall Down

Ppractically danced into the kitchen the next morning, my bare feet tapping lightly on the linoleum tile. I was still in my baby blue pajama shorts and tank top. My six-year-old brother sat at the table making *zoom* noises as he raced a red Hot Wheel Ferrari around his glass of milk. My dad had on his signature gray sweats and white T-shirt that he wore every Sunday. He leaned against the counter, his caramel-color hair sticking up in all directions, and a cup of coffee held close to his heart as if it was the only thing keeping him upright.

"Good morning," I chirped.

The bell on the toaster rang, and the toast sprang up. I grabbed a plate from the cabinet and looked at Chase. "You want jelly?"

"Grape," he replied without looking away from his toy car.

I smothered each slice of toast with butter and jelly and set the plate in front of Chase before asking Dad if he'd like a couple of slices.

"Please." He took a seat across from Chase and turned on the small twelve-inch television with the remote.

I put two more slices of bread in the toaster and grabbed a glass from the cabinet. "Did you have fun at the park yesterday?" I asked, knowing very well my brother always had fun when he went there.

"Yep!" Chase replied through a mouth full of toast. "You should have come with us. I found a dead crow with its bill and feet yanked off."

"That's gross!" The image of a mangled crow flashed in my mind, followed closely by the memory of the rabbit from the night before. My stomach lurched in disgust.

"It was awesome!" Chase assured me.

"That poor bird." I looked at Dad. "You didn't let him touch it?"

"Sure, and we brought it home so we can boil it up for dinner." Dad rolled his eyes. "Of course I didn't let him touch it."

Okay, I probably should have given him more credit and not accused him of letting Chase play with a thing like that. I poured myself a glass of orange juice and started buttering the toast.

"How was your night?" Dad asked, changing the subject.

"It was okay." I could have done without seeing Paige, but meeting Isaac certainly made up for that. "It was fun," I admitted out loud.

I handed Dad his toast and took a seat next to Chase.

"Thanks," Dad replied.

"No problem."

My heart did a tap dance in my chest just thinking about Isaac. I could picture him perfectly. His easy smile. The way he looked at me. Paige holding his hand as she scribbled her number across his palm. I should have admitted I was jealous. Maybe then Isaac would have spit in his hand and wiped it clean on his jeans.

The meteorologist on television promised a beautiful day. Sunny, mid-sixties. This made me realize I still had Isaac's jacket. I made a mental note to grab it before I left the house. To paint. I must have been out of my mind when I had volunteered to help.

I looked up and interrupted the conversation I hadn't been aware was taking place. "Did you know someone moved into the house across the street from Josh Corey's family?"

"Mrs. Lawson's old place?" Dad asked.

I nodded. "The new owners have a son."

"Oh?" Dad puckered his lips as if he'd just sucked on a lemon. "And from that smile I'm guessing you like him," he added before taking a large bite out of his toast.

"He's nice. I'm helping him paint today." I checked the clock on the microwave. I still had time before Isaac would be here to pick me up.

Dad choked on the food in his mouth, and Chase stopped drawing squiggly lines in his jelly.

"What?" I asked. You would have thought I'd just told them I was going to dance at a strip club. Talk about overreacting.

My dad gulped his coffee to push down the toast stuck in his throat. "You're painting?"

"With paint?" Chase added. "Daddy, quick, where's my hat?"

"We're painting at his house," I said and gently shoved Chase. "Just because I spilled a little paint on you *one time* doesn't mean I can't paint."

"It was a can of paint, and it took a week to get it out of my hair!"

I tickled his waist, causing him to squeal with laughter. "Chase Michael Riley, it was half a can," I said, "and it only took one day." And five baths. In Chase's mind that was a week's worth of baths. "Anyway, he promised his parents he'd help them paint, and he asked if I'd like to lend a hand."

Over Chase's head, I saw a picture of Mrs. Lawson in the right-hand corner of the television. I grabbed the remote from the table and turned up the volume.

"Here's Maria Sanchez with more," Peter Goodie, morning anchorman, said.

"Thank you, Peter." Maria Sanchez stood in front of a sprawling red brick building where Mrs. Lawson lived, the entrance to the assisted living facility some twenty yards behind her. "Nurses at Sunshine Village said that Annabelle Lawson's health had been deteriorating at an alarming rate since her arrival just one month ago. Doctors are still unsure what the ninety-three-year-old woman, who was reported in perfect health by her family physician back in March of this year, contracted. She was found dead on top of the covers in her one-bedroom apartment."

"Are any of the other residents at risk?" anchorman Peter Goodie asked.

"The doctors here don't believe that Mrs. Lawson was contagious, but they are keeping a close eye on those who had contact with her."

"Thank you, Maria." Maria nodded, and the view switched back to the newsroom. "The date and time of the funeral services has yet to be announced."

I lowered the volume. "I can't believe she's gone."

Dad got up to refill his coffee cup. "A lot of people knew her. She'll be missed."

I nodded and set the remote in front of him, dismissing the sad news for the time being to tend to more immediate matters—like the shower I desperately needed after a night at the beach—and headed upstairs.

It was ridiculous how long it took me to figure out what to wear over to Isaac's. It was the second time I'd be seeing him, and his parents were likely to be there. I didn't want to look like I didn't care what I wore. My sweats and oversized T-shirt were out. And I was too paint-challenged to wear something I would ever want to wear again. I finally settled for a pair of semi-old jeans and a purple T-shirt.

Isaac pulled up in front of my house at precisely ten o'clock. He drove a dark green Jeep Rubicon that looked like it could roll over Kaylee's MINI Cooper. He got out and opened the passenger door for me.

"It's not too late to change your mind," he said as I climbed in.

"No chance." I smiled to show I meant it. "I like painting."

Chase, who had found his hat and come to the screen door to get a look at my new friend, burst out laughing. As soon as Isaac walked around to the driver's side, I shot Chase my *Shut up or I'll kill you* glance and drew an imaginary line in front of my neck for emphasis.

I was excited to see Isaac again. There was something different about him that made him a mystery waiting to be unraveled. He chose his words carefully, as if he had a secret he didn't want to accidentally let slip. It thrilled me to think of the possibilities. Maybe his family were undercover agents for the government or secretly wealthy and Isaac was looking for someone to travel the world with. My mind came up with all sorts of exciting scenarios. At least it did until I thought of a few negative ones. What if he sold drugs? I didn't think I could date someone who did that, no matter how cute or nice he was. Worse, what if he'd been the stud at his old school? The guy who'd dated every pretty girl only to dump them once he'd gotten what he wanted. Maybe that was why he watched what he said. Maybe he didn't want to accidentally mention someone else. What if I was the newest addition to his harem?

I knew that thought should have upset me, but instead it made me giddy because, if it was true, I was the one he'd chosen to spend the day with.

I couldn't get my hands to stop shaking, so I tucked them under his jacket. I smiled at Isaac when he got in and did my best not to stare at him. It was hard. The morning light highlighted a thin crescent-shaped scar on his right cheek that left the healed skin pearly white. He had a similar scar on his chin. I shifted in my seat so that I'd be able to see him better.

"How'd you get the scars?" I touched my cheek and chin to indicate where on his face I meant. I'd never seen scars heal quite like his.

Isaac gave me a sideways glance that sent my heart into a frenzy of quick beats. I had to get a hold of myself. He was just a guy, a damn cute one, but a guy all the same.

After a moment, he said, "Difference of opinion between me and another guy."

"Ohh." I let the word drag out while I thought about asking for more details. There was something exciting about a guy who had scars. Something almost dangerous. Maybe that was why my heart raced the way it did. Maybe it was warning me to be careful. I didn't voice any of this out loud. Instead, I held up the olive green jacket I was carrying. "I brought your jacket back."

"Thanks."

"So, what are we painting?" I asked as he weaved his way through the streets of Gloucester. Maybe I'd get lucky and it would be the garage.

"My mom wants the dining room painted. She hates the teal paint in there now."

Okay, it wasn't the garage or even just the trim outside, where it wouldn't matter as much if I dripped paint on the ground. But I would at least still be painting on a flat surface. "Sounds like a plan."

Isaac navigated the side streets as if he'd been doing it all his life. The warm autumn air brushed my cheeks and sent my ponytail flying behind me. He glanced over at me and smiled, the left side of his lips higher than the right. I reminded myself to breathe.

"Hungry?" he asked. "I could stop and pick us up something."

My stomach was a tangled mess of emotions: excited to be seeing Isaac again, nervous that we might not have anything in common and would end up painting in silence, and scared that he would turn out to be a dream or, worse, a frog like in the fairy tales. I didn't think I could eat a thing.

"I ate at home," I lied. Isaac looked a little disappointed, so I added, "I wouldn't mind a latte."

We swung by a coffee shop near Isaac's house, and armed with four cups of specialty drinks and a box of muffins, we pulled into his tree-lined driveway and drove under a leafy umbrella of burnt orange and red. The house, a mocha two-story with brown shutters and cream trim, had every window open.

I followed Isaac up the walk and through the front door. Inside, the smell of fresh paint and pine cleaner fought to overpower each other. The living room and dining room were on either side of the foyer. Both rooms had dark hardwood floors. The dining room table, chairs, and china cabinet sat in the middle of the living room along with several unpacked boxes. A gallon of paint and a ladder were propped against the wall. Straight ahead was the staircase.

"Let's give my parents their coffee, and then we'll get to work."

Isaac led the way upstairs, where we found his mom standing on a ladder, edging the master bedroom in a glossy camel color. She wore paint-splattered overalls and a scarf covering her short auburn hair. The furniture had been pushed to the center of the room. His father had his back to us as he rolled paint onto the wall.

"We brought caffeine," Isaac said. "And breakfast."

I stood a little behind Isaac and smoothed my hair with my fingers, hoping to make a good first impression.

His father put down the roller and came over to shake my hand. "You must be Madison. It's very nice of you to come over to help, but there's been a change of plans."

I held out my hand, ready for it to disappear in his father's, but when our palms brushed, I got shocked by static electricity.

"Ow!" I yanked my hand back, my fingers curled into a fist.

He exchanged a quick glance with Isaac. "Sorry, I'm always shuffling my feet. Shock Lisa all the time."

"It's true," his mom confirmed, looking at Isaac. I turned my attention back to him, but he was busy placing two coffees and a couple of muffins on the floor near an empty water bottle.

"It's okay," I reassured them. "What's the change of plans?"

His mom waved her paintbrush in the air absentmindedly and said, "I'm not happy with the paint we bought for the dining room. So I was hoping you two wouldn't mind doing some unpacking instead."

"Sure." I shrugged, secretly thanking his mom for hating the color. It was better for everyone that I wasn't trusted with a gallon of paint in a room that had real hardwood floors.

Isaac leaned closer to me and whispered loudly enough for everyone to hear, "This is her way of getting me to set up my room."

"Can you blame me?" She laughed. "If I didn't, you'd just live out of the boxes."

"Really, I don't mind," I said before Isaac could argue.

Isaac gave me a quick tour of the upstairs, which included two bedrooms stuffed with boxes and miscellaneous furniture and a bathroom with a skylight.

"Where's your room?" I asked.

"Downstairs. Wait till you see it."

His bedroom only added to his mystique. The basement door was common wood, but the passage beyond was far from ordinary. I ran my hand along the rough brick wall where a railing would normally be and made my way down the curved stone stairs. Every couple of steps, there was a nook in the wall and a half-burned candle to occupy it. Dried wax dripped from a few. Musk and spice beckoned to me, pulling me forward.

"It needs a little work," Isaac admitted.

The basement wasn't big. The walls were the same brick and the floor the same stone as I'd seen on the way down. An iron ring the height of a chair rail wrapped its way around the circular room. Isaac had his bed pushed against the far wall, the black comforter thrown on it haphazardly. There were several boxes cluttered in front of a low black bookshelf and more in front of a rectangular nook that looked like the closet. The only door, this one with iron hinges and hardware, belonged to a small bathroom. A wrought iron chandelier — the old fashioned kind with candles instead of light bulbs — dangled from the ceiling. Add shackles and bars, and you'd have one hell of a dungeon. Despite the obviously dark tones, his room was cool in an unusual way.

"I like it," I said.

Isaac used his foot to push a few boxes out of his way. "I couldn't have designed it better if I'd tried."

I wondered if he would have seriously designed his bedroom with stone floors and iron accents and somehow doubted it.

I hooked my fingers through my belt loops. "So, where do you want to start?"

"Over here." Isaac used his hand to clear away a large cobweb that blocked one corner of the rectangular nook, wiping the thin strands on the bottom of his jeans afterward. "I want to put up a bar so I have a place to hang my clothes."

He gave me four screws.

"Are these iron?" I asked, surprised at the weight of them.

"Matches everything else." He picked up a bracket and a cordless screwdriver. "Don't ask me where my dad found them."

My job was to hand him the screws, which left me plenty of time to watch the muscles in his back and arms flex as he forced them into the stone wall. Once the first bracket was in place, he set up a step stool.

"I'll need you to help hold the bar so I can make sure it's straight."

"Sure." I climbed the three steps up the ladder.

Isaac had just lifted the bar in place when a large black spider spun down from the ceiling and landed on my shoulder. I screamed and, forgetting I was on a ladder, jumped backward. Before I fully knew what happened, I was on the floor with my right arm twisted under my body.

Isaac put down the bar and hurried to my side. "Are you okay?"

I was mortified, sprawled across his floor like a clumsy child. I wanted to disappear, but that wasn't an option.

"Yeah, I'm fine." I tried to push myself up, but as soon as I put pressure on my right hand, pain shot through my wrist and triceps like a million needles stabbing me, and I fell back down. "Ouch!"

Isaac wrapped an arm around my waist and helped me into a sitting position. He gingerly took my forearm in his hands and frowned.

"I think I may have broken it." I bit my bottom lip to keep from cringing in pain.

He ran his fingers from my elbow to my fingertips as he examined my wrist closer. The warmth of his touch was soothing in a maybe-something-good-can-come-out-of-being-a-klutz sort of way. After all, it did give me Isaac's undivided attention. He was so close I could smell vanilla and spearmint—his shampoo, I guessed.

"I'm sorry," he said, like it was his fault I had forgotten I was standing on a ladder. "I should have got the vacuum like my father always does and made sure I got the spider too."

"It's okay."

Isaac continued to rub my arm with long strokes from my elbow to my fingertips.

"I may need to go to the hospital." It was the last place I wanted to spend my Saturday, but with the amount of pain I felt when I tried to get up I was sure I'd broken something. I would have wiggled my hand to see if I could move it if Isaac hadn't had it in such a vise grip.

"That's not necessary," Isaac replied, a strange edge to his voice. After what seemed like several long minutes, he then eventually asked, "How's it feel now?"

I moved my hand up and down like a hinge. Surprisingly, my wrist didn't hurt as badly as when I'd first fallen. It was like his massage had eased all the pain and soreness away, or I was in too deep a state of shock and embarrassment to feel pain right then. I was sure it was the latter and I'd be begging my dad to take me to the emergency room when I got home.

"Better. Thanks," I finally replied.

He helped me stand. "Do you still want to help me unpack, or would you rather I take you home?"

I didn't hear him at first. I was too busy looking for the spider. Then the words *take you home* bounced around my head. Weird, but I had a hard time thinking straight with him standing so close to me.

"No. I'm good."

Isaac's mouth perked up into that crooked smile of his. He removed a pile of jackets, clothes, and I'm not sure what else from the sphere-shaped chair and insisted I sit. He finished putting up the bar by himself.

I curled my legs under me and watched him work. A silver chain slipped from beneath his navy blue T-shirt. From it hung a charm about the size of a quarter with an image of what looked like an old man's face. I cocked my head to the side and squinted as I tried to get a better look at it.

"That's an interesting necklace."

"It was my grandfather's. He gave it to me before he died." He tucked the charm back under his shirt before opening one of the boxes and grabbing a stack of socks from inside it.

"What's on it?"

"The Green Man." The socks went into the top dresser drawer. "According to my grandfather, it represents birth, death, and rebirth."

I nodded, understanding the importance of an item like that. My mom had never made it out of the hospital after my brother had been born. And I think she'd known she hadn't had much time left. One day, when I'd been visiting, she'd patted the bed, indicating for me to sit next to her. She'd removed the diamond journey necklace my dad had given her for Christmas and fastened it around my neck.

"So you remember that I'll always be with you, no matter where life takes you," she had said.

The chain was so delicate. I had been afraid I'd lose it, and while I know it's silly, I had been afraid that if I did lose it my mom wouldn't be able to stay with me. So, after her funeral, I had hung the necklace from the top of the lampshade near my bed. It's been there ever since.

Most of Isaac's clothes were still on hangers or folded and separated by the dresser drawer they went in. He was surprisingly organized for a guy, and I wondered if his mom had packed his stuff. The closet was filled and the dresser full in no time.

"It would have taken my dad a week to unpack that many boxes, and he wouldn't be able to find anything the next day," I commented when he had finished.

"I was kind of anal when I packed," he admitted with a shrug.

Isaac really didn't need my help, but when he reached the boxes near the bookshelf, I got up and knelt on the floor next to him.

His gaze moved to my arm.

"I'm fine." I rolled my wrist to show him and astounded myself when there wasn't even an inkling of pain. "It's not even sprained."

Satisfied, he let me organize his movies and music while he hooked up the stereo.

He had a large mix of alternative and rap music, and mostly male singers, so when I hit a country CD with a blonde on the cover I held it up.

"Taylor Swift?" I asked.

"What?" A red flush crept into his cheeks. "I had a crush on her."

I looked at the cover. Maybe that was his secret. Maybe he was into blondes. What if I was an experiment to see if they really did have more fun? My dark chestnut hair was about as far from Goldilocks as it could get.

He reached for the CD, but I raised my arm over my head before he could grab it.

"I was young," he said, lunging forward and missing my hand.

"And you're so old and wise now," I teased, moving the CD behind my back.

He grabbed for it, his body practically on top of mine as he tried to catch my hand. I leaned back, laughing.

"Maybe we should play it," I said, squirming to keep him from being able to reach it.

He wrapped an arm around my back, pulling me closer. "Let's not."

We were a jumbled mass of arms and legs. His belt buckle rubbed the bare skin of my stomach, and his neck was in perfect kissing distance. My gaze traveled to his lips. His close proximity had me forgetting I was winning the game of keep-away until he snatched the case from me.

We both laughed as we disentangled ourselves. He tossed Taylor Swift over his shoulder, and the CD conveniently landed on the bed.

"You can tell me the truth." I went back to his collection, hoping to find something else incriminating. "You're a little bit country."

He gave me a sidelong look that said, *Puh-lease*. "What do you listen to?" he asked as he plugged cables into the stereo.

"I like a mix of music, really. Except heavy metal and rap. R&B's cool." I held up a couple artists as examples of my taste.

"Eminem is rap," he said, looking at the cases in my hand.

"But this one features Rihanna, and she's R&B."

"That doesn't make the song R&B."

I shrugged. "Sure it does."

He smiled, shaking his head. "Admit it, you like the bad boys."

When he took a CD from the selection I held, it was a rock band. He popped it into the player, and "So Much to Say" drifted out of the one speaker he had connected.

It was after three in the afternoon when I placed the last DVD on the shelf.

Isaac broke down the box I'd unpacked as he confessed, "I'm glad my mom hated the paint."

There was something in the way he'd said it that sent an elated shiver through me. Not because I was nervous to be alone with him, but because I had a sudden urge to cover his mouth with mine. That would be so unlike me, but at that moment I wanted to grab the front of his shirt and pull him closer. It took me a second to compose myself, and I had to focus on my words to get them out in something that resembled a calm tone.

"Oh, really?" I glanced around his dungeon-like room. I'd happily be his prisoner.

"Really." Isaac crouched down, one hand resting on the floor on either side of me, his smile devious. "Aren't you in the least bit curious why?"

My pulse raced in a mix of excitement and longing. His cologne combined with the scents of his room and made my head spin. My reply came out weaker than I meant it to.

"Why?"

"First, it gave me an excuse to get you down here." He ran his hand over my ponytail, giving it a gentle tug before placing his hand back on the floor next to me. He was enjoying himself. "And second, now I can do this."

His lips brushed mine in the softest kiss I'd ever felt. Then — too soon for my racing thoughts that urged me to reach up and run my fingers over the muscles in his arm — he broke our kiss and fell back on his butt, his legs stretched out in front of him and crossed at the ankles.

I didn't move. Couldn't, really. I was mesmerized by his feather-soft kiss. He fought back a smile, and I hoped I didn't have a stupid expression on my face.

"Josh was right about you," he said.

"You talked about me?" That snapped me out of my stupor. I probably shouldn't have been surprised since it was Josh and Kaylee who had set us up. "What did he say?"

Isaac shook his head. "I can't tell you that, but I can say it was nothing bad."

I stuck my bottom lip out to pout. I didn't like it when people talked about me, and I had no idea what Josh would have said. I crossed my arms over my chest, which made Isaac laugh.

"Okay," he said through his laughter. "If it's going to eat at you, I'll tell you this. He said there was something special about you, and he was right."

I opened my mouth to reply but didn't really know what to say to that. Josh was my best friend's boyfriend. He wasn't supposed to think there was anything special about me. Nothing.

Isaac cleared his throat in an effort to stop his guffaw. It took a minute, but he managed to rearrange his face to be more serious. "You're cute when you're being all righteous."

"I'm not being—"

He leaned in closer to me. His eyes were a shimmering, deep brown, but there was a speck of ocean blue at the edge of his right iris. I couldn't remember what I was about to say. My heart did a pirouette in my chest, and my breath caught in my throat. I closed the distance between us. His lips were firm and warm, and I wanted to kiss him forever.

Until my stomach interrupted with a loud rumble, protesting that I hadn't fed it anything that day. I cursed its timing.

Isaac sat back; a look of concern took over his expression. "Maybe we should eat."

"I'm not hungry." But my stomach made another embarrassing growl that said otherwise.

He stood and offered me his hand, which I took. He pulled me to my feet. "It's my treat."

Chapter 3

The Grill

Isaac put on a clean pair of jeans and a collared shirt before driving me home so that I could change. My dad and Chase were in the family room when we got there.

"Do not do anything to embarrass me," I half ordered, half begged my dad before introducing Isaac to him and Chase. I knew my dad well enough to know that if I didn't say anything and if he didn't like Isaac he'd pull out my grandfather's old hunting rifle and start to clean it hoping to scare Isaac off. And if my dad did like Isaac, he'd be asking him what he planned on doing with his life.

The fear of what they might talk about while I was gone caused my adrenaline to take over. I took the fastest shower in my history of showers, towel-dried my hair, dressed in jeans and a sweater, and made it back downstairs in less than fifteen minutes. I'm not sure I'll ever be able to do that again.

Dad and Isaac were sitting on the edge of our worn leather couch watching football when I checked on them. Chase was driving a shiny black Porsche through his Matchbox carwash, glancing up at the television every now and then. Seeing them absorbed in the game helped me to relax, and since it seemed like conversation wasn't top priority for Dad or Isaac, I took a minute to call Josh and Kaylee and ask them if they wanted to meet us at The Grill.

When I got off the phone, I watched the back of Isaac's head from the doorway of the family room. Perhaps Kaylee had been right when she'd said it was time to put Kevin in the past and move on. Maybe I had been holding on to what we had because it was easier than putting myself out there and giving someone else a chance to get to know me.

Isaac was easy to talk to and fun to be around, and I was dying to know what his arms would feel like wrapped around me. I mentally rolled my eyes, thinking that I was a little pathetic. But then again, I didn't care. If I was going to start fresh, I could be anything I wanted to be, and right now I was okay with giddy schoolgirl with a crush on an older man. Besides, if I had to jump back into dating, why shouldn't it be with the hot new mystery guy?

I cleared my throat. Isaac and Dad looked at me.

"Ready?" I asked.

Isaac got up and faced my father. "It was nice to meet you." He patted Chase on the head as he walked by him. "Later, dude."

"See ya," Chase replied in a tone that told me he hoped he did see Isaac again.

"I won't be late." I grabbed my purse.

Dad nodded and told us to have fun.

Isaac followed me outside.

"Your family's nice," he said when we got in the Jeep.

"Thanks." Then, realizing a comment like that would mean some conversation had to have taken place while I was in the shower, I asked, "So, what did you talk about?"

"Gloucester and your mom, mostly."

"My mom?" Of all the things they could have talked about in the few minutes I was gone, I didn't expect it to be her.

"I was looking at the pictures on the mantel; you have her smile." He took a left out of my neighborhood. "Chase mentioned she passed away. I'm sorry."

I knew the picture he was talking about. I was ten, and my mom was pregnant with Chase. It had been taken in our backyard a few months before she died.

Isaac placed his hand over mine and gave a squeeze. A tingling sensation drifted through me. "I didn't mean to upset you."

"It was a long time ago." My mom was not a topic I discussed with many people, and I certainly didn't want to be spilling my life story to the guy I'd just met.

Isaac nodded and changed the subject. "Are Josh and Kaylee meeting us at The Grill?"

"They'll probably beat us there, actually. They said they'd save a table."

The Grill was a small restaurant in a renovated house along the main road. It was crowded, like it was every night. Both pool tables were in use, and every stool in front of the soda bar was taken. The jukebox rang out over the hum of voices. I scanned the tables to the left looking for Kaylee.

"There they are," Isaac said, pointing to our right. "In the back."

We made our way around half a dozen small square tables.

"Hi." I took a seat next to Kaylee.

"How was your day?" Kaylee then lowered her voice so only I could hear her. "It had to be good or you wouldn't still be hanging out with him."

"It was fun." I knew I was smiling like the Cheshire Cat in *Alice and Wonderland*, but I didn't care.

It was hard not to inhale my burger, something I would have done if it were just Kaylee, Josh and me. Halfway through my meal, Kaylee grabbed my hand and pulled me to my feet. "Let's pick out some music."

I resisted the urge to grab a handful of fries to eat on the way to the jukebox.

"So, what did you two do all day?" Kaylee asked as she read the long list of songs.

"Set up his room. It's pretty cool. It's in the basement."

She put her money in the machine. "Did you kiss him?"

I must have grinned or looked as if I was ready to burst at the seams to squeal *YES!* or something, because Kaylee grabbed my wrist. "You did! Is he a good kisser? I bet he is."

Our kiss had been so brief and soft, and I could still feel his lips on mine. Unconsciously, I touched my mouth with my fingertips, which was answer enough for Kaylee.

"I knew it," she said. "I can still remember the first time Josh and I kissed. There were fireworks."

Their first date was on the Fourth of July. The whole town saw fireworks, but Kaylee swears it was Josh's lips on hers and not the bursts of red, white, and blue lights being shot into the sky.

"Soo…" She moved closer to me, so that our arms were touching as we leaned over the jukebox pretending to look for the perfect song. "What else did you do? Come on. I want the dirty details."

"There aren't any dirty details." I glanced over my shoulder to make sure we were still alone.

"You want me to believe you and Sexy over there" —she indicated with a tilt of her head in Isaac's direction— "were alone in his bedroom, and there was no cuddling or touching?"

"Sorry to disappoint, but it was just a brief kiss."

She looked more disappointed than I had been at the time. "I bet he's just being a gentleman. Wait till he drops you off tonight. I bet he sticks his tongue down your throat."

"Kaylee!"

She cracked up laughing and punched in the numbers to her favorite songs, and we headed back to the table. We were gone long enough for a couple of Josh's friends to take our seats. Mark, a lanky guy with cheeks that resembled a chipmunk's and enough freckles to make a cloudless night sky jealous, shoved the rest of my fries in his mouth, while Ben, a guy built more like a compact sumo wrestler than a teenager, chatted excitedly.

"What are they doing here?" I whispered. This was supposed to be a double date.

"You know they have a way of finding Josh. They're better trackers than hound dogs. Besides, Mark likes you."

I stiffened. "No he doesn't. And he's dating Emma."

"To get you jealous," she said.

"That's ridiculous." I had known Mark since grade school, but we'd never hung out. The only time I saw him outside of school was when he happened to be with Josh.

Kaylee grabbed my arm and waited for me to face her. "Come on, Madison. You can't be that blind. Mark has been trailing behind Josh ever since Kevin moved, hoping to get your attention."

I shook my head and walked toward our table. Mark did not like me. We'd talk if we happened to be in the same place at the same time. We were friends because of mutual friends. That was all.

Mark jumped up when he saw me. "Hi, Madison. How's it going?"

"Good." I sat, and Mark grabbed an empty chair from the table behind him. Kaylee took a seat on Josh's knee. To prove to Kaylee that she was wrong, that Mark wasn't following Josh hoping to see me, I asked, "What are you guys doing here?"

"We saw Josh's car," Mark said, giving Isaac a sideways glance. Or maybe I imagined that.

Kaylee and I exchanged a look. Mine said, *HA! He's not looking for me.* Hers said, *I told you so.* Only, she was wrong and just didn't want to admit it.

Ben sucked the last of his soda through a straw with a slurp. "Yeah, and we had to come in and see if you were here."

All the smugness I'd felt a moment ago drained out of me in one big *whoosh.* Kaylee's eyebrows disappeared under her bangs, and she mouthed, *See.*

"How about a game of pool?" Ben asked, oblivious to the tension building around the table.

"I'm in," Mark said. He looked at Isaac and in a dry tone asked, "You want to play?"

"Thanks," Isaac rested his hand over mine, which was on the table, "but I'll pass."

"Another time," Josh said, wrapping his arms around Kaylee and giving her a squeeze as if to remind Mark and Ben they were here with us.

One of Kaylee's songs blared over the speakers. She hopped up, dragging Josh to his feet as she did so. "Dance with me." She grabbed Isaac's and my hands next. "You two aren't getting off that easy."

Isaac looked helplessly at Josh as he stood. Josh shrugged, a goofy smirk on his face, and followed Kaylee. Ben ate a few fries off Kaylee's plate. Mark just frowned.

Isaac and Josh sort of shuffled their feet as we danced. My back rubbed Isaac's chest as I shimmied in front of him. He was as comfortable on the dance floor as I would have been walking a tightrope, which made it all the more fun when I turned to face him, arms raised over my head. His eyes followed my hands as they trailed down my torso, stopping on my thighs as I wiggled my hips and bent my knees until I was crouching. Then I was up again, and Kaylee and I bumped hips and continued moving to the pulse of the music around the guys. They made it through one-and-a-half songs before Josh tugged Kaylee off the dance floor.

Isaac's arms encircled my waist. "You ready to get out of here?"

I nodded and took his hand, ignoring the sting of static electricity. We stopped at the table first. Mark and Ben were gone.

"We're leaving," Isaac said to Josh and Kaylee.

Josh tossed some money on the table and replied, "We better be going too."

"Isaac, your keys." Kaylee held up a set of keys by its bright red carabiner.

"Those aren't mine," Isaac replied.

"They're Mark's." I remembered seeing the bulky set of keys—with the brass black widow hanging from it—clipped to his belt loop before.

Kaylee held onto them. We kept an eye open for Mark as we left but didn't see him.

"Josh can give him a call and let him know I have them." She clipped the keys around the strap of her purse.

The night was cool and the sky clear, but the air felt wrong somehow. Thick. It crawled over my skin, leaving goose bumps in its wake. I hugged my elbows and glanced anxiously around me, not sure what I expected to see.

Josh cursed, pulling my attention away from our surroundings. I followed his gaze.

"Damn it!" He kicked at one of the flat tires on his silver Mustang.

Isaac walked around to the passenger side. "The tires on this side are okay. We can fix it."

The sole of Josh's gym shoe slammed against the tire again. He hissed, "I only have one spare."

Isaac walked back around the car and placed a hand on Josh's shoulder. "The front tire doesn't look bad."

I craned my neck to get a better look at the front tire, which I would have sworn was as flat as the back tire, but Isaac was in front of me placing his keys in my hand. "The Jeep is a couple of cars down. Why don't you and Kaylee wait for us there?"

When I opened my mouth to protest, he added, "You look like you're freezing, and Kaylee does too."

Kaylee had her hands wrapped around her arms and was shifting her weight from one foot to the other. She did look cold.

"Thanks." I took the keys and motioned for Kaylee to follow me.

When we reached the Jeep, I held the remote up so that I could see it better, pressing the button with the picture of an open lock. The double beep of the doors unlocking was almost drowned out by Kaylee's gasp. She grabbed my wrist. Her nails dug into my skin.

"Ow!" I tried to tug free. "You're hurting me."

Kaylee's fingers tightened like a vise as she took a step closer to me so that our shoulders touched. Kaylee's eyes were wide and focused on the far end of the parking lot. My gaze followed hers. "What is it?"

The street lamp flickered on and off, creating odd shadows among the cars parked there.

"Who is that?" Kaylee whispered.

I squinted, looking between and inside the distant vehicles. "Who's who?"

She raised her free hand and pointed toward the darkness in front of us. "Right there, standing in front of the pick-up truck."

It was one of those work trucks with the racks for ladders.

"Kaylee, there's no one there." And even though I couldn't see anyone, I was still freaked out. "Come on. Let's get in the Jeep."

We did. I started the engine and cranked the heat.

"Where'd he go?" Kaylee kept shifting in her seat so that she could look behind us and next to us. Between her behavior, what I'd felt when we walked outside, and the fact that someone had slashed Josh's tires, I really didn't feel safe sitting in a Jeep with a soft top that didn't offer all that much protection from a psycho with a knife.

Behind us, a street lamp grew brighter, illuminating the rusted out minivan beneath it; it sparked, and then only the orange glow of the filament could be seen.

"What if that guy sees Josh or Isaac?" Kaylee reached for the door handle. "We have to warn them!"

"I didn't see anyone." I grabbed her wrist before she could bolt out of the car. "The guys are fine." Only, as sure as I was that *I* didn't see anyone, I wasn't so sure that *she* didn't see someone. What if she was right and this guy went after Josh or Isaac? What if he was waiting for Kaylee or me to step out of the Jeep? I scanned the back of the parking lot looking for movement. There was none.

A car's engine roared to life, making it impossible to hear if someone were to approach.

Something then tapped against the metal of the Jeep. Kaylee and I grabbed each other's hand. *Tap. Scrape.* Neither of us moved. When my door swung open, I jumped. Kaylee screamed.

"Sorry," Isaac said. "I didn't mean to scare you. Tire's changed."

Josh pulled up behind us, and Kaylee got out. "I'll see you later," she said and ran to his Mustang.

I climbed over the stick shift to the passenger seat, and Isaac waited for Kaylee to be safe inside Josh's car before he got in. I wondered if she felt as unsafe as I did being in a car with a vinyl top.

"Does Josh have any idea who'd slash his tires?" I asked.

"They weren't slashed." Isaac backed out of the parking spot. "He probably ran over a nail or something."

I would have sworn on my mother's grave I'd seen a gash in one of the tires, but, then again, maybe what I had seen was the nail sticking out of the sidewall. "How'd you fix the front tire?"

When Isaac didn't reply right away, I thought he was going to deny that both tires had been flat, and I couldn't imagine why. Unless he thought someone had done this to Josh's car to make a point that hanging out with Isaac was not a good idea. Didn't Isaac tell me just this morning that he'd gotten into a fight with someone? What if that person held a grudge? What if Isaac's family hadn't moved because his father was tired of driving from Amesbury to Rowley? What if they'd moved because this other guy still had it out for Isaac?

"The front wasn't as bad as the back," Isaac finally said. "Josh will be able to drop Kaylee off at home and make it to his house. His dad has an air compressor in the garage. He can fill it there."

I wasn't buying that Josh had just so happened to get nails in two tires. He was very particular about where he drove that car. He'd drive ten miles out of the way if it meant he could avoid road construction and damn near came to a complete stop over railroad tracks because he didn't want to mess up his suspension.

I was afraid to ask Isaac if he knew what really happened back there. Not because I was afraid of the answer but because I was afraid he'd get mad at me for prying into his business. If he wanted to tell me, he would. And just because Isaac had gotten into a fight with some guy didn't mean that he'd hurt me. Right?

As we drove to my house, I decided not to let my imagination get the better of me.

"Thanks for dinner," I said when we were parked in my driveway.

"Thanks for helping today." Isaac looked at me, his eyes smoldering as he leaned over the stick shift and brushed my lips with one of his feather-soft kisses that sent a warm tingling sensation all the way to my toes.

No one who could get my heart beating as fast as it was with such a brief kiss could possibly be bad. I was sure of it.

"Sweet dreams," he added.

And that's exactly what I planned on having that night: steamy, sweet dreams of him.

Chapter 4

School

"I had the worst night's sleep," Kaylee said when I got in her car the next morning. She had dark circles under her eyes. "I kept dreaming that Freddie Krueger was after me. In my dreams I was doing everything possible not to fall asleep, and then when I finally woke up I couldn't fall back to sleep. Madison, I swear someone was in that parking lot last night."

Kaylee didn't scare easily. She was the one who loved to see the latest horror movies at the theater. I didn't like seeing her upset.

I rested a hand on her arm in reassurance. "Kaylee, I didn't see anyone. You had to have seen a shadow of a lamp post or antenna, or maybe there was something in the back of the pick-up truck." I was trying to remember if there were any pipes or brooms or even a ladder.

She glanced at me, her expression hopeful. "Do you really think so?"

"Yes." I didn't sleep well either, but it wasn't monsters from the movies that kept me up. "I need caffeine if I'm going to make it through Mr. Chapin's class. It's my treat."

"Coffee works for me." Kaylee took a right at the light, heading toward the strip mall.

I had so many questions about what had happened at The Grill, questions I was sure Isaac would brush off with a smirk and too few words. Like how he and Josh had managed to change the tire in a matter of minutes; only a pit crew at the Indy 500 could work that quickly. Not to mention, I would have bet my entire savings—all nine hundred and two dollars of it—that the front tire had been as flat as the back. And how had Isaac's four little words—*We can fix it*—managed to calm Josh so quickly? There was only one thing Josh loved more than that Mustang, and she was sitting next to me.

"Did Josh say anything about his car when he drove you home last night?"

Kaylee shook her head. "Not much, why?"

"I don't know. Just curious, I guess."

I had to be reading too much into nothing. Kaylee wasn't worried about the tires, so I told myself that I shouldn't be either.

We drove through the drive-up window at the coffee shop, then sped to school. Kaylee parked a few cars down from Josh's Mustang.

She grabbed her backpack off the seat behind her. "We better hurry. We're late."

We arrived to first period ten minutes after the bell. Mr. Chapin, who had been leaning against the front of his desk, talking to the class when we got there, stopped teaching and watched us take our seats.

"Ladies, I trust this will be the last time you show up to my class tardy."

I nodded. Kaylee smiled apologetically.

"And I trust you've read the assigned pages in *Death of a Salesman*." It wasn't a question.

Kaylee nodded this time. I swallowed and hoped my expression didn't give away that I was already behind on the assignment.

"Good," Mr. Chapin said. "Because I just finished telling your classmates that the book report counts for fifty percent of your grade this quarter and the quizzes another twenty-five."

Mr. Chapin was known for his love of American literature, crazy long essay assignments, and pop quizzes—three things I could have done without my entire life and still been perfectly happy. Not to mention, I didn't need to be reminded just how far behind I was first thing in the morning.

I sank lower in my chair. I'd only taken Chapin's class so that Kaylee and I would have the same first period. I held my cup under my nose and breathed in the scent of pumpkin spice syrup, knowing it was the only thing that was going to make the next hour bearable.

The caffeine kicked in by the end of class, and I was feeling much more alive. It seemed to do wonders for Kaylee too.

"Oh!" She unclipped the bulky set of keys with the ugly spider from her purse. "Give these to Mark."

I held them up by the carabiner. "Do you think he uses all these keys or just carries them around to look important?"

Kaylee and I giggled as we left the classroom.

"I'll see you in History," she said as she headed in the opposite direction.

I walked slowly through the halls to my second period Food class, hoping I'd run into Isaac. I had no such luck. Mark was in class, though, so I gave him his keys. At lunch, I thought I saw Isaac waiting in line a few people ahead of me, but when I tapped the guy on the shoulder, he turned out to be a tall freshman with spiked brown hair like Isaac's. By the end of the day I was tired, disappointed, and couldn't wait to get home.

"Madison, just call him," Kaylee said when she pulled up to my house.

"I'll seem too anxious." Besides, I told myself, maybe he didn't want to talk to me. I didn't want to call him and make a fool of myself.

"You are anxious," Kaylee pointed out. When I shot daggers at her with my eyes, she rested her hand on my arm. "How about I call Josh and have him call Isaac. That way you can find out what he's up to."

"No," I said stubbornly. "I'm serious Kaylee, don't tell Josh that I'm going crazy waiting for a call. Promise me."

She rolled her eyes as she drew a cross over her heart, and I knew she'd keep her promise. "At least come over and hang out."

"I can't. I told my dad I'd watch Chase. I'm taking him to the park. Come with us? We're going to play Hot Lava." Kaylee's company would make the time go by more quickly, and Chase loved having her around. We'd all benefit.

"Tempting," she said. "But if you're not going to come over, then I might as well catch up on my reading before Chapin asks me a question I can't answer."

I sighed. I should really be reading too. I opened the car door and got out. "I'll see you tomorrow."

As soon as Kaylee pulled away, I regretted not taking her up on her offer to have Josh call Isaac. I unlocked the front door and stepped inside to find Chase sitting at the bottom of the stairs, shoes and baseball cap on.

"Hey, squirt." I tugged on the brim of his cap. "Where's Dad?"

"In the kitchen, talking to Officer Zimmerman."

"Let me go say hi, and then we'll go to the park." I dropped my backpack on the floor in the foyer.

Chase nodded.

Officer Zimmerman's voice drifted out of the kitchen. I stopped in the hallway and listened.

"Never seen anything like it. Coroner's been asked to re-examine the body. Make sure nothing was missed the first time around."

"They think there was foul play?" Dad asked.

"Won't know until the report's in, but it would explain a few things."

"I thought she died in her sleep. Joe, she was in her nineties."

"And as spry as a woman in her fifties, until recently," Officer Zimmerman retorted. "I was one of the first on the scene when the center called. I didn't think too much of it at the time, her being as old as she was, but the veins in her face and arms created a roadmap just under her skin. With what people liked to say about her…" There was a pause, then Officer Zimmerman added, "Do us both a favor and keep your kids inside. Okay?"

"Sure," Dad agreed.

After a few seconds of silence, I took the last few steps into the kitchen. They sat at the table, two open cans of Pepsi in front of them.

"Hey," I said.

"Madison." Officer Zimmerman inclined his head in way of greeting. "How's school?"

"Good." I smiled and looked at my dad.

"Well." Officer Zimmerman stood and grabbed his hat off the table. "I better get going."

I raised my hand in a half-wave goodbye. As soon as I heard the front screen door close, I asked my dad, "Was he talking about Mrs. Lawson?"

Dad opened the refrigerator and grabbed a beer. The owner of his own business, he never drank before going to paint someone's house. I knew then that whatever it was had my dad worried.

He chugged half the bottle. "They found a suspicious area in the woods not far from where you kids like to get together. It looked like someone was sacrificing animals or something."

"What does that have to do with Mrs. Lawson?"

The news reporter had said she was found in her room, not outside in the middle of trees.

"Detectives found a locket that belonged to her in the brush. Mrs. Lawson's nurse said she never took it off." Dad finished the rest of his beer. "I want you to be careful who you're hanging out with, you got that?"

"Sure." It wasn't a hard promise to make; I was always with Kaylee when I was out. "Dad, no one was hacked up or anything, were they?"

"Joe couldn't say much, but I don't think so." Dad grabbed another beer. "I'm going with you and Chase to the park."

"Won't that put you behind schedule with your clients?" October was one of my dad's busiest seasons because that was the time of year people realized their house really did need a fresh coat of paint before winter.

"You let me worry about that."

I almost told him that if he was going to take Chase to the park, then I would stay home and do homework, but I didn't. I got the feeling he needed to be with both of us for a little while.

In the short time it took us to walk the three blocks to the park, I had convinced myself I'd hear from Isaac before dinner, but he didn't call or text me. I checked caller ID on our house phone as soon as we got home, in case he called there instead of my cell. Nothing. I kept both phones near me the rest of the night. He never called.

Isaac didn't call Tuesday either.

By Wednesday, I was ornery and working hard not to take my bad mood out on Kaylee.

"Josh said he's been busy helping his parents," Kaylee told me on the way to English. "I bet if he knew you wanted to see him again —"

I blocked the classroom doorway. "Don't you dare tell Josh to have him call me."

"Madison, you're being ridiculous," Kaylee whispered back. "Just call him, then."

"I don't want to come across as desperate or a pest or obsessive." I turned and walked into the classroom.

Kaylee followed so closely behind me that she stepped on the back of my Converse sneakers twice. When I turned to tell her to be careful, she hissed, "It's been three days. Wait a couple more and the only thing you're going to come across as is uninterested."

"Ugh!" I sunk into my seat. She was right, which annoyed me. I really wanted Isaac to call me. I wanted him to be thinking about me as much as I was thinking about him, which was obviously not the case or he'd have tracked me down on Monday. "Fine. If I don't run into him by the end of the day, I'll call him."

"Good," Kaylee said, "because you're driving me nuts."

"Whatever," I mumbled.

I took a different way to my second period Food class, hoping I'd run into Isaac and save myself from having to call him. I was almost to the classroom when I saw him. Even with his back to me, I recognized his olive green jacket. He was talking to Paige.

Damn her. Why did she have to go after Isaac?

The worst part was she was laughing — it looked sort of sinister to me, but since I hated her I probably shouldn't have passed judgment. I'd never really taken a good look at Paige since she'd changed her look, but the black clothes, pale face, and dark make-up worked for her. Her skin was smooth and her eyes big. I still preferred the shy, plain-looking girl I used to know, though, the one who had actually been my friend.

Isaac leaned in closer to her and said something I couldn't hear. She listened, wetting her lips.

Oh! If he kisses her!

I bit down on the inside of my cheek to keep from screaming in frustration. The corner of Paige's mouth rose to a smirk.

Kaylee was right; the only thing I was coming across as was uninterested. I'd given Paige three days to move in on the guy I liked. I was such an idiot. Tears welled up in my eyes, and I fought to calm my breathing. I couldn't break down and cry in the middle of the hallway. Not where Isaac would see me. Not in front of Paige. I ducked into the nearest classroom as Paige stepped around him.

"You know where to find me," Paige called over her shoulder as she walked by my hiding spot.

I didn't notice the twenty-some sets of eyes watching me until the bell rang. I feigned a smile and mumbled an apology to the teacher of whatever class I had just interrupted. As embarrassed as I was, I didn't rush out of the classroom. I peeked first to make sure Isaac wasn't still standing by the lockers.

I wasn't even sure if I had a right to be mad or jealous or whatever I was. Isaac and I had spent a day together. That didn't make us exclusive. I tried to remind myself that he'd only met a few people in Gloucester. Who was to say he wouldn't meet other girls he'd want to date?

For one, me!

I couldn't have imagined his interest in me, could I? Maybe he brought girls to his house all the time, invited them into his bedroom, and kissed them. Maybe he hated how I kissed.

I so wasn't making myself feel better.

And I was late now. I didn't think the morning could get any worse.

As soon as I walked into Foods it did.

"Madison," Mark whispered and waved me over to the table he was sitting at. "I saved you a seat."

"Thanks." I dropped my backpack on the floor between us.

Mrs. Sheppard continued her lesson as if I hadn't walked in late. Something smelled like day-old garbage or some sort of really strong spice. I hoped we weren't making anything with onions or garlic.

"You look terrible," Mark whispered a little too happily. "Bad morning?"

I exhaled loudly. This was the fourth time this week I'd been late to one of my classes. It was only a matter of time before the school called my dad to inform him of my poor attendance. Dad would freak and no doubt lecture me on how I was ruining my good attendance record or drone on about how I needed to be more responsible. The guy I liked wasn't as into me as I was into him. *And* I looked like hell. Wonderful.

"I have a headache," I said to Mark.

Mark nodded, and I realized that awful smell was coming from him.

"Are you wearing cologne or something?" I asked.

Mark's pudgy cheeks flushed red, nearly hiding his freckles. "It's new. Do you like it?"

"Um, yeah," I lied, not wanting to hurt his feelings.

Mark sat up a little straighter, and I noticed that his button-down shirt had deep creases — the sort that come right out of the package. "Want to hang out Friday? We could see that new movie."

I should have seen that one coming. He had saved me a seat. He was wearing cologne. He had put on a new shirt. I was blind, as Kaylee so elegantly put it the other night.

"Thanks," I said sincerely. "But I can't Friday."

I offered him an apologetic smile before turning my attention to Mrs. Sheppard. Did Mark know Isaac and Paige were dating? Was I the only one that had missed the news? The thought of Isaac looking at Paige the way he had looked at me had me close to hyperventilating. I nearly fell off my seat when Mark touched my arm.

He waited patiently, and I had the distinct feeling I'd just missed something.

"What?"

"How about Saturday?" Mark fidgeted with his pencil as he waited for my answer.

"Thanks. Really," I said, "but — "

"You don't like me that way," he finished for me.

It was true, I didn't like him that way, but I didn't want to be mean and come right out and say it.

"Mark, you're a really nice guy, but we're friends, and I wouldn't want to ruin that." I could have hit myself in the head for giving such a lame excuse, but it was the best I could do on short notice. And it was true. Then it occurred to me: "Aren't you dating Emma?"

"We broke up." His eyes went to his lap, and his shoulders slumped forward. He reached into his back pocket and pulled out a thin silver chain. He placed it on the table in front of me.

"I'd like you to have it. No strings, just friends."

I picked it up and studied the black onyx. It was set in an intricate silver knot. I ran my finger over the stone. It was beautiful.

"Mark, I can't —"

"I don't want it back, and I spent too much money on it to just throw it out. Please. You'd be doing me a favor by taking it."

He looked so sad. I couldn't help but feel sorry for him. I slipped the long silver chain over my neck. "I'll hold it for you. Um, maybe we can see a movie another time." The words were out of my mouth before I could stop them. "As friends," I added, hoping he'd understand.

Mark spent the rest of the period glancing at me every few minutes, which I might have been able to ignore if I wasn't stuck in the same kitchen unit as him.

And we made French onion soup. There should be a limit to what we are expected to cook before nine o'clock in the morning.

The rest of the day I kept my head down and made a beeline for each classroom. I didn't want to see Isaac making yet another girl laugh or Mark, who would be expecting me to say yes to the next time he suggested we hang out.

The end of eighth period couldn't have come soon enough. Kaylee found me at my locker.

"Hi," she said. The word gushed with excitement. For a second I wanted to trade places with her so that I could be that happy, but then she added, "We have to hurry."

"Hurry where?" I asked. I was too upset to hurry anywhere if it wasn't home to my pajamas and a pint of mocha-almond-fudge ice cream.

"Our first Harvest Festival meeting, of course." When I didn't jump for joy, she added, "Madison, I told you we had a meeting today."

"No, you didn't. Kaylee, I want to go home." I stomped my foot for emphasis.

"You promised." She stared at me with big round eyes that I really needed to learn to say no to.

"Okay," I conceded and held my arm out to the side. "Lead the way."

"Thank you." She beamed. "I'll make it up to you. I promise."

Unless she was somehow going to make this meeting as exciting as planning an escape to someplace fun, I highly doubted she'd be able to make it up to me any time soon — not with how screwed up my day had turned out to be — but whatever.

She looked at the black onyx charm hanging around my neck. "Where'd you get that?"

"From Mark. It's a long story."

Kaylee stepped in front of me, mouth set in a straight line and eyebrows raised.

I'd just agreed to go to a meeting I didn't want to be at; I shouldn't have had to explain my accessories too. However, I could tell Kaylee had no intentions of budging until I did.

"We're just friends." When her eyes grew wider in disbelief, I added, "I'm just holding it for him."

"Uh-huh." She picked up the stone and examined it. "It's pretty."

I gathered my hair in my hands and smoothed it to one side. I went to slip the necklace over my head. "Here, you wear it."

Kaylee placed a hand on mine before I could get the thing off. "Yeah. I'd love to, after the meeting. We're late."

The committee consisted of eight students and two staff members. The desks had been pushed aside and several chairs moved to the center of the room to form a circle. The others were already seated and talking among themselves when we got there.

It didn't surprise me that Natalie Parker and Lauren Richards were there. Natalie, a petite girl with dark brown hair and a pixyish face, was about a head shorter than Lauren, who couldn't have been taller than five-foot-four in heels. Paige was there too, of course. Her mom was one of the staff on the committee. Sarah Johnson, my second oldest friend (Kaylee being my first), made six. Sarah and I didn't hang out like we used to when we were young, but I knew I could count on her whenever I needed her, just like she knew she could count on me.

I grabbed Kaylee's wrist when I saw Mark and Ben. "Why didn't you tell me they were on the committee?"

"Because I just found out this morning," she whispered back. "They must have signed up after I did. Do you believe Mark likes you yet, or do you need more proof?"

"Shut up."

The last two seats were between Natalie and Mark. I practically knocked Kaylee over in my haste to get the seat next to Natalie.

Mrs. Parris, a middle-aged woman with a small prim mouth and thick ankles, clapped her hands together, and silence fell around us. "Now that everyone is here, I would like to get started. The first thing we have to figure out is how much money we'll need."

Sarah raised a dainty hand. When Mrs. Parris inclined her head, indicating for her to go ahead, Sarah tucked her shiny blond hair behind her ears. "We should be able to re-use most of the decorations from last year."

"Ben and I can help with that," Mark offered.

Mrs. Parris nodded, her hands neatly folded in her lap as she listened. Mrs. Osborne straightened her navy jacket, tapped the point of her pen to her tongue, and jotted notes in a tan planner with an expression much too serious for a meeting about scarecrows and hot dogs.

Sarah continued, "And I bet we can get Mr. Hoffman to give us a good price on cornstalks and bales of hay."

Lauren spoke up next. "Maybe we could have a bake sale this year. It will help raise cash for future events. We can put up fliers. I bet the Food class will participate if we asked them."

Then everyone started to jump in with suggestions. I even managed to forget my problems for a few minutes, and to my surprise, being stuck in the same room with Paige wasn't as bad as I would have thought it would be. For the first time in weeks, she was friendly to everyone. It was toward the end of the meeting when I started to think there might be a reason she was so happy. What if she was dating Isaac? It wasn't until that moment that I actually believed it could be true. My stomach tightened, and I wanted to be sick. Her eyes met mine, and the corners of her mouth rose into a wicked smirk. The fingers of my right hand curled into a fist.

Mark reached over Kaylee and placed a hand on my arm.

"Are you okay?" he whispered.

I forced a smile and nodded in reply.

Paige's smile disappeared as her eyes fell to Mark's hand on my arm and then to the chain around my neck. The weight of the stone pressed against my chest bone, and I found myself turning my head to look at Lauren, purposely making my hair hide the necklace.

Shortly after that, Mrs. Osborne and Mrs. Parris said we had made enough progress for one day.

Kaylee and I followed Natalie, Lauren, and Paige out of the classroom. Josh was waiting in the hallway with Isaac, who looked even better than he had on Sunday. First thing that came to my mind was, *Finally, he tracked me down*, but then I realized he might not be waiting for me. My heart, which had twirled excitedly in my chest just from seeing him, slammed into a wall of ice.

I wasn't sure Isaac would be happy to see me. Maybe he was there because Josh was and not because he was looking for me. The image of Isaac and Paige huddled together in the hall replayed in my head in enhanced 3D. Had Paige asked him to meet her here? I slowed my pace as Isaac's velvet brown eyes scanned those leaving the meeting. His expression hardened when he saw me, or maybe he was looking at Paige, who was a step ahead of me. I nearly ran into her when she stopped walking. Isaac's eyes closed for the briefest of moments as his head moved ever so slightly from left to right. I would have sworn I heard Paige say, "We'll see." Then again, having your heart smashed against an iceberg can make you imagine things.

I stopped breathing and had to tell myself to inhale before I passed out. Josh draped an arm over Kaylee's shoulder.

Isaac pushed off the locker. "I was hoping I'd find you here."

His words melted the frost inside me and freed my heart. He was waiting for me. Overtaken by relief, I completely forgot how to speak. In my peripheral vision, I saw Mark scowl and stalk away with Ben in tow.

Isaac stepped forward and brushed his hand over my sleeve. "Are you all right?"

"Yeah." I squashed all thoughts of Paige from my mind. "How have your first few days been?"

"Not bad. Most my classes are blow-offs," he admitted. "How's your week been?"

It's getting better. Out loud, I said, "Okay."

We walked to the parking lot with Josh and Kaylee. When we reached their three cars, I took the necklace off and slipped it over Kaylee's head.

"Just don't let Mark see it," I whispered. "He may get mad if he finds out I gave it to you."

"Kaylee?" Isaac asked. "Do you mind if I steal Madison from you?"

I was about to point out that he should be asking me if I wanted to be stolen. It wasn't like I was a child or couldn't speak for myself. Well, most of the time.

But before I could say anything, Kaylee replied, "I think I can get by."

Isaac shifted so that I could walk by him to the passenger side of his Jeep. Kaylee took this opportunity to wink at me. And, because I did want to spend time with Isaac, I obligingly climbed in.

Chapter 5

Nearly Dead

The doors were off the Jeep, allowing the cool autumn breeze to rush past us as we cruised down the street. The sweet scent of burning wood filled the air.

Isaac held the gearshift as he drove. I reached for the radio, planning to nonchalantly brush my hand against his as I went to change the station; only, he moved his hand to the steering wheel. I ended up surfing through the channels until I found a decent song, which just so happened to be the same song that had been playing on the other station. So much for smooth moves.

Several questions warred with my excitement about being with Isaac. I didn't want to ruin the afternoon playing inquisitor, but I wanted answers. Certainly some of my questions wouldn't cause him to turn the car around and take me home. *Where have you been?* seemed innocent enough. *Is there something between you and Paige?* seemed like something I should know. *Are you playing with my emotions?* was the question on the tip of my tongue.

I never would've asked him the last one, but I did wonder. Damn near three days had gone by without a word from him, and then he shows up and whisks me away. What was I supposed to think?

One question couldn't hurt. If Isaac said he was out on dates with other girls, what right did I have to be upset? This was only our second date, if it was a date. He might not have liked me that way.

Maybe after spending a day with me he'd realized we'd be better off as friends. Maybe that was why he had disappeared for three days.

Please don't let that be it, I prayed. I tucked my hands under my thighs to keep them from shaking.

"Do anything interesting the last couple of days?" I finally asked.

"I was in Amesbury with my dad. We had a few things to grab from our old house."

I wanted to scream *YES!* I didn't. I nodded to show my interest.

He *had* helped his parents, like Josh had said. He hadn't been out with Paige or anyone else. I believed Isaac. I'm not sure why, maybe because he didn't have a reason to lie. I really needed to stop letting my imagination run away with me or I was going to drive myself crazy.

When Isaac reached Washington Street, I asked, "Where are we going?"

"I want to show you something."

That was all he said until we pulled up to Annisquam Lighthouse, which I'd seen more than a dozen times. You don't live in Gloucester with a father who wished he painted murals instead of buildings and not have seen the lighthouses. Isaac parked in the fifteen-minute parking lot and got out.

"Did you want to take a picture of it?" I asked, knowing that was all a person could do with limited time there.

He gave me one of his dazzling smiles and turned toward the lighthouse. "Come on."

He didn't take my hand, just showed the way. Our footsteps thudded softly over the ramp that led to a large wooden door. Isaac's hand hesitated over the doorknob before he quickly turned it. To my surprise, it wasn't locked.

"My father's friends with a couple guys from the Coast Guard," he explained. "I like to come here to clear my mind."

Inside, we made our way up the long, winding stairs, through the trapdoor that led to the top, and out on the balcony. The white light flashed inside the tower every seven-plus seconds, warning ships and boats to stay clear of the rocks below. I kept one hand on the dark bricks of the tower and looked out past the black iron railing. My head swam as my stomach tightened. I pressed my back against one of the windows.

"Are you afraid of heights?" Isaac asked.

"A little," I confessed.

A stillness filled the air, a calm serenity that wrapped around me like the wings of an angel. A moment later, Isaac's strong arms circled me, pinning my back to his chest. His breath smelled of spearmint. It brushed the side of my neck and sent an excited shiver through my entire body.

"Better?" he asked.

"Much." And not just because I felt safe nestled in his arms. His gallant behavior had to mean he hadn't dragged me to the top of a tower to give me the old *It's not you, it's me* speech. I melted into him, knowing he didn't want to be just friends.

He guided me forward, stopping when we were peering out over Annisquam Harbor. We were hidden from view of the parking lot now.

I glanced over my shoulder and up into his sultry brown eyes. "It's beautiful."

"Yeah." He gave me a little squeeze. "View's not bad either."

I smiled and looked back at the bay. Seagulls soared gracefully, following the shoreline and settling on the rocks below us. The water glistened like diamonds in the sunlight. The view was stunning.

"I could get used to coming here," I admitted.

"I'm going to hold you to that."

Isaac released his grip on my waist, taking my hand before he sat down, and I settled next to him. I'd never seen the harbor from this height. I knew from maps that it connected Ipswich Bay to the Annisquam River but hadn't had an opportunity to see it for myself. "I find it relaxing. The water, the air, it—" Isaac stopped, seeming to consider his words. When he spoke, he did it slowly, as if weighing his response before saying it. "I always feel renewed when I come here. Recharged."

In the distance, boats glided across the smooth surface of the river. With my arms behind me, I dropped my head back and let the sun's warmth wash over my face. The breeze, like long fingers, played with my hair.

"You know this town has a history?" he went on, his voice far away as if deep in thought. "Every town in Essex County does. You can find the particulars if you do a little research. Most just choose not to."

I opened one eye quizzically.

He smiled. "My parents were history majors. You don't grow up in their house and not develop a hunger for the past."

"My mom liked history. Salem's especially. She was always reading some old book on it. My dad was an art major. They met in college."

Isaac appeared to watch me with admiration. "There's a magic around you in this light."

I smiled and let myself get lost in his gaze. His hand ran the length of my arm in a lazy movement, sending a familiar tingling sensation all the way to my toes. Instinctively, we leaned closer to each other. His fingers trailed their way up to my shoulder, along my cheek, and over my mouth. My breath caught in my throat, and my heart went into a sprint. Our lips met naturally. His tongue brushed mine with just enough tenderness to awaken all my senses. Time seemed to stand still, but I'm pretty sure our kiss lasted only a few seconds. Isaac kissed my forehead before pulling me closer so that my back was against his chest.

It took my brain a moment to start working again. No one had ever managed to jumble up my thoughts with one kiss, not even Kevin. I knew it was too late. I'd already fallen for Isaac. It scared me, wanting this much to be with someone I'd just met. One kiss and I felt as if I couldn't live without him. It was silly and exciting and unsettling and wonderful all at the same time.

A satiny caress—like the softest feathers—encompassed me. The air even seemed alive. I'd heard people say that everything around them had disappeared when they'd kissed their special someone, but I had never experienced it until now.

Isaac intertwined his fingers in mine. "Is your father originally from Boston?"

"Boston?" I couldn't imagine where he'd gotten the idea my dad was from Massachusetts. If anything, his accent was more Chicago-meets-Kentucky.

"That's where you said he went to college. Right? I wasn't sure if he was from the Boston area, then."

I honestly didn't remember saying where my parents went to college. Being with Isaac was making my mind all loopy. "No. He's from Illinois, but he wanted to go to school out east. He felt there'd be more inspiration for his paintings. As it turned out, he does better with latex paint and large walls than he did with oils and canvas. Still, my mom used to joke that the magic of Essex County pulled him here." I laughed at the memory and how absurd a statement like that was.

"Well, I'm glad he ended up here."

My cheeks grew warm, hoping he meant what I thought he did. I wanted to hear what he'd say, so I asked, "Why's that?"

"Because if he hadn't, you wouldn't be here."

Those few words were like icing on a cake, sweet and delicious.

The sun singed the harbor as we descended the wooden stairs. I was so elated I could have danced to the Jeep.

There was a sheet of paper in the middle of the kitchen table when I got home. Scrawled across the top of it in red ink read, *Kaylee called,* then below that were three ticks to say, *Three times.* I checked my cell phone. No missed calls. I plopped down onto one of the wooden chairs with a plate of leftover pizza, a bottle of water, and the phone.

"Not so fast," my dad said before I could dial. "The school called."

Uh-oh. I put on my best innocent expression.

He placed his hands on the table and bent forward so that his face was inches from mine. "You've been late to three classes this week."

It was actually four. I wondered which teacher hadn't ratted me out to the attendance office.

"Madison, I don't want you ruining your attendance record."

"I was only a few minutes late. I didn't miss anything."

"That's not the point, young lady." He scowled. "You better not be late again. Do you understand me?"

"Yeah." I understood I'd be grounded if I didn't manage to get to my classes on time, at least for the next few weeks.

After spending the next twenty-gazillion minutes reiterating this to me, he stalked out of the kitchen. I dialed Kaylee, and she answered on the second ring.

"You will not believe what happened," she said. She didn't even say hello. And here I'd thought she'd called to see how my afternoon with Isaac went.

There was silence on the other end of the line. I could practically see Kaylee drumming her fingers on her leg waiting impatiently for a reply.

"What happened?" I asked dutifully and took a bite of pizza.

"A truck nearly turned me and my MINI into scrap metal. That's what happened."

I choked. A girl needs warning not to have her mouth full of food when someone's about to tell her that her best friend could have died. After downing a third of my bottle of water to get the half-chewed food pushed to my stomach, I screamed into the phone, "Omigod! Kaylee, what happened? Are you okay? Why didn't you call me?"

"Because, as it turns out, I'm okay, and Josh was there, and I didn't think they had a phone at the top of the lighthouse."

She knew damn well I meant on my cell phone, but since she was all right I didn't point this out.

"How'd you know where we went?" I asked.

"Josh."

I rolled my eyes. Of course Josh would know. He would have told Isaac where to find me after school. That still didn't tell me what had happened with Kaylee. She didn't weave in and out of traffic, let alone cut in front of eighteen-wheelers.

"Well, spill!"

"Damn car was acting up. Sputtering. Jerking forward. About halfway home it seemed like it was finally running right when *bam*, the steering sticks and the brakes go out. Next thing I know, I'm in the middle of an intersection, and all I can see out my driver side window is the grill of a semi-truck. I should be dead. Seriously Madison, my life flashed before my eyes, and for a moment I—" She paused. "Never mind, forget it."

"You what?"

"It's silly now that I think about it, but for a moment I thought I saw a dark hooded figure. You know, the ones that schlep souls to the afterlife."

"A reaper?" I asked. We were definitely laying off horror films.

"Yeah. But that's totally ridiculous, right?" She let out a nervous laugh. "Because when I looked again, there was a group of kids with skateboards. One of them had on a hooded sweatshirt."

Or it was ridiculous because reapers aren't exactly strolling down Main Street with the living. I kept that thought to myself.

"Kaylee, I'm sure it was one of the boys." When she didn't say anything else about it, I asked, "Where's your car now?"

"Josh had it towed to his house. His guess is the computer shorted out. His uncle's a mechanic. He's going to have him give it a once-over this weekend."

"Are you okay? Do you want me to come over? I can probably borrow my dad's truck and be there in ten minutes."

"I'm a little shaken, but I'm okay. I'm going to go to bed. Look, Josh's picking me up tomorrow. We'll swing by and get you before school. Okay?"

"Sure. Kaylee?"

"Yeah?"

"Are you sure you're okay? If you need me, I'll ride my bike over if I have to." I was pretty sure it was buried in the garage under my dad's tent and Chase's pitcher's net, behind the cooler, old crates, and other treasures my family no longer used.

"I'm fine. Really. We'll be by at the normal time."

Kaylee hung up. I hadn't gotten to tell her about my afternoon, but that seemed insignificant now.

Chapter 6

Deception

In the morning, two sharp honks let me know my ride had arrived. I grabbed a slice of toast from the table, tousled Chase's hair, and said goodbye to my dad on my way to the front door. With the toast clenched between my teeth, purse slung over my shoulder, and backpack dangling from my elbow, I stepped outside and froze when I saw the deep green Jeep waiting in front of my house.

I had to be a sight, and not in a beautiful goddess way. I looked through a veil of wet hair and tried to straighten my top, bounce my backpack up to my shoulder, and walk with some dignity to the passenger door. I'd forgotten about the toast sticking out of my mouth until I was sitting next to him and went to say hi. I quickly removed it.

"Hi." Isaac fought back a chuckle. "I take it you're not a morning person."

"I was expecting Josh and Kaylee." And I wanted to hit myself in the forehead for saying that out loud.

"Josh told me what happened with Kaylee's car. I hope you don't mind, but I told him I'd pick you up."

"Not at all." My heart danced in my chest to confirm it.

"I was going to ask if you'd like to grab a latte and a muffin or something, but I see you already have breakfast." He indicated with his chin to the toast in my hand.

I looked at the meager piece of wheat toast, opened the door, and tossed it out.

Isaac let out a hearty laugh that wrapped me in its joy. He shifted into drive. "The coffee house it is."

I could get used to Isaac picking me up in the morning. We walked into school hand in hand. We were greeted by several curious stares from our classmates. Isaac didn't seem to notice or care. For me, it marked a step forward in our relationship. It was public, which made it all the more real.

Isaac leaned down and gave me a soft kiss. "I'll see you after school."

I made it to English class with four seconds to spare. Kaylee was already there.

"You should have told me Isaac was picking me up," I scolded. "I would have at least dried my hair."

"I didn't know until Josh drove right by your street. I was going to call you, but my phone's dead, and Josh wouldn't give me his. He insisted I let Isaac surprise you."

I dropped my backpack on the floor and tried to get my bagel out of the bag as quietly as I could while the rest of the class settled into their seats.

"Want half?" I offered to Kaylee.

She stared blankly at my outstretched hand.

"I got you jelly," I added, knowing she never ate a bagel plain. When she continued to watch my hand with intrigue, I said, "Earth to Kaylee?"

She wrinkled her nose and shook her head. I shrugged, guessing she'd already eaten at home.

Sarah Johnson took a seat at the desk in front of Kaylee. "I spoke to Mr. Hoffman." She looked so excited you would have thought he was a jewelry broker and not a farmer. "He'll sell us as many cornstalks and bales of hay as we need for seventy percent off. He even offered to deliver it. I'm going to ask Mrs. Sheppard if her Food classes can do some baking for us. Did you check the props?"

Kaylee and I had been assigned prop-duty with Mark and Ben less than twenty-four hours earlier. I wasn't sure when Miss Sunshine thought we would have had time to check them, and I wanted to know what she drank in the morning, because she had enough energy to fuel the seniors at the old folks' home for a week.

"We're going to check at lunch today," I answered with as much enthusiasm as I could muster before noon. "And I have Mrs. Sheppard next period; I can mention the bake sale to her."

Mr. Chapin called class to order, which left me to enjoy my latte and bagel in peace.

I spoke to Mrs. Sheppard right when I got to second period. Mark was there, a little out of breath, pointing to the stool next to him. I wondered if he had run to second period to get there before I did so he could save me a seat. I sighed and sat down.

"Are you okay?" he blurted.

"Yeah, why?"

"I ran into Paige on my way to class. She told me about Kaylee's car. You guys could have been killed."

"How did Paige know about that?" I asked. It wasn't like Kaylee was advertising to the world that her life had almost ended the previous night.

"I think Isaac told her. I'm not sure. Madison, that car's nothing but a sardine can on wheels. You guys need something safer. Like a truck or a—"

"Tank?" I asked.

Mark looked like he might hyperventilate at any moment. "Yeah."

"First of all, I wasn't in the car with Kaylee. Second, she's fine, and Josh is going to have someone take a look at her car before she drives it again."

"Oh, well, that's good." Mark blushed, apparently embarrassed he didn't have the whole scoop.

I pulled out a pencil and notebook. I wanted to know when Isaac saw Paige. Here I was, falling foolishly head over heels for him, and I might not have been the only one he was dating. I reminded myself that Isaac and I hadn't known each other long enough for me to be in love with him. No. Definitely not. I was in love with the new relationship. I had to be careful or I'd get my heart broken. And Paige would delight in seeing me get crushed. That had to be her plan, to wait for me to need Isaac so much that I didn't want to be without him, and then she'd steal him away from me.

Or maybe Isaac knew what he was doing. Maybe he liked to have two girls crazy about him. Maybe it made him feel superior. He had to like me, though. Why else would he pick me up for school?

Mark tapped my arm.

"What?" I snapped but then forced a smile. It wasn't Mark's fault I had issues.

"I said that Ben and I got to school early. We checked last year's props, and with a little paint and some twine we'll be all set."

I flicked my hair out of my eyes and asked, "Twine?"

"The scarecrow's been decapitated. We'll have to stitch its head back on."

I nodded, and because I had to get my mind off Isaac and Paige, I said, "Sarah spoke to Mr. Hoffman, and he's giving us a great price on the cornstalks and hay, and I just asked Mrs. Sheppard about helping out. She's more than happy to. She figures if all her classes bake cookies a day or two before the festival we'll have more than enough for the bake sale."

"Great."

I actually welcomed the test in Foods that day. It meant I didn't have to talk anymore and didn't have time to think about anything but the questions.

Third period afterward was torturously long because I was dying to get to History. I needed to talk to Kaylee. I needed her to tell me I was letting my imagination get the better of me, that Paige wasn't waiting for me to be comfortable in my relationship with Isaac just to steal him away. I needed to hear that Isaac wasn't a jerk. She might even know how Isaac felt about me — that is, if he'd said something to Josh, who in turn would have told Kaylee. God, this was turning into middle school again.

I marched into History, glad to see Kaylee.

"Has Josh said anything about Isaac?" I plopped down in the hard plastic chair and dug in my backpack until I found my History book and pen. "Kaylee?"

Kaylee sat perfectly still, her back straight, hands on her book, and eyes on the chalkboard.

I rested my hand on hers. "Kaylee? Are you okay?"

Mechanically, she turned to face me.

She was really scaring me. I inched my desk closer to hers and asked, "What is it?"

She shook her head. "Nothing. I'm fine. What did you say?"

But I only saw a ghost of the friend I knew behind those deep brown eyes. "Nothing. You sure you're okay?"

"Yeah."

Mrs. Parris told everyone to listen up, then droned on about the Civil War. Until Kaylee's blood-curdling scream startled half the class, including me.

"Kaylee," Mrs. Parris said. "What is the matter with you?"

Kaylee was crouched on top of her chair staring at her backpack, which was on the floor between us. "Get away from me!"

"Kaylee Bishop, that is quite enough," Mrs. Parris demanded. "Get down from there!"

Kaylee screamed another earsplitting cry in response.

I watched in horror along with the rest of my History class. Kaylee continued to stare at her backpack, shrieking loud, piercing screams all of Essex County could hear, and seeing something no one else did. Books, papers, and pens landed on the floor with thuds and clanks as she shoved them aside and kicked the chair away in her haste to scramble on top of her desk. The chair's metal legs screeched as it skidded several inches across the tile, and Kaylee looked at it as if it was on fire.

Mrs. Parris pushed her way out of the room through a throng of students who had already arrived from other classrooms. They gasped at the sight of a hundred-and-ten-pound junior crouched like a cat on top of a desk, screaming as if her life depended on someone, anyone, helping her.

Kaylee pointed frantically at the History book in front of me, shouting what sounded like "Madison, give me the book!" but I wasn't sure. As I watched my best friend on top of that desk, I wasn't sure of anything.

Paige snickered and handed Kaylee her book instead. Kaylee swatted at the imaginary fire or thing or whatever she thought was in front of her. Her short brown hair hung in her eyes. When the book slipped from her hand, she frantically looked for another. My eyes caught shy Natalie Parker's tear-filled ones while several other students snickered.

Emma went to hand Kaylee another book. This snapped me out of my stupor. I jumped up and knocked the book from Emma's hands, sending it flying across the room.

"Stop it!" I screamed to every laughing jerk in the room before facing Kaylee. With both hands held out to help her, I said, "Kaylee, come down from there."

Kaylee hopped on top of her desk like a frightened bird trying to escape. I was afraid she'd fall off.

"Please, Kaylee, let me help you." I ignored the warm tears that streaked my face and took a step closer. Kaylee's eyes darted all around me as her whole body shook. I could hear Josh yelling for others to get out of his way.

"Kaylee, can you hear me?" I asked. "It's okay, I'm here."

Kaylee sprang backward, evidently forgetting she was crouched atop a three-by-four-foot perch. I lunged toward her, knowing there was no way I could keep her from falling, but Josh caught her and pulled her to him. His muscular arms pinned her to his chest.

My gaze met Josh's golden brown eyes. Fear and confusion penetrated his, as if to ask, *What happened?*

"Get them off of me!" Kaylee kicked both legs. Josh held her tighter.

I didn't know what I was supposed to get off her, but I brushed the imaginary intruders from her jeans and arms. All the while, Josh whispered in her ear, "It's all right, babe, I got you now."

Finally, I combed my fingers through her tangled web of hair, brushing it away from her eyes, and rested my forehead against hers. "You're okay. I promise."

Mrs. Parris came back with Mr. Stoughton, the Economics teacher and an ex-football player.

"You got her?" Mr. Stoughton asked, almost as if to say that if Josh didn't, he would.

Mrs. Parris put a shaky hand on Josh's shoulder. "We better get her to the nurse."

Josh nodded. With his arms still wrapped around Kaylee, he guided her out of the classroom. I pretended not to see the numb expressions around me and grabbed mine and Kaylee's things before following the odd procession into the hall. The other students were back in their classrooms. The click of Mrs. Parris's heels stopped just outside the doorway, leaving us to be enveloped in an eerie silence.

In the nurse's office, they tried to get Kaylee to lie down. They wanted to speak to Josh and me in private, but they wouldn't get the chance. Kaylee trembled each time Josh let go of her. It was like he was the glue holding her together, the person keeping her from screaming and jumping on more furniture. Kaylee needed me too; she held my hand so tightly I thought my bones would break. Tears stained both our faces.

"What did she take?" Principal Douglas asked.

While I didn't know what was wrong with Kaylee, I did know one thing. "She doesn't do drugs."

Principal Douglas wiped the sweat from his forehead with a handkerchief and sighed. "I know she's your friend, but we can't help her if we don't know what she took."

Kaylee spoke, the first words since we'd left the classroom, only she sounded more like a parrot than a girl in control. "I don't do drugs."

Josh smoothed the hair away from her forehead and kissed the top of her head. "She's not on anything."

Principal Douglas pressed on. "Look at her. She's shaking like a leaf, she's clammy, and she can barely talk. Maybe she's a closet addict."

"No. She's not," Josh and I replied at the same time.

I didn't need our principal telling me what Kaylee was; I could see for myself, and even though I knew he was trying to help, he was making me angry.

Two men in blue EMT uniforms walked in, one holding a black leather bag. The taller of the two knelt down in front of Kaylee and shined a light in her eyes.

"Pupils are normal." He proceeded to take her blood pressure, which was elevated. Her temperature was normal. He stood back up. "She's not showing the common symptoms of someone who's under the influence. We'll take her to the hospital. I'm sure they'll want to do blood work."

I could have told them what the blood work was going to show. Nothing. Something else was wrong; why didn't they see that?

"I'll get the stretcher," the second paramedic said.

"I can walk." Kaylee stood.

Josh and I followed her lead, our fingers laced through hers. She trembled. Josh switched which hand he used to hold hers and wrapped his arm around her waist for support.

The paramedics exchanged looks. After a moment, the first nodded.

Kaylee pulled Josh and me closer. "Don't leave me."

"Never," Josh whispered to Kaylee. Louder, he said, "We're coming."

I half expected someone to tell us we couldn't go, but no one did.

The taller paramedic led the way out of school. His partner followed. When we reached the ambulance, the first paramedic turned to us. "You'll have to follow us in your car."

Kaylee squeezed my hand even harder. I yelped. Josh placed his hand under her chin and tilted her face up to his. "We will be right behind you. I promise."

She nodded and let the paramedic help her into the ambulance.

At the hospital, a pert nurse stopped us just outside of Kaylee's examining room and asked, "You are?"

"Her brother and sister," I replied quickly, hoping if she thought we were related to Kaylee she wouldn't make us stay in the waiting room. It worked.

Kaylee's parents arrived shortly after us.

The whole afternoon was surreal. Kaylee kept a tight grip on either Josh's or my hand at all times. Her eyes never stopped roaming the room. They ran test after test, but wouldn't tell us anything. It was unnerving, so Josh and I resorted to eavesdropping on her parents' conversation.

"The MRI didn't show any abnormalities," we heard her father saying to her mother, "and the initial blood work came back negative. Her doctor is wondering if she's having some type of post trauma from her near-death experience with the semi."

There was a pause, and then her mother blew her nose and asked the question that was on the tip of my tongue. "Can that happen?"

"I don't know," her father replied. "The chief of medicine still believes it's some type of drug."

Josh and I kept the promise we'd made to Kaylee at school: we didn't leave her alone. We sat in stiff hospital chairs as she rested, eyes closed. For a few minutes, she actually appeared to be getting better. Then her eyes popped open, and fear overtook her face.

"Get them off me!" Kaylee pushed the cover away from her. "Help me!"

Josh and I brushed and patted and swatted at the unseen. We wanted to help her, but there seemed to be no way how. The doctor came in with two burly orderlies. The orderlies held Kaylee down while the doctor slammed a needle into her butt. Kaylee went limp.

Now she was on drugs.

After that, the doctor insisted Josh and I go home. The sedative would make Kaylee sleep. He felt that if it were something she had taken, it would be out of her system by morning. He assured us they'd take good care of her. With no other choice, Josh drove me home.

It took me forever to fall asleep. Around two, I was jarred awake by Kaylee's screams, only to realize it was a dream. It seemed so real. After that, I slept lightly, too afraid of what my imagination had in store for me.

I woke Friday morning in need of aspirin and a shower, which I had respectively.

Josh picked me up a little after eight. We had no intention of going to school.

"Isaac said to tell you he'd meet up with you later," Josh said. "He's going to talk to Kaylee's second and third period teachers."

I nodded. "I don't get it, Josh. She was fine in English yesterday. What could have happened in just a few hours?"

"I'm not sure." Josh ran a hand through his wet mop of black hair. "But Kaylee didn't do this to herself."

"You think someone did this to her on purpose? Like drugged her or something?"

"I'm going with *something*," Josh mumbled in a low growl.

Between the lack of sleep and trying to make sense of the previous day, my head hurt so badly it was buzzing like a swarm of angry bees. Kaylee had to be better. She just had to be.

"I'll bet she's fine this morning," I said with forced confidence. "Let's stop at the coffee house on the way to the hospital. A mocha always cheers her up."

We walked down the sterile halls of the hospital, armed with three large coffees and a bag of muffins. Josh and I had managed to convince ourselves everything would be back to normal. Kaylee would be sitting up in bed, smiling at us.

We couldn't have been more wrong. My latte nearly slipped from my grip when I saw the black straps around Kaylee's wrists.

A nurse, who had been adjusting the drip on the IV, whispered, "She had a slight setback."

"Setback?" I choked out. "What type of setback gets a person strapped to her bed?"

Josh set his and Kaylee's coffee on the small tray near the window. "What happened?"

"She woke around two, screaming. When we came into her room, she was standing on the bed, hitting the wall and bed frame with her pillow." The nurse patted Kaylee's hand. "The straps are just a precaution. We don't want her to injure herself."

So much for normal.

I fixed the collar on Kaylee's pink pajamas and untangled a few strands of her hair that were caught in the clasp of the onyx necklace. Josh pushed a couple of chairs closer to the bed before he leaned over and kissed her forehead. She opened her eyes and squeezed our hands.

"Hey." I swallowed the lump that had formed in my throat. "How are you doing?"

Kaylee gave a sad sort of smile. She squeezed our hands again and closed her eyes. The beep of the heart monitor was steady. Josh and I, unsure if she was resting or asleep, talked about anything we could think of, hoping it would bring back our Kaylee. I drank my latte, praying the caffeine would chase away the pounding in the back of my head. Josh and I picked at the muffins, more for something to do than because we were hungry.

Her parents came into the room, carrying Styrofoam cups of coffee from the hospital cafeteria. Her mother's brunette hair lay flat against her head; dark shadows lined her eyes. Her father's salt and pepper hair stuck out like a shaggy dog's. Their clothes were wrinkled. They had clearly spent the night at the hospital.

We took turns staying with Kaylee. I preferred when she slept, and I hated myself for that, but when Kaylee was awake, her eyes roamed the room, eventually locking onto some unseen force, and her heart would begin to race.

The doctors still didn't know what was wrong with her. She wasn't sick. I didn't know how I knew that, but I did. I could feel that much.

Chapter 7

Searching

It was late afternoon when Josh dropped me off at my house. I called Isaac, but he didn't answer his phone. My dad tried to get me to join him and Chase for dinner, but I couldn't eat. I was too worried about Kaylee.

Saturday turned out to be a repeat of Friday.

By Sunday morning, I wanted answers. I needed to do something to help Kaylee. So I decided to research her symptoms myself. I turned on the computer in the corner of our family room before going into the kitchen to grab a cola from the fridge.

"Don't spill that on the keyboard," Dad said.

"I won't."

I twisted off the top and took a long swig while I walked back to the family room. I sat in our old swivel desk chair, pulled my knees to my chest, and waited for the computer to finish booting up. It was at times like these I wished we had a newer computer with a high-speed connection.

I really didn't know where to begin, so I started to type in the illnesses I'd overheard while at the hospital. Each one resulted in thousands of possible links. I quickly found which sites offered the most concise explanation of the diseases along with symptoms and common treatments; I couldn't help wondering how doctors kept it all straight. A couple hours must have gone by, and I was no closer to helping Kaylee than the doctors were.

"Try panic attacks," Dad said from behind me.

Panic disorder came up.

My dad read over my shoulder. "The symptoms match."

"But the causes don't," I said, deflated. "Besides, her parents would know if her family had a history of panic disorder, and Kaylee is the least stressed person on the planet."

"Keep searching." He patted my shoulder. "You'll find something. I have to get your brother dressed."

I just kept clicking on different links. One led me to *mental illness*, and I started to check the history of these diseases. There was data going back to the sixteen hundreds.

All of the articles mentioned witchcraft. One of them included a picture of two girls, maybe twelve or fourteen, dressed in nightgowns like those worn in the seventeenth century. One of the girls crouched in a corner pulling at her hair. The other stood on a bed, apparently trying to climb the wall. Their eyes were haunted. Either one of them could have been Kaylee.

The caption below the picture read:

A properly cast curse will leave its victim defenseless and often a danger to herself. Medicine is frequently given to sedate the victim.

I followed a link to another site. If I believed what I read, a curse was cast of the dark, drawing from the powers of evil, costing the spell-giver a piece of their soul.

I clicked on link after link. Passages seemed to leap from the screen:

There are two types of witches: the ones who call upon outside forces to give them power and the natural witch whose powers lie dormant within them until they are awakened.

And,

Natural witches are rarely evil and have the ability to recognize one another through simple touch.

I kept reading, thinking that this just couldn't be real. Magic was a trick of the eye. A skill that used illusion to give the appearance that the impossible was possible. As I read on, though, my skepticism wavered. The sites I found had me thinking there was much more to magic than pulling a rabbit out of a hat. I'd heard that people only use a fraction of their brain. What if someone could tap into that unused portion and harness power from within themselves, and then use that power to do their bidding? Hadn't I woken determined to do whatever I could to help Kaylee? Maybe that meant believing in the obscure.

Besides, Kaylee had gone from happy and confident to miserable and schizophrenic in minutes. Her symptoms certainly fit the actions of a person who has been cursed.

I drank in the pictures and the words with a hunger that grew into vengeance. Believing more and more that I'd found what ailed Kaylee, I wondered how this could have happened and who would wish something so evil on her.

Several sites warned about witches who brought destruction and bad fortune wherever they went, claiming these witches would draw to them the people they hurt. Another site felt a witch who used her powers carelessly would be easy for other witches to recognize. Power would leak from their very pores and bleed into every word they spoke, tainting the air with magic that could be tasted and felt.

The more I read, the more I believed people really could have powers. Something about the idea resonated through me. It felt exactly right.

Eventually, it was as if the words screamed at me: *souls condemned, elements, the power of three times three, talismans, hexes, circle, sigil…*

The last site had my heart pumping:

Test the powers within you with a simple spell.

I slid the mouse up and to the left. The cursor followed — highlighting the picture of a printer — and I clicked on it. Our inkjet woke from sleep mode and churned out the article I'd been reading. I printed a few of the others before shutting it down.

If witchcraft was real and someone did curse Kaylee, they were going to pay. One way or another I would see to that.

The steady grumble of my dad's old lawn mower could be heard coming from the front yard. Good for me, because I needed a few things from the kitchen, and there was no way he'd let me take seasonings, stemware, and cutlery upstairs without asking me what I was doing. I already knew how crazy I'd look.

With the stack of newly printed papers clenched in my hand, I raced to the kitchen. Chase was pulling a full gallon of milk out of the fridge, clutching the flimsy plastic container with both hands.

"Let me get that." I managed to hook a finger under the handle before he dropped it.

Chase's cups were in the same cabinet as the stemware. The spell called for a chalice, but we were fresh out. I set one of my mom's delicate wine glasses on the counter and grabbed a Lightning Mc-Queen mug for Chase.

"Is Kaylee better yet?" he asked.

"I hope so." I wasn't about to tell my six-year-old brother the doctors didn't even know what was wrong with her.

"I made her a card." He pointed to the table. It looked like an art store had exploded in that corner of the kitchen. There were as many pieces of brightly colored construction paper stuck to the top of the table as were glued to the white paper he used for the base of his card. Crayons were everywhere. His plastic zigzag scissors were on the floor under his chair.

"She's going to love it," I said.

"I bet she ate at that hotdog stand near the pet store. Remember how sick I got from their food?"

"I do." Chase had thrown up half the night after eating a cheese dog and fries there.

I handed him the cup of milk, put the gallon back in the fridge, then rummaged around in the silverware drawer for a knife. I decided the long bread knife was overkill, yet a butter knife didn't seem to have any mystical power to it. I needed something that resembled a small dagger. The carving knife drying in the dish rack near the sink caught my eye.

I'd just wrapped my fingers around the black handle when Chase asked, "What are you doing?"

What was I doing? Preparing an altar to perform magic? Like it was real. Like people went around blinking or pointing a finger or waving a wand and *poof*, whatever they were thinking at that very moment came true. If life were that easy, there'd be no need to work for anything.

Lack of sleep finally caught up with me. I slid the knife into the drawer. While I had spent hours surfing the Internet looking for a magical cure, Kaylee was alone, laid up in the hospital. Nice friend I was.

"I gotta go," I said to Chase before racing to the front door.

Chase trailed behind me. "Are you going to see Kaylee? Can I come?"

"Not this time."

He frowned. Instead of arguing, though, he held out his hand. "Can you give her this?"

"Yeah." I took the colorful card from him, snatched my dad's keys off the small table near the stairs, and dashed outside.

Hoping Dad didn't need to go anywhere that day, I waved my arms over my head to get his attention. He cut the engine on the lawn mower and walked over to me.

"Can I borrow your truck?" I asked.

He looked past me at his pick-up truck. It was one of those extended cab deals with a shiny silver lockbox that held his tools and a hard cover over the bed to hide the ladders and poles and other bulky supplies Dad used on a regular basis. The thing was a monster and his entire business on wheels. And I wasn't the greatest at parking it.

"Just be careful and park away from other cars."

"I will."

Kaylee had to be suffering from a type of panic disorder. It was the only explanation for her sudden outbursts. She wasn't getting better because she was scared, and who wouldn't be scared not knowing what was happening to them? The article Dad and I had found said that a person who suffers from panic disorders often worries about when the next attack will occur. Kaylee was probably consumed with fear, wondering when her symptoms would flare up again. The pressure to remain calm and in control would cause anyone to lose it. If Kaylee understood what was happening to her, she would be able to relax. She'd get better.

I laughed out loud at how simple it was. How the doctors were missing the obvious. If they'd just stop sedating her and take the time to address the problem, Kaylee would be home thinking about homework and the festival and, of course, the guys.

I turned up the radio and sang along. The sun peeked out from behind puffy white clouds, promising a bright and cheery day. I should have grabbed a deck of cards before I left the house. Kaylee had to be sick of being cooped up in a sterile room with nothing to do.

I pulled into a parking space at the back of the visitors' lot, well clear of any other vehicles to keep Dad happy, and once inside the hospital, I made a quick stop at the gift shop. Minutes later I was riding the cramped elevator to the seventh floor, the latest copy of *Cosmopolitan* tucked under my arm and Raisinets and Jelly Bellies tucked in my purse. I wished I'd thought to grab a pint of Chunky Monkey ice cream—Kaylee's favorite.

The doors slid open, revealing a tiny waiting area. Four navy blue vinyl chairs sat across from public restrooms. The corridor to my left led to patients suffering from different neurological disorders, which I knew from a conversation I'd overheard the other day on my way up. Kaylee was straight through the waiting area, down a similar corridor. I'd walked this route so many times in the past few days, I could have found her room with my eyes closed. I hoped this day would be the last time.

A nurse in a light pink lab coat smiled as I walked by her. When I turned the corner, I saw a guy with short dark hair leaving Kaylee's room, which was at the far end of the hall. He went in the opposite direction. I squinted, trying to get a better look at him.

"Isaac!" I half yelled.

The guy didn't even flinch. He was tall, wearing faded jeans and a dark sweatshirt. I couldn't see his face, but the back of his head really looked like Isaac's.

I picked up my pace and called his name again. A nurse poked her head out of one of the rooms, her nose scrunched up in a disapproving manner.

"Sorry," I mumbled as I rushed past her.

The guy was in the elevator when I reached the end of the corridor, his shoulder the only visible part of him.

"Wait! Hold the—"

A piercing scream echoed from behind me, bouncing off the bright white walls and stopping me in my tracks. "Kaylee."

Her name had barely made it out of my mouth as I watched the elevator door close. If that *had* been Isaac, he would have rushed back out. No way could he not have heard the frantic cry for help. I bolted back the way I came, reaching Kaylee's room at the same time as a slew of hospital workers, including a burly male security guard.

Kaylee bucked in her bed, back arched, trying to get as much of her body off the mattress as the straps around her wrist would allow.

"Get her doctor!" a nurse yelled over her shoulder. She stood next to Kaylee's bed, looking afraid to touch her. Mrs. Bishop was on the other side of the bed, face as white as a ghost and eyes red from the tears that just wouldn't come anymore. The security guard went to take a step forward, but I jumped in front of him, pushing the nurse aside on my way to Kaylee.

"These straps are just scaring her more!" I screamed.

What was wrong with them? Since when do the people who are supposed to heal the sick resort to tying patients to beds? The whole situation infuriated me.

"Kaylee, it's okay." I grabbed her shoulders and looked deep into her eyes. "You're okay. I promise." I ran my hand over her bed, smoothing the sheet and moving the covers out of the way. "Calm down so I can get the straps off you."

The nurse started to protest, but I shot her a look that dared her to try and stop me. Anger trickled through my limbs, giving me the feeling that I could take her and the security guard if they messed with me. Kaylee's doctor entered the room with another nurse behind him. The nurse carried a long needle and a bottle of clear liquid. My gaze met her doctor's.

"She's fine." I assured him. Kaylee had settled back onto her bed, her fists balled around the sheet. "Waking up this way just startled her." I tugged at a strap to show what I meant.

The doctor walked over to the bed. Kaylee grabbed my hand and squeezed. I bit back a yelp from her pressure while the doctor checked her pupils and pulse. Satisfied with what he saw, he directed the others to leave. Mrs. Bishop still hadn't moved.

"Help me get these things off her." I removed the leather binding around Kaylee's left wrist while her mom worked on the one on her right.

"How'd you know what was wrong?" Mrs. Bishop asked.

"If you woke up in a strange room tied to a bed, wouldn't you scream?"

"I suppose."

"Don't you think that all this security is scaring your daughter? How is she supposed to believe that she's okay if everyone is treating her like a psych patient? This is Kaylee we're talking about."

Mrs. Bishop didn't say anything, but she did free Kaylee's other arm.

"I'll stay with her," I offered. "Why don't you go home for a couple hours, grab something to eat and change."

Mrs. Bishop had on the same navy pants and cream sweater she'd been wearing Saturday. Dark bags haunted her eyes. She ran her fingers through her chopped hair, her nails snagging on a few knots. "I could use a shower."

"Kaylee will be fine."

Kaylee, who seemed to be absorbing the conversation, nodded.

I walked Mrs. Bishop to the door and whispered, "I won't leave her alone."

I then plopped down on the bed, purposely bumping Kaylee's hip with mine. She scooted over.

"What's happening to me?"

I pulled the covers up to our waists.

"You've had a rough few days," I replied. "The doctors think that the shock of the near accident with that truck caught up to you. I should have come over that night. I never should have let you be alone."

Kaylee twitched a shoulder. It told me she was more traumatized by the event than she had admitted. I felt horrible for not realizing that before. I was her best friend. I know her better than anyone else. I should have known she needed me. I should have shown up on her doorstep with my pillow and a hug. I wouldn't make that mistake again.

I pulled the card my brother had made out of my purse and handed it to her with the Jelly Bellies. "Chase made this for you."

She looked at the brightly colored get-well wishes, a smile stretching over her face. "Tell him thanks and I love it."

"Will do." I ripped open the box of chocolate-covered raisins. "Want to talk about it?"

Her eyes roamed the room as if checking that we were alone. "I can't," she whispered.

"Maybe if you just tell me everything that happened with the MINI, every last detail, it will help you feel better," I pushed, recalling one of the treatments for schizophrenia is therapy. Letting a person discuss her fears. I could only imagine how terrified Kaylee must have been in an out-of-control car that was no taller than the tires of a big rig.

"It was the weirdest thing. You and I have been all over Massachusetts in the MINI and it's never let us down." She popped a Jelly

Belly into her mouth. "It didn't really want to go at first, you know? I'd press the gas, the engine would rev, but I wasn't moving any faster. Josh just happened to be behind me when we were leaving school, so he followed me home."

I knew the rest. Her car had sputtered for several minutes before the engine warmed up, and it had seemed to be running like normal. She'd been on the main road when the brakes had gone out and the steering stuck. The MINI had stalled on her in the middle of an intersection. She swore it hadn't rolled to a stop but had abruptly come to a halt. (I was sure that was a matter of perception, but didn't say so. Instead, I gave her leg a gentle squeeze to say it was okay.) The grill of a semi had been kissing the chrome door handle of the car before it was all over. I let Kaylee recount the event in her own words: from the guy in a sports car honking at her for driving twenty under the speed limit to the bugs splattered against the grill of the truck, to not feeling like she was okay until she'd been in Josh's arms. He had been the one to call a tow truck. Last I heard, the MINI was still parked in his driveway.

Kaylee's shoulders relaxed. She stopped looking around the room as if expecting someone to pop up from behind the spare chair. By the time the nurse came to check on her, Kaylee and I were talking about how much homework Mr. Chapin gave. We were laughing and chatting, and it was like old times. The nurse even took the straps out of the room.

Her doctor said that she had to remain at the hospital for the next forty-eight hours for observation to make sure she was really past the worst of it. I knew she was. Right then, sitting on the bed with the rough sheets under the hum of the fluorescent light above her headboard, Kaylee was back to herself.

"You know something?" I inquired, waiting until she asked what before continuing. "You really need a toothbrush and a comb."

"Hah!" Kaylee belted out a laugh, then covered her mouth with her hand. "Why didn't you say something sooner?" She ran to the bathroom.

"Because I was enjoying hanging out too much," I called after her.

I grabbed my cell phone and quickly typed a message to Josh, letting him know the good news about Kaylee's condition. My thumb hovered over *Send* when a loud crash—like the sound of breaking glass—came from the bathroom.

Chapter 8

The Test

Pieces of the bathroom mirror lay scattered on the sink and floor around Kaylee's bare feet. She clenched her arm close to her chest. I stood in the doorway, a hand on each side of the doorframe, gaping at her.

"Are you all right?" I managed to ask, secretly hoping that the mirror somehow jumped off the wall while she was brushing her hair. Then I saw a stream of blood running down her forearm. My eyes traveled up to her bleeding knuckles. I grabbed a towel and wrapped it around her hand. "Did you punch the mirror?"

Kaylee didn't reply.

"What happened?" a voice said from behind us.

We both jumped. Mrs. Bishop couldn't have come back to the hospital at a worst time. She missed all the joking and chatting. She didn't get to see her daughter acting like a carefree teenager.

"I don't know," I admitted.

And just like that, Kaylee was back to square one. The doctors ran more tests. A specialist was called in. I was told to go home.

Dad and Chase were tossing a ball in the front yard when I got to the house. I felt dejected. I'd failed Kaylee again. I dropped my purse on the floor next to the stairs and trudged to the kitchen, sinking into a chair and giving in to the tears I'd suppressed since her relapse. I'd been so sure she'd simply needed to talk through what was bothering her and she'd be fine.

After a while, there weren't any tears left. I wiped my cheeks dry with the palm of my hand as I opened the refrigerator. I saw the wine glass I'd taken out earlier in my peripheral vision. The articles I'd printed that morning were stacked in a neat pile next to it.

Deep in my heart I knew Kaylee wasn't crazy. Nothing inside of her had snapped as she walked from third period to fourth period. Some outside force was at play, and I planned to find out what it was. As impossible as witchcraft seemed, I had to try it.

Chase's voice drifted in the front door, reminding me that I wasn't as alone as I felt. If I didn't move quickly, I'd be trying to explain what I was doing to my dad, and there was no way he'd understand my desperation.

Without wasting another moment, I grabbed the wine glass, papers, a knife, a lunch plate, and a container of salt from the cabinets. In the hall closet, I found a shoebox filled with candles and added a bag of white tea lights to the pile. Next, I sprinted up the stairs and into my room, dropped everything on my bed, and prepared for my spell.

Resorting to witchcraft. God, I had to be going insane to believe that magic could be the cause of Kaylee's illness.

I went to the bathroom and splashed cold water on my face.

No, crazy was my best friend being afraid of her shadow or thinking she was schizophrenic. It was watching her condition get worse with each day that passed and not being willing to try the unbelievable.

I told my reflection that I was perfectly and undeniably sane.

"Yeah, right," I mumbled. "Sane people always believe they can cast spells."

The website said to find peace within yourself. The hazel eyes that stared back at me were anything but peaceful. Skepticism, confusion, fear, and anger clung to each other in the eyes I saw. Those were the only emotions I had left in me, and they were the only emotions I had to work with. I filled the wine glass halfway with water and went back to my room.

Thankful that the tea lights came in their own casing, I placed them on the carpet in a circle around me. I sat cross-legged in the center of the candles with the rest of the items I'd taken from downstairs beside me and the instructions to the spell in my lap.

I felt ridiculous sitting in my room like this. I took three deep breaths to calm myself.

"The worst thing that can happen is nothing at all," I reminded myself.

I began by setting the plate on the carpet in front of me. The wine glass, or *chalice*, as the website had referred to it, went to its right. I poured a small pile of salt onto the plate and set the knife and the last candle near the salt.

Next, I was to draw the power within me — if there was any — to the surface. I wasn't sure what that meant, but maybe it was like meditating, concentrating all my thoughts and energy on what I wished for. So I placed my hands palms-up on my knees and closed my eyes. *For Kaylee.* To find out what's going on. To know if someone had intentionally singled her out wanting to hurt her. To find that person and make them fix this.

When I opened my eyes, the air felt thick and tasted of copper. I immediately remembered the Internet site that had said magic could be tasted and felt. In that moment, I knew I had to try my best to cast away all fear and skepticism, to will myself to believe something like this could really work. It had to.

I leaned closer to the items in front of me, whispered, "Ignite," and blew gently on the candle, which remained as unlit as it had been when I'd started. I began again, breathing in deeply and forcing myself to believe.

But just in case my breath alone wouldn't be enough to light the candles, I decided to light the first one the old-fashioned way, the mortal way. I struck a wooden match against the black strip, lighting it, and held its flame to the candle on the plate.

"Ignite."

The wick caught fire and then one by one the candles around me lit without the need of the match. Their flames were soft at first, but grew in strength like the fury bottled up within me. They reached upward in bright determination. It was all the proof I finally needed to accept that magic existed. That people could be witches. That someone had cursed my best friend and they would pay.

The flames of the candles licked the air as if it were gasoline, gaining in power and size until I was trapped in the circle I'd created. Until I was afraid I'd burn down the house.

My fear was back. How had the Internet described it? *Threefold.* That was the word I'd seen. My fear was back threefold. I blew at the candle on the plate, hoping if I extinguished it the others would go out as well. Only, when the flame of that candle was doused, the others grew. Their heat had me dripping sweat and gasping for air that wasn't there. Even with the immediate threat of being burned alive, I couldn't get myself to move. Who would help Kaylee now? Through the confusion of my panic, I heard one word, spoken loud and strong and with authority.

"Obliterate!"

Isaac stood in the doorway, his arm raised, the palm of his hand facing me. Power poured from him, smothering the fire around me, and with his power came the oxygen my lungs craved. The smell of copper was gone, replaced with the sweet scent of vanilla and spearmint that was Isaac.

My chest heaved as if I'd run a hundred miles. Isaac's eyes penetrated me, leaving me feeling vulnerable and a little silly. He stepped into my room and swept his hand sideways. The candles that formed my circle flew to the wastebasket in the corner of my room. The plate, glass, and other items vanished, reappearing on my dresser. He closed the door behind him.

My face was not only wet with sweat, but with tears as well. I'd just seen with my own eyes that magic was real, but I still couldn't believe it. Isaac trembled visibly; his hands balled into fists at his sides like someone trying their best to control their temper. I felt like I had to say something. Since I was still trying to process what had happened, I settled for the only other thing I could think of.

"My dad isn't going to like us being in my room with the door closed."

"He sent me up here to try to cheer you up."

"Oh."

He spoke his next words slowly, each with emphasis. "You cannot practice magic when your emotions are running wild."

His comment cleared the fog in my brain, allowing the recent events to fall into place like the pieces of a puzzle.

I'd been so stupid.

Every blasted shock that happened when Isaac touched me. The hints that Gloucester had a history. The weight of the air around me when I was with him. He was a witch, and he knew about his powers. He would have felt mine and known what it was. The night of the bonfire came back to me. When his hand had brushed the back of my neck, he'd begun to ask, "Are you——?" only I hadn't let him finish his sentence. My response would have told him I hadn't known about my powers, and there was only one reason not to mention them to me. He was one of the witches the Internet had warned about. One who drew others to him. It wasn't love I felt for Isaac, it was his powers pulling me to him. His magic casting a spell over me. I'd been such a fool.

"You," I accused. "How could you?" I lunged for him, pounding my fists on his chest. "Kaylee doesn't deserve this. She doesn't have any powers. How could you do this to her?"

Isaac grabbed my wrists. His magic wrapped around me like thick ropes tying my arms tightly to my chest and binding my legs together so that I couldn't move.

"Madison, calm down. Your father will hear you."

"I will not calm down!" I screamed, figuring I'd better get the words out before he sealed my mouth shut with invisible tape. "What were you doing at the hospital today? What did you do to Kaylee?"

"I was trying to help her."

"Right. That's why she became hysterical seconds after you left her room." I struggled to move my leg so that I could knee him in the groin. It didn't work.

"She was dreaming, squirming like a fish out of water while I was there. I couldn't help her, and I couldn't stand to see her like that any longer. I went home to read through more books, hoping to find a counter spell."

"You're lying!"

Mrs. Bishop would have told me if Kaylee had been thrashing in her sleep. She wouldn't have let me undo the straps around her wrists. She wouldn't have left the hospital to go home and take a shower.

Isaac covered my mouth with his hand instead. "Listen to me. I didn't hurt Kaylee. You have to calm down."

I bit his hand. He swore and yanked it away. My unseen bonds gripped me tighter.

Isaac glanced at the door. With a wave of his hand I became weightless vapors. I tried to scream, but there wasn't enough left of me to form the sound. A moment later, I was sitting on my bed next to Isaac, his arm around my shoulders. It all had happened too fast. Then the door to my room swung open, and my dad was there, panting.

"I heard a scream?" he said. "Are you okay?"

Isaac patted my shoulder. "She broke down talking about Kaylee."

I opened my mouth to scream *LIAR*, but the word came out gargled. I glared at Isaac. He kissed my forehead. I would have smacked him if I could have moved.

"We all understand," Isaac said. "It's okay."

I pursed my lips and squinted. *Bastard*, I thought, hoping he could hear the unspoken word.

My dad dragged his hand through his hair. "Why does it smell like something's burning in here?"

Isaac nodded toward the nightstand where a single two-wick candle burned. The box of matches I'd used earlier was next to it.

"Yeah, well, leave the door open. Okay?" And my dad left. If I wasn't so angry, I might have been scared to be alone with Isaac.

Isaac waited a moment before closing the door halfway with a wave of his hand. He picked up the stack of papers I had printed from my bed. He remained calm—arrogant, in my opinion.

"I see you've embraced your powers," he said.

I would have replied, *Bite me,* if he'd released my voice. I made another fruitless attempt to break free of my bindings.

He scanned a page as he talked. "You're right that Kaylee's been cursed. I could feel its power when I visited the hospital. What I don't understand is how the curse still has the hold on her that it does."

The answer to that question was simple. He was good. He knew how to cast a curse. If I ever regained the use of my hands I was going to claw his eyes out. I closed mine, trying to find my center and the power I had called upon earlier. Maybe if I concentrated hard enough I could set Isaac on fire. When I peeked, he was reading one of the articles. To my disappointment, he wasn't engulfed in flames.

After a minute, his velvet brown eyes looked up at me, and I hated that he still had the power to make my heart beat faster.

"I'm not the one who cursed her."

I followed his gaze back to the paper and saw his finger just above a passage I'd read earlier: *Natural witches are rarely evil and have the ability to recognize one another through simple touch.* Though my thoughts were in chaos, I somehow knew then that Isaac was a natural witch. He didn't feel evil. Not really. And his magic didn't taste evil.

Some of my anger toward him faded, and his spell slipped away. "Why should I believe you?" I could finally ask.

"Madison, you know I'm not the bad guy."

I knew I didn't want him to be the bad guy. But he had a past, one I knew little about. He had enemies, or at least one he'd gotten in a fight with before moving to Gloucester. The weird events around town, the thing with the MINI, and Kaylee's panic attacks had all started after we'd met Isaac. He'd have to do more than tell me he hadn't hurt my best friend for me to believe I had the wrong person.

"If you're so innocent, then why didn't you tell me about these powers, about being a witch?"

"Because you may not have wanted them, and once you know what you are, you have little choice but to embrace them."

"That's stupid. How can I choose if I don't know my options?"

"Some people never know, and they live long, happy, normal lives." He pinched the bridge of his nose, his eyes locked on the ceiling. "Had I known you were going to embrace your powers with anger and vengeance, I would have told you. You could have killed yourself."

"I didn't embrace them with anger and vengeance." I'd just tapped into those feelings to help kick-start the spell.

His jaw set tight. His voice strained. "The only thing coming from you was negative emotions. Don't deny it. Your magic tasted like old pennies. You have to promise me you won't do any more spells until you're shown how."

Seeing as I had almost roasted myself alive, it was a promise I could live with.

"I—"

Isaac put his finger to my lips. "From this moment forward, your promise is your word. With your powers awakened, your word is binding. Be sure to mean what you say."

I swallowed audibly. "You mean if I said to my dad, 'Cross my heart and hope to die,' and I'm lying, I might actually die."

"That's exactly what I mean."

I studied Isaac's face for any sign that he was joking, waiting for him to say, *Of course you won't drop dead.* He never did. All I saw was sincerity, understanding, and wisdom I might never have myself. Either he was a very good actor, or he was telling the truth. The calm serenity I'd felt at the lighthouse was back, and it encircled me like a down blanket. I realized I had always been able to feel Isaac's magic.

I reached out and touched his hand. The shock of electricity—power—didn't surprise me this time. The tingly sensation I'd felt whenever Isaac touched me traveled up my arm and through my body.

"Do you feel that?" I asked.

"I've been able to feel your magic since the day we met."

"Why is it I don't always feel the pinch of electricity?"

"That would be our powers colliding. After the night at the bonfire, I've been using my magic to hide it from you."

That was why he always paused before he kissed me. It made sense. I nodded. "But you couldn't hide it completely. I could still feel your magic trickle through me."

He raised his free hand up and smoothed my hair. His touch was warm, minus any jolt of power. "I didn't want to block everything. I've been careful to only withdraw enough of my powers to keep us from getting shocked."

And then I wondered again how much of what I felt when I was with Isaac was our powers playing with my head. Maybe what I deemed as affection was nothing more than magic twisting my thoughts into lust. I wanted him to be telling me the truth. That he was a good witch. That he didn't use magic to harm the people around him. That once Kaylee was better, we'd go back to being a couple. While my heart begged me not to pursue the conversation, my mouth spilled my fears.

"That means what I feel when I'm with you isn't real. It's just a trick of our magic making me, I don't know, believe I feel one way when I don't."

Isaac's smile reached his eyes. "Oh, I'd guess our attraction to each other is some sort of magic, but nothing to do with our powers messing with our heads."

He'd said *our*. That meant I wasn't the only who had fallen quickly for someone I'd just met.

Isaac leaned closer to me, but I pulled away. There was one more thing I needed from him before I'd let myself become too excited.

"Prove to me that you didn't put Kaylee in the hospital, and I promise I won't use my magic until I'm shown how."

He inclined his head. "Deal."

A tinge of guilt overtook me. As I sat arguing with Isaac—possibly the only person who could help me—Kaylee remained in the hospital, held captive by a curse the doctors could do nothing about.

"What do we do now?" I asked.

"I prove to you that I'm telling the truth, and then we find out how Kaylee is being trapped by the curse. Once we know that, we can break it. Then we find who's targeting her." Isaac stood, pulling me to my feet with him. When I didn't willingly follow, he added, "I promise what I'm about to show you will be all the proof you need."

It was a bold statement to make, only there didn't seem to be any consequence if he was lying.

"Cross your heart and hope to die?" I asked in a teasing tone, but if we really were bound to our word and he was on the up and up, then he'd repeat the words back to me.

His expression hardened: a man on a mission or a man about to hang himself. I waited.

"Cross my heart and hope to die." He even drew an X over his chest.

I figured he had a damn good card up his sleeve, and I couldn't wait to find out what it was. "Let's go."

Chapter 9

Truth

By the time we reached Isaac's house, the sky had ripped open. Rain pelted the hood of the Jeep, bouncing off the metal with a hollow *ting*. I covered my head with my arms and ran to the front door behind him.

Once inside, Isaac shook his head, and a spray of water flew off his hair. We wiped our shoes on the front rug and headed to the basement stairs. A light had been left on; its amber glow seeped toward the stairs. Vanilla and spice beckoned to me as it had the last time I'd been here. Isaac led the way, and as he passed the first nook in the stone wall, its candle ignited.

I stopped to stare at it, then at the next and the next as each candle awakened at his passing. When Isaac reached the bottom of the stairs, he glanced over his shoulder and asked, "Are you coming?"

I descended the remaining steps to see Josh sitting on the floor with books all around him.

My gaze met Isaac's. Josh knew what Isaac was. He knew about magic and curses and what ailed Kaylee. He had to or he wouldn't have been there. By the amount of reading material sprawled around the room, it was obvious they were searching for a cure. I didn't know what to say. Isaac broke the silence.

"We good?"

I nodded.

"We're three strong now," he said to Josh. "You find anything?"

"No. There are too many curses with the same symptoms. It'll take forever to perform each of the counter spells." Josh looked at me. "Hi, Madison. I take it Isaac explained everything to you?"

"Not yet." Isaac touched the iron ring that circled the walls. In response, the ring glowed orange for a couple of seconds. A low hum reverberated through the room. "I'm reinforcing my protection spells, or *wards*, to use the correct magical term," he explained. "I really couldn't've built this room better if I did it myself. The stone floor and brick walls are all made from the earth and help maintain the strength of the spells. The iron ring distributes it evenly around the room, not to mention keeps unwanted visitors out."

"Unwanted visitors?" I repeated and wondered, if school had an iron ring around it, would it keep Paige out?

"Some forces are allergic to iron," Josh said, closing the book in front of him.

"Of course," I muttered, not really understanding and still waiting for my new knowledge about the powers to fully sink in. "Are you expecting trouble? Is that why you have the, what did you call them?"

"Wards," Isaac said. "No, I wasn't expecting trouble. Most of them were for practice."

"And now?" I asked, not missing his use of past tense.

"Now they will be put to the test. My intention ward will stop anyone with ill intent from being able to come down here."

"Wait," I interrupted. "How can a spell know what someone is planning and then stop them from marching right into your room and doing it?"

Isaac took a moment to answer. "Say you wanted to steal from me. The ward would sense this and put up an invisible barrier. You'd be able to see the stairs, even think there's nothing unusual about them, but you wouldn't be able to cross the threshold. A wall of magic would stop you."

"It'd be like walking into a sliding glass door you didn't realize was closed," Josh added.

I cocked my head to the side as I considered this. "Does it only stop those who have powers?"

Isaac shook his head. "It works on everyone."

"And the other wards?" I asked, fascinated by what magic could do.

"The concealment ward will hide our powers from others. They won't be able to sense our magic. There are a few others as well."

I nodded. It was a lot to absorb in one afternoon, but after witnessing the type of magic Isaac could do, I didn't need to question his ability to cast these wards.

"And you're a witch?" I asked Josh.

"Not as strong as Isaac. Both his parents have powers. My mom doesn't."

I walked over to Josh and placed my hand on his bare arm. Sure enough, a jolt of power, like static electricity, shot into my hand.

I looked back at Isaac. "And your parents practice magic? Like family hocus-pocus time?"

Isaac remained near the wall. I got the feeling he was studying me, trying to gauge my reaction to all of this. "They taught me what I know and are members of a coven in Amesbury. They don't use their powers unless they have to."

"What about Kaylee? Does she have powers?"

Josh shook his head. He looked miserable, and his guilt at not being able to help her coursed through me. It was awful, choking me from the inside.

I hugged myself and took a seat on the edge of the bed. "How long have you known about each other?"

Isaac sat next to me. "Since the day I moved in. The energy in the air when our fathers shook hands was too powerful to ignore. After Josh passed the test of my intention ward, I invited him to add one of his own. It allows him to enter the basement when I'm not here. It also gives him a safe haven, should he ever need one."

The day I'd helped Isaac set up his room, he'd been glad that his mom hadn't liked the paint for the dining room. He'd said it had given him an excuse to get me down here. "Is that why you were happy to have a reason to invite me into your bedroom, to test my intentions?"

Isaac smiled sheepishly. "Past events have taught me to be careful and probably less trusting than most. I had to be sure you weren't pretending not to know about your powers."

There's a test I passed with flying colors. If only English class were that easy.

"Does anyone else I know have powers?" I knew the answer, though, before Isaac even replied. It seemed so obvious now.

"Paige," Isaac said. "And she has little to no control over hiding it. Her powers ooze from her pores like puss from an open wound."

"And someone at the bonfire was using," Josh added. "The air reeked of it."

"Using?" I asked.

"Magic," Isaac explained. "That's what you call it when someone casts a spell."

"Oh. So you mean Paige was using at the bonfire, don't you?"

Isaac shook his head. "She was using when she introduced herself, so I know what her magic feels and smells like. She's not a natural witch, which is probably why her powers reminded me of worms or fish. The magic we smelled later that night, though, made me think of rotten eggs or sulfur. Besides, Paige's powers definitely aren't strong enough to give off the type of energy we felt."

I would have preferred that answer to be, *Yes, it was Paige,* because that would have meant we knew who hurt Kaylee. We could demand she make things right. Once she did, I'd yank out a handful of dark red hair to make myself feel better.

"Does she know about you and Josh?" I asked.

"Me, yes," Isaac replied, "but I don't think she realizes Josh has powers too."

It was a relief to finally have some answers. Isaac's powers had to be the secret behind his throaty laughs and sly smile. They were the reason he chose his words carefully. There was one important question left. "How do we help Kaylee?"

"Josh, Paige, and then you," Isaac said. "It had me wondering how much power is in Gloucester. Most people never discover what they are. Hell, even those who have embraced their powers know they need to keep them a secret. It's not something people wear on their sleeves. It would be the Salem Witch Trials all over again; only this time it would be death by lethal injection instead of hanging or burning. Always remember, people fear what they don't understand."

I would never forget the image of Isaac standing in my bedroom doorway with his hand extended in front of him, canceling my out-of-control spell as if he were blowing out a candle. He'd bound me without so much as a word. Moved me from where I'd stood to my bed without touching me. People had a very good reason to fear power like that. In the wrong hands, it could be dangerous.

"We've been digging into our past," Josh said. "Isaac's was the easiest. His parents had already researched their family, so he just had to ask them. I was able to trace my family back to Gerald and Margaret Corey, who lived in Salem in the seventeen hundreds."

"And they were witches?"

"We know they were accused. Considering my father and I have powers, I'd have to say at least one of them was a witch."

"We did a little digging into your mom's past too," Isaac confessed.

"My mom?" I asked. "How would you know where to begin?"

"Your dad mentioned her family was from the area that day Chase told me she passed away." Isaac pulled out a notebook. "We believe your mom's family goes back to the Salem Bassets. We can't be sure without the names of your great-grandparents, however."

"Do you think she possessed the powers?"

"They're passed down through blood, so it would make sense that she did."

"But wouldn't I have known if my mom could move things with her mind?" I thought back to when Mom had been alive, and I couldn't think of anything magical that had happened. Objects hadn't moved by themselves. Fires hadn't started without manual intervention. And the only scent that had lingered around my mom was the jasmine perfume she'd wear.

Isaac shrugged. "She may not have known what she was."

They gave me a few minutes to process it all. If what Isaac and Josh were saying was true, a lot of people in Gloucester, maybe even Essex County, could have powers. It was a scary thought, really, knowing that your friends and neighbors could do terrible things to one another. What would tip the scale in favor of the good guys?

"When we came down here, you said we were three strong," I said. "What does that mean?"

Isaac answered, "A spell performed by a coven is always stronger than a spell cast by a single witch. It means our coven has the power of three."

"So, how do we help Kaylee?"

"That's what I don't understand." Isaac rubbed the back of his neck as he studied a spot on the wall near the stairs. "This morning, when I was at the hospital, I couldn't help noticing the curse is as strong as it was on Saturday, like it was just cast."

"How's that possible?" From the reading I'd done in the morning, I knew a curse's power came from its source. Kaylee had been cursed three days ago. Since then, her parents hadn't wanted a lot of people seeing her like this. They'd requested limited visitors, and the only ones they approved were in this room. So the person who did this to Kaylee couldn't have gotten near her—not even to visit.

"We don't know." Josh punched the stone floor; blood trickled from his knuckles. "Not one of these books says it's possible without some cursed object holding its victim prisoner."

"You mean like a hex bag or voodoo doll?"

Isaac nodded. "It can be anything, but Josh took her clothes from the hospital, and you have her purse and backpack."

Josh's head fell forward into his hands. "The only things she has that are hers are the pajamas her parents brought her and the necklace you gave her."

A wave of dread pushed through me.

I had done this to Kaylee.

I swallowed the scream building in my throat and said, "I know what it is."

Chapter 10

The Fifth Floor

Isaac drove us to the hospital.

"But I saw you give her the necklace," Josh said from the back seat.

"Mark gave it to me," I mumbled. I played with the strap of my purse, concentrating on twisting it around my index finger only to untwist it and start over again so that I didn't have to look at either of them. I knew the only thing dumber than taking the necklace from Mark was telling the guy I liked that I'd accepted jewelry from someone else, but what choice did I have? Kaylee's sanity depended on my honesty. I kept telling myself I hadn't exactly *taken* the necklace, I'd offered to hold it, but that didn't make me feel better about the whole situation.

Out of the corner of my eye, I saw Isaac give me a sidelong glance.

"I know," I moaned. "It was stupid."

Josh bounced his head off the backseat. "Can't you drive any faster?"

The tires on the Jeep screeched against the pavement as Isaac took the turn into the hospital parking lot. He pulled into the first available space he saw, and we piled out of the Jeep and ran to the doors. The necklace had to be what was holding the curse to Kaylee, which meant Mark was a witch. His keys probably had a spell on them too, and the man Kaylee had thought she'd seen in the parking lot at The Grill had been a product of his magic. It also meant Mark wasn't trying to harm Kaylee; he was trying to harm me.

The elevator ticked by each floor at an annoyingly slow rate that was made even more painful by stopping to let people on and off at the different floors. I was ready to scream by the time we reached the seventh floor, and I didn't know if I should then feel relief or panic when I saw Kaylee's bed neatly made with clean linens. The color drained from Josh's face.

Isaac placed a hand on his shoulder. "You would have felt it if she'd gotten worse, like you did at school when this whole thing started. Remember, your feelings for each other make you a part of each other. They connect you to her. You need to remain strong, for her."

Josh spoke through clenched teeth. "Then where the hell is she?"

"They've moved her," said a young nurse standing behind us. "She's on the fifth floor."

"Why?" I asked, stepping aside so that she could get by me and refusing to let myself think the worse.

"They can take better care of her there." She set a clean bedpan and water pitcher near the bed.

We sprinted back to the elevators and punched the *five* button. Josh drummed his fingers against his leg as the elevator descended two floors.

"This can't be good," I mumbled.

Isaac took my hand in his. Josh looked as if he was ready to jump out of his skin as the light in front of us highlighted the number five. The doors opened into a dingy white hallway. There was a small waiting room to our immediate right and double glass doors to our left. A blue and white sign above the door read, *All visitors must check in at the Nurse's Station.* Isaac held the door open. An air of despair and hopelessness engulfed me as a middle-aged woman in a motorized wheelchair rolled past, muttering something about being late for the party.

"This has to be wrong," I whispered. "Kaylee shouldn't be here."

Isaac coaxed me forward. "Come on. Let's find out what's going on."

We stopped at the nurse's station. A bored looking woman looked up from her magazine. "May I help you?"

"We're here to see Kaylee Bishop," Josh said. "We were told she was moved to the fifth floor?"

I didn't like it here. In the room across from the station, a man stared intently at his hands, and in the room next to him another man was busy stacking and restacking checkers. First, the red were in one pile and the black in another. Then he'd scatter the piles and restack them one at a time so that they were every other color. I kept hoping we had the wrong floor. Maybe we got out on four by mistake. They couldn't have put Kaylee with these people. She wasn't crazy. Didn't they see that?

"Names," the nurse said curtly.

Isaac answered for all of us.

She checked our IDs, typed our names into the computer, and said, "She's in room twenty-three. Down the hall, third door on the left."

The good news was she wasn't behind the solid white door with extra locks and a bright red sign that read, *Psychiatric Ward*. Josh jogged down the hall. Isaac and I followed behind him.

Mrs. Bishop was asleep in a chair in the corner of the tiny private room. Her mascara was smudged, making it hard to tell where her makeup ended and the dark circles of someone who hasn't been sleeping well began. She clutched a rosary tightly in her hand.

My eyes wandered elsewhere. There were bars on the outside of the windows, and the bed frame was padded with thick white cushions. I tried to tell myself it could be worse: it could have resembled a prison cell. Wide black straps held Kaylee to the bed by her wrists, ankles, and waist.

"Don't move," she whispered, her voice raspy, her eyes bloodshot, and her face damn near gray.

Josh took a step forward, stopping when Kaylee pleaded.

"Please." A tear slid down her temple. "You'll wake them."

Her eyes moved to the empty corner of the room.

Isaac whispered, "She's seeing demons."

I couldn't take it any longer. How much more could Kaylee bear before she really went over the edge? What if we were already too late?

We moved at the same time. Josh went for the necklace, tearing it from her neck and crushing the stone in his hand with a blast of power. His magic tasted different than Isaac's. It was more like hot apple cider with a touch of tin, although I'm pretty sure the tin was an emotion he wasn't supposed to use to fuel his powers. I went for the strap around Kaylee's waist, fumbling with the buckle. Isaac went for the ones around her ankles, releasing her feet with a wave of his hand.

"Madison, let me get that," Isaac said.

I moved, and in less than a second he had her waist and wrists freed.

Josh discarded the remains of the necklace onto the floor, scooped Kaylee up in his arms, and sat on the bed, holding her tight. She looked small curled against him, like a child. I watched his magic pour out of him in a delicate golden web that wrapped itself around her like a cocoon before fading and becoming invisible.

I was afraid to touch her, fearing she'd break. But crouching down in front of them, I dared to brush her bangs away from her eyes with my fingertips. "Kaylee, honey, are you okay?"

Before Kaylee could answer, Mrs. Bishop was on her feet. "What are you doing?"

"Taking Kaylee out of this place," Josh growled. "She doesn't belong here."

Mrs. Bishop's voice shook as she spoke. "She needs help."

"You call this helping her?" Josh stood with Kaylee cradled in his arms. Kaylee clung to him.

Mrs. Bishop stepped toward them. "Josh Corey, you put my daughter back on that bed."

I stood up and blocked her path so she couldn't get any closer to Kaylee. "Mrs. Bishop, this is not helping her." I waved my hand at the room for emphasis. "She is not insane."

Mrs. Bishop went for the door next, but Isaac beat her there. He rested a hand on her arm, his mouth moving fast and forming unspoken words. I could feel his powers. Then, loud and clear, he said, "We're supposed to take Kaylee with us."

"Yes," Mrs. Bishop said as she twisted her hands together. "You should take her with you."

Isaac guided her back to the chair. "You don't want to tell anyone we were here."

"No." Mrs. Bishop agreed. "Certainly not."

"And you were sleeping," Isaac added. "Remember?"

Mrs. Bishop sat down and closed her eyes.

Josh headed for the door, but Isaac grabbed his shoulder, stopping him before he could open it. "We can't carry her out of here. The nurses will call security."

I didn't see why not. "Can't you do whatever it is you just did to Mrs. Bishop to the nurses?"

"I can't cast a confusion spell on the entire floor. Josh, put Kaylee down and create a glamour."

"A what?" I asked.

"A glamour," Isaac said as he bent down to pick up the necklace. "It's like an illusion, only a glamour is done on a person to change their appearance."

"Babe," Josh whispered in Kaylee's ear. "I need you to walk. Can you do that?"

"I shouldn't leave." Kaylee's eyes met his. "They'll kill me. They said they could find me wherever I go."

Oh my God, she still thought demons were after her; we were too late. My vision blurred, and I had to wipe my eyes. Josh kissed the top of her head, looking like he was on the brink of tears himself.

"You're safe now," he said, "and I will do everything in my power to keep you that way."

He put her down so that she was standing next to him. He kept an arm around her waist and closed his eyes. Kaylee's pajamas were replaced with blue jeans and a white sweater. Sneakers covered her once bare feet. Her hair was combed back, her eyelids were brushed blue, and her cheeks had a healthy glow to them.

My mouth fell open in awe.

Isaac nodded in approval. "We need to be quick. Madison, count to thirty before following us; this way the nurse only sees three of us walking out of here."

I met them in the lobby. We walked casually out of the hospital to Isaac's Jeep. Kaylee kept looking nervously over her shoulder mumbling, "They'll find me."

As soon as we were in the Jeep, I asked, "With the necklace destroyed, shouldn't she be better?"

Isaac started the engine, then looked over his shoulder at Kaylee. The glamour was gone. Her hair hung limp around her pale face, and she was wearing the pajamas her parents had brought to the hospital. "We need to get her something to eat and somewhere she can rest."

Something to eat ended up being a burger to go from the first fast food restaurant we passed, and a place to rest turned out to be Isaac's house, in his basement. He gave me a pair of sweatpants and a sweatshirt before the guys went upstairs to grab drinks. I helped Kaylee to the bathroom and started a warm shower.

She grabbed my wrist. "Don't leave me."

"I'm not going anywhere."

I found a clean towel and washcloth under the sink. I handed the washcloth to Kaylee in the shower and took a seat on the toilet, lid down.

I had to know if this was over, if Kaylee was back to herself. I filled my lungs with air and prayed destroying the necklace had worked. "Do you feel better?"

"You know, it's weird, but I do," she said, and I released the breath I was holding. "As soon as I was in Josh's arms I felt safe. Crazy, I know, but the demons don't like him. They tend to leave me alone when he's around."

It wasn't crazy. Josh had destroyed the onyx charm and enveloped her in his powers. I knew how it felt to have someone else's power wrapped around me.

"The demons didn't come until I was strapped to the bed, you know," she said. "The doctors made me an easy target. I couldn't run. Couldn't move. I begged the nurses to untie me. They wouldn't, and my parents wouldn't. Do you think the demons got to them too? Maybe that's why they left me tied up. Maybe the demons threatened them. I'm lucky they didn't get to you or Josh."

Kaylee reached out of the shower curtain. I handed her the towel.

"I knew they had to be demons by the dreadful things they did," she continued. "Once I was tied down, they sent more than just spiders and snakes after me. They'd run their hands and tongues over my arms and face. Their saliva burned too." She looked at her arms as if expecting to see welts or scorched skin. "They were getting ready to do worse."

My God, what did Mark do to her? My eyes were wide and my mouth open in silent horror as Kaylee described what she'd been through. Tears ran down the length of my cheeks and onto the floor.

How do you tell someone the past few days didn't really happen? How do you tell them that they were under a curse that caused hallucinations?

"Kaylee, what do you know about magic?" I asked.

She pulled the sweatshirt over her head and asked innocently, "You mean like abracadabra and I-put-a-spell-on-you type stuff?"

"Sort of, yeah," I replied, realizing she didn't get that I was implying magic was the cause of all her problems. I tried to think of a delicate way to explain everything to her.

"I know it makes good movies," she said.

Screw being subtle. "Kaylee, you were under a curse. No one is after you. There was nothing at school or in the hospital. It was all an illusion created by magic."

Kaylee giggled nervously. "And they said *I* was crazy." But she looked as if she was giving it serious consideration.

Josh knocked on the bathroom door. "How are you doing in there?"

Kaylee flung the door open and threw her arms around his neck. "Thanks for getting me out of that place."

Josh smiled the first real smile I'd seen from him in days. "Don't mention it."

"What should I do with her pajamas?" I asked.

"Give them to me." Isaac held out his hand. "I want to burn them. She doesn't need anything to remind her of the last few days." Isaac took the pajamas and disappeared back up the stairs. I wondered if he was actually going to burn them.

Kaylee's eyes darted around the room, and for a moment I thought she saw her demons.

"Where are we?" she asked, her voice soft.

"Isaac's house," Josh said. "How are you feeling?"

"Tired and hungry."

Josh took the burgers out of the fast food bag and handed one to Kaylee and one to me. We sat on the floor to eat, the bag torn open so that we could share the fries.

"Did you save me one?" Isaac asked when he rejoined us.

Josh handed him a burger.

Kaylee was halfway through hers before she said anything else. "They'll come for me. They'll find me and then they'll punish me." She bit her bottom lip nervously.

Please, don't let us be too late. The fact that she hadn't begun to scream hysterically since Josh had crushed the onyx charm, however, gave me hope.

"Kaylee, you have to listen to me." I put down my food and took her hands. "Nothing is coming for you. It was all a hallucination. What you saw at school. What you saw at the hospital. None of it was real."

"But the spiders in the classroom, they crawled out of my backpack. Hundreds of them were coming after me."

I shook my head and gripped her hands tighter, willing her to believe me. "There were no spiders."

Kaylee looked at Josh.

"Nothing was there," he confirmed.

Kaylee's brow furrowed. "And you didn't see those people at the hospital? The ones with red eyes and the markings on their skin?"

Josh shook his head. "They weren't real."

"How do you know?" Kaylee asked, her whole body trembling. "They spoke to me. They said they'd find me no matter where I went."

Kaylee looked around the room. It was like we'd lost her, like she'd never be the same person.

"Nothing can get to you down here, not with my wards in place," Isaac said.

"Your what?" she asked.

Isaac started at the beginning and explained about his powers, about Josh's and mine too. He even produced blue flames in the palm of his hand to show her. He then explained how he had different wards guarding his room. How no one who intended to harm us would be able to come down the stairs. How outside forces wouldn't be able to feel our magic.

"You haven't seen any spiders or demons since I crushed that necklace, have you?" Josh asked.

Kaylee shook her head.

"That necklace was cursed," he said. "As long as you had it on, it controlled your thoughts. It made you see those things." Josh placed a hand under Kaylee's chin. His powers rippled through the air.

Kaylee touched her arms. "Are you doing that? It feels like being wrapped in silk."

Josh grinned. "That's me." He removed the metal cross from around his neck.

"Another necklace?" I asked skeptically.

"I've put some of my magic into this one." Josh put the necklace on Kaylee. "As long as you're wearing it, no one will be able to put you under another spell."

Kaylee ran her thumb over the cross. "Thanks."

"Don't take it off," Isaac instructed. "There's too much power in Gloucester. If the person who put the curse on the onyx necklace realizes Josh has powers, that we all have powers, and that we interfered with their spell, they may come after you again."

"Why didn't the necklace affect me?" I asked. "I'd worn it too."

"The curse could have needed to be triggered," Josh offered.

"Or your powers provided a level of protection," Isaac said. "Like the difference between a table made out of pine and one out of oak. The oak is naturally stronger. Had you worn the necklace longer, though, I'm sure it would have gotten to you too."

I couldn't help realizing Kaylee was the weakest person in our group. She couldn't protect herself from outside forces. Not that I knew how to protect myself either yet. But I had powers in me. I could learn. I would be able to protect myself. I could even do harm to anyone who tried to hurt my friends or family.

Just knowing this warmed my blood. It filled me with the sort of anxious energy I got before parties or festivals. I felt as if I could transfer my energy into a tangible form. Without really thinking, I held the palm of my hand up in front of me. The air above it sizzled and hissed. My powers moved down my arm to my fingertips like millions of army ants marching away from their colony. The taste of copper filled my mouth. Then, almost as quickly as this wonderfully delectable feeling came, everything stopped, and a sharp sting burned my outstretched hand.

Isaac—eyes narrowed and dark—frowned at me. His expression scared me, and I looked away.

"That wasn't nice," I told him. My fingers curled into a fist trying to block the pain.

"That wasn't me," he replied. "That was your powers yielding to the promise you made."

Damn, my hand stung. Imagine holding your palm over a lighter, and when you can't stand the heat anymore, you leave it there. Geesh! A little warning about the consequences of breaking my promise would have been nice. I'd just figured it meant I shouldn't do spells, not that I wouldn't be able to. A, *Hey, magic will be painful if you try to use your powers before I show you how,* would have been nice. And it was true: if he had told me even accidental spells wouldn't work but would leave a wicked sting, I might not have made the promise.

Give me a break; I couldn't control my emotions one hundred percent of the time, let alone the powers I unleashed.

Sorry, I should say the powers I *embraced.*

What was more annoying than my throbbing hand was that Isaac seemed to be able to read my mind.

"It only stings because you used your anger to fuel the spell," he said.

"I—" I was going to say, *I did not,* but Isaac fixed me with a shrewd glare—one eyebrow raised. "I didn't do it on purpose," I snarled instead.

"Control," Isaac said. "You must be in command of your thoughts when you cast."

"He's big on that." Josh handed me a bottle of water. Its coolness felt good against my skin. "But I know how you feel."

"Thanks."

Kaylee couldn't stop looking around us. Yet no screaming at least meant she didn't see her demons, the spiders, or maybe something worse. "Why me? What did I do for someone to—" She didn't seem able to say the word *curse.*

"They weren't after you," I mumbled.

To think I'd almost ruined my best friend's life. Not that I'd known anything about the powers before this morning or that I had done it intentionally, but I should have told Mark no when he gave me the necklace. What had I been thinking? Then again, I never would have guessed Mark could be so cruel. So evil. It wasn't like we'd gone out and I'd dumped him for Isaac. There never was a Mark and me.

Never.

"There was no way Mark could have known I'd give Kaylee the necklace." I pulled my knees to my chest and wrapped my arms around my shins. "That curse was meant for me."

"Mark has powers?" Kaylee asked. "He's so, I don't know, average."

"He must," I moaned into my legs. "I'm so sorry, Kaylee."

"Don't be silly," she said, stifling a yawn. "You didn't know the necklace was cursed."

"That weasel," Josh growled. "What are we going to do about him?"

"March up to him and punch him in the face," I said, pounding my right fist into my left hand. "Hard. And I want to be the one to do it."

"We bind him." Isaac reached into his pocket and pulled out what remained of the onyx necklace. "This will be the base of our spell. Using an item he put his own powers into will make our spell stronger. We'll need some of his hair, and a piece of his clothing would help."

I smirked. "I'll gladly yank out his hair and rip off a piece of his shirt, right after I hit him."

"No one will be punching Mark," Isaac said.

"Give me one good reason why I shouldn't," I asked. Seriously, I wanted to see Isaac stop me, and I already knew not to promise I wouldn't.

"If he knows we're onto him, he'll do everything in his power to stop us, including a spell to keep others from binding him," Isaac said. "I know *I* would, if I were in his shoes."

Kaylee shuddered. "I don't want to see him. I can't handle it, not yet."

"That's not a problem," Josh said. He looked sideways at Isaac, who wore an apologetic expression. "We didn't exactly ask permission to take you from the hospital. I'm pretty sure the nurses have noticed you're gone by now."

Kaylee's bloodshot eyes grew wide. "My parents will be worried sick. I should call them."

When she looked to her right, I knew she was looking for her purse, which was still at my house on the floor next to her backpack.

"You can't," Josh said. "Isaac and I already talked about that. Your mom won't remember we were there. The hospital won't know exactly what happened to you. We're hoping the doctors think your mom undid the straps to make you more comfortable and that you just wandered off. They'll search the hospital first. It will buy us some time."

"What happens when their search comes up empty?" I asked.

"They'll contact the police."

Kaylee giggled under her breath and stifled another yawn. "I've been kidnapped."

Isaac's bedroom *would* make the perfect place to hold someone prisoner.

"In the meantime, the safest place for you is here," Isaac said. "My parents have wards on the house. Their faith ward will be to our advantage. Even if the police come to the door, they'll believe what I tell them. If I say I visited you at the hospital and left when you fell asleep, they'll nod, jot it down in their notepad, and leave. My wards will help keep others with powers from sensing you're down here, and if they try to come down to take a look for themselves, they won't be able to. At this time, looking for you is the same as intent to do harm. As long as I believe that, it shall be, and my wards won't budge."

Kaylee nodded.

"You need some sleep," Josh said.

"I don't want to sleep." Kaylee moved to the foot of the bed and curled up. "I'll just rest here while you guys come up with a plan."

Kaylee was asleep almost as soon as she lay down.

And the planning turned out to be the most fun I'd had in days.

Chapter 11

Fire and Water

Josh tossed what remained of our dinner away. He came back and stood a few feet from Isaac. With me a few feet in front of them, we formed a loose circle—triangle really, but in magic you always draw a circle, so if you connected us with lines, they'd have to be curved.

"Where do we begin?" I asked them.

"With your powers," Isaac said, "you don't have to be in our coven. Josh and I discussed it already, and we would welcome you if you chose to join, but it is your choice. I'll show you how to use your powers no matter what you decide."

Josh was like a brother to me, and Isaac and I had a connection, one I hoped went beyond powers. Together we could stop Mark from hurting anyone else. "I want to join."

Isaac nodded.

Josh closed his eyes and shook his arms the way a person does when he is trying to relax.

"You want to clear your mind before practicing magic," Isaac explained and copied Josh.

I did the same, although I peeked a few times just to make sure I wasn't taking too long to clear my mind. I opened my eyes when I heard Isaac's sangfroid voice.

"You will be our air and Kaylee our earth."

I'd read about elements on the Internet. When I had tested my own powers, I'd had something representing each element in my circle: the wine glass for water, candle for fire, salt for earth, and knife for air. The website mentioned that covens often assign each member to an element.

"Kaylee doesn't have powers," I said. "How can she represent earth?"

"Magic is at its strongest when all the elements are represented," Isaac explained. "Kaylee has an emotional bond to you and Josh. By her representing earth, she will help to ground us to the here and now. By her being a part of our coven, when she's strong again, we can transfer some of our power to her. She won't be helpless to defend herself from magical forces."

"I thought if someone who's not a natural witch called upon outside forces, they would call upon demons or something dark."

"Many do," Josh said.

"And in doing so they stain their soul," Isaac added. "Mess around with a big enough demon, and you could lose your soul. Natural witches risk this too. You need to understand your powers before you use them. They are a part of you and everything around you. They are the stones beneath your feet and the air that you breathe."

"Everything is connected," Josh said. "I remember when I first embraced my powers, I was eight. My father made me promise I'd keep them a secret. He said as I got older I would learn to taste others' powers and know without a doubt who I could trust with my secret."

Powers are a part of everything, check. *Keep them a secret*, check. *Trust few*, check.

I nodded to let them know I understood.

"When you use," Isaac said, "you're taking from these powers and transferring the energy into your spell. If you're not in control of your thoughts and emotions when you cast, your spell will end up out of control like the fire at your house."

"The first spell you did was fire?" Josh asked, a mixture of astonishment and surprise in his expression.

I frowned. "I lit a few candles."

"And almost burned down the house," Isaac so kindly reminded me.

Josh let out a low whistle.

Isaac continued, "Now that you've embraced your power, you'll start to see the things around you with more clarity."

"It's almost as if everything is crisper," Josh said. "Like watching a movie in high def. You'll be able to see and feel things you couldn't before."

"Like how I can taste your magic?" I asked.

"Exactly like that," Isaac replied. "And the taste of someone's magic can tell you a lot about the person. Your magic reminded me of dirty pennies. That's how I knew the energy that went into it was fueled with negative emotions."

Great. I reminded the guy I liked of pennies, and not just any pennies, dirty ones. I had to work to keep my disappointment from showing in my expression.

Isaac went on. "Power is easy to bend to your will. As you get stronger, you will be able to absorb power from trees, grass, people, even the air around you."

Isaac held his hands in front of him as if he were holding an imaginary basketball. The air around him crackled. The vanilla and spearmint that was his magic suffused the space between us. I could actually see a ball of energy, translucent and pulsing, in his hands. Josh held a hand in front of him, and the ball of energy stretched and shifted until it was a long tube that connected his hand to Isaac's.

I felt like a child who'd just seen a magician pull a quarter out of her ear.

Isaac and Josh pulled their hands away from the tube, and it vanished. I reached out in front of me, feeling the remains of their power in the air. Lush like velvet, it caressed my skin.

"Magic is often subtle." Josh flicked his forefinger off of his thumb like he was flicking a crumb off a table, and a burst of air brushed past my cheek. "Or it can be forceful." This time he held his hand to the side, palm out toward Isaac's closet. A moment later, the clothes were pushed in as if someone had fallen against them.

"And it can be countered," Isaac said. "Like I did at your house. Are you ready to try?"

Was I ever!

"Yes," I said in a voice much smaller than I'd meant to use.

"Then let's create our bond and see what you can do."

Isaac and Josh raised their arms above their heads and looked at me. I raised mine.

"By the power of water," Josh said, an expression of complete calm set in his features.

"By the power of fire." Isaac's eyes were suddenly alight with a fire of their own.

And since they both were looking at me, I took my cue and said, "By the power of air."

Isaac and Josh said the next part together: "We shall cast with the powers of three times three."

I wasn't sure if I was supposed to say it too. Just in case, I muttered, "Um, what they said."

The corners of Josh's mouth tugged upward for a brief moment.

We relaxed our arms, and I waited to see what I should do next. Several of the stones on the floor around us glowed translucent orange. Our circle.

Isaac put his hand out in front of him — like someone does before saying, *Tah-dah!* — and produced blue flames. Josh did the same, only he produced a perfect drop of water that looked as if it had dripped from a large faucet; it dangled suspended above his palm.

"Your turn," Josh said.

So if Isaac represented fire and in turn produced fire, and Josh represented water and produced water, was I supposed to produce air? And how the heck was *air* supposed to look? My brow furrowed together. I held my hand out and concentrated, focusing on the air in my palm. Absolutely nothing happened.

"What are you trying for?" Isaac asked. I was relieved that he really couldn't read my mind.

"I'm not sure," I confessed. "What would air look like?"

Isaac stifled a laugh by coughing.

"I only did water because I didn't want to copy," Josh said with a stupid grin on his face. He closed his hand, then reopened it, turning his drop of water into fire.

I ignored the heat of embarrassment that rose to my cheeks and tried again. Seemed no matter how hard I stared at my hand, I wasn't going to produce the lovely pale blue flames they had.

Isaac canceled his spell and came closer to me. "You don't have laser eyes." He put his hands on my waist. His powers glided over my skin as they wrapped around me. There was something behind his usual vanilla and spearmint scent. It was subtle like the spray from the ocean or maybe a breeze through the forest. Outdoorsy. Cologne mixed with magic. I inhaled, my back hitting Isaac's solid chest.

I could get used to being this close to Isaac. Yet I had to force myself to ignore the feel of his magic against my arms and listen to his voice. It wasn't easy. His warm breath teased my neck as he spoke.

"You should feel your power building within you, flowing into your hand and into the spell."

I had felt that before. It was easy when I was angry. I closed my eyes and focused on my breathing. I focused on each beat of my heart. As I did, I could feel the air in the room charged with Isaac's and Josh's powers. I wanted it to be charged with mine too. The taste of strawberries and chocolate kissed my tongue. My powers danced to the tips of my fingers, tickling my skin from the inside. I beamed with sheer delight as fire appeared in my palm. I didn't create the pale blue flames Isaac and Josh had, though. Mine were the vibrant violet-blue of a tanzanite gem.

"Now throw it," Isaac said.

"What?" I couldn't have heard him right.

"Throw it at Josh."

"Don't worry," Josh taunted. "Your little fire won't burn me."

I liked my flames and really didn't want to throw them, but Josh kept staring at me, wiggling his finger to tell me, *Come on.* I couldn't pass up the challenge. I brought my arm back, saw Isaac grinning like a proud cat behind me, and whipped my flames at Josh, who lazily held his hand in front of him. My spell died with a faint hiss.

It was a little pathetic how easily he'd canceled it.

We continued to practice. It was a good thing Isaac and Josh only threw balls of air and large drops of water at me, because countering spells wasn't as easy as they'd made it look. If they had used fire, I would have had third-degree burns.

At some point, Isaac's father called us upstairs. Isaac spun a funnel of warm air around me. It not only felt wonderful — it dried my hair and clothes.

Two police officers stood in the foyer. They were looking for Kaylee and were very disappointed when they discovered Josh was with Isaac and me.

"We were hoping she was with you," the officer admitted to Josh. "Are you sure she hasn't gotten in touch with you?"

"I'd know if I talked to my girlfriend." Josh ran a worried hand over his face as he shook his head. "How could this have happened?" He looked as if he could barely hold himself together. His eyes were the red of someone who hadn't slept. He looked nothing like he had in the basement. Boy, was he quick with a glamour. He'd managed this one while he had walked up the stairs, and he deserved an Emmy for his performance.

Just like Isaac had said would happen, the officer nodded, jotted notes in his notepad, and thanked us for our time.

After that, I called my dad and asked him if I could spend the night at Sarah's, using the excuse that I wanted to be with friends. I then called Sarah and asked her to cover for me in case my dad called there to check up.

"Sure, no problem," Sarah said. "How's Kaylee?"

"She's better," I replied. "But do me a favor and don't tell anyone we talked, okay? I can't really explain now."

"Sure. If you need anything…" Sarah left the sentence hanging.

"You know you're the first person I'll call."

We practiced into the early morning hours. I got the hang of calling upon my powers, and while I was only able to counter a small percentage of Isaac's and Josh's spells, I could block just about all of them. By the time I lay down next to Kaylee, I felt as if I'd undergone a rigorous exercise regimen.

Isaac and Josh tossed a bunch of pillows and blankets into piles on the floor, but I don't remember them lying down. I must have passed out as soon as my head had hit the pillow. I woke hours later with Kaylee's hand on my face.

Chapter 12

The Plan

"So, what's the plan for today?" Kaylee asked. She looked rested; the pink was back in her cheeks, and her eyes no longer had the haunted look of a person afraid of everything around her. She took a big bite out of a bagel.

Isaac, Josh, and I had worked out the details of our plan while we'd practiced the previous night. The key was to act natural and move through the day as if we were worried sick about Kaylee. We didn't know if everyone at school would know she was missing—like the doctors and police believed—or if they'd think she was still at the hospital and not allowed visitors, so we were left playing that piece by ear.

"Madison and I are going to school," Josh said. "Isaac's going to tell his parents he's not feeling well. He'll stay here with you."

"Josh and I will get the things we need for the spell and hurry back here after school."

I hated having to wait until the entire school day went by, but the guys had insisted it would look suspicious if Josh and I drove to school together, yanked out Mark's hair, ripped his shirt to pieces, and left. I felt we could claim temporary insanity. Whatever.

Kaylee nodded.

We set our plan into motion after that. Josh dropped me off a few houses down from mine so that it would look like I was walking home from Sarah's. My dad was in the shower, and Chase was eating breakfast in the kitchen when I got in. I hurried to my room and stuffed a clean pair of jeans, a long-sleeved T-shirt, socks, and sneakers into Kaylee's backpack before opening my window. The cool morning air rushed in.

Josh was already standing below and looked up at me. "Just let go of it."

I dropped the stuffed backpack along with Kaylee's purse down to him.

"I'll be back in thirty." He cut through the backyard and out of sight.

As soon as my dad was done in the bathroom, I brushed my teeth, showered, and tried to get a brush through my tangled hair. I couldn't help but curse—a lot—as the brush got caught on knot after knot. My dad's voice bellowed up the stairs as he yelled for me to watch my mouth. It was comforting to know some things were still normal; it made me want to run up to my dad and give him a hug for just being him. A giggle bubbled up my throat as I imagined the surprised expression I'd get for thanking him after he'd yelled at me.

Before I went downstairs, I placed a few loose threads into the folds of one of my dad's handkerchiefs and tucked it in my purse for later.

Dad looked up from the morning paper when I walked into the kitchen. "How are you doing, sweetheart?"

"I'm holding it together." I poured myself a glass of orange juice and took a seat next to Chase.

"Is Kaylee home?" Chase asked. He knew Kaylee was sick, but none of the details. My dad and I didn't know how to explain to a six-year-old that someone who was young and happy one day could be seeing things that weren't there the next.

"Not yet, but we're hoping she will be soon." I ruffled his hair and forced a grin. My dad had no idea I knew where Kaylee was. He only knew the police had stopped by looking for her.

"Any word?" he asked, his question cryptic.

"No." I finished my juice and rinsed the glass out in the sink, purposely making my hand shake so I'd seem rattled. If I were too calm, my dad would be sitting me in a chair, shining a bright light in my face, and insisting I 'fess-up and tell him where Kaylee was.

I had to keep up the act. "Josh is picking me up. I'm hoping he's heard something."

As if we'd synchronized our watches, Josh's horn sounded with one long blast.

"I'll see you later." I waved over my shoulder as my dad and brother said goodbye.

Outside, I ran down the walk to the curb where Josh had parked and got in his car. His dark hair was slick and shiny, still wet from his shower. He had a latte waiting for me. It smelled of pumpkin spice, heavenly.

"Thanks."

"No problem." Josh pulled away from my house. "Kaylee wanted me to thank you for the clothes and her stuff. She feels a whole lot better not wearing Isaac's sweats."

"I knew she would. What are they doing today?"

"Isaac is going to explain the powers to her. The more she understands them, the safer she'll be. Even without any of her own, she'll know what to watch for and what can protect her."

I nodded and took a sip of my latte, instantly feeling a little better about the day ahead.

It was harder to be at school than I had expected, though. Everyone asked about Kaylee. The good news was that no one knew the nurses had lost her. That meant the hospital and police were keeping it quiet.

In English, I didn't even make it to my seat before Natalie Parker cornered me.

"How's Kaylee?" She chewed on the nail of her index finger.

"She's about the same," I said, sticking to the words Josh and I had agreed to use.

"I'm really sorry." Natalie paused for a moment, looking as uncomfortable as I felt, then took her seat.

I recited my line several more times before Mr. Chapin called the class to order. When there were only five minutes left to first period, he called me to his desk.

"I heard about Kaylee," he said. "I know how difficult it can be when a friend's in trouble, but as a friend, it's our responsibility to help them."

I wasn't sure what he expected me to say to that, but he watched me expectantly, so I said, "I know."

"Do you?" He paused, giving me one of those looks adults like to give when they don't believe you: eyebrows raised and mouth in a thin line. "Sometimes it means telling a teacher or a doctor something you may have promised you'd keep a secret."

I opened my mouth then closed it. He thought Kaylee did drugs. That meant most of the staff thought she did drugs. How was Kaylee supposed to face her teachers and classmates if everyone thought she was a junkie? It wasn't fair.

"She didn't take anything, Mr. Chapin," I said, fighting to keep my voice calm. "I'm sure she'll be okay."

"You're a good friend, Madison. Still, if you need someone to talk to, I have fourth period free, and I'll be in my classroom."

I turned on my heels and stormed back to my desk. Even after we bound Mark, his reputation would be unscathed. To everyone else, he'd still be that awkward but sweet freckled-faced boy. No one would know he had caused Kaylee's hallucinations.

I tossed my things in my backpack and headed to Foods. Several "Kaylee's about the same" and "I'll tell her you said hi and to get well soon" were said as I made my way to class.

I followed two chatty sophomores into the classroom and almost lost what little control I had left over my emotions when I saw Mark sitting at our table. I was sure my face turned a few shades of red as I fought the urge to throw something at him and snarled, "Hello." I should have asked Josh and Isaac to show me how to create a glamour. It took me a few seconds, but I managed to pull myself together after that. This would be my only chance to yank out Mark's hair. The thought cheered me up.

"How's Kaylee?" he asked when I sat down.

"Like you care," I hissed, too quietly for him to hear. I forced a smile, hoping he'd mistake my anger for worry. "About the same."

"I heard what happened." He was wearing that stinky cologne he'd had on the other day, *Essence of Jerk*. "They're saying she was on acid or something, but—"

"She didn't take anything," I snapped.

"That's what I was going to say, that I didn't believe them. Were the doctors able to figure out what's wrong with her?"

"No." I could taste my anger building, literally, as if I'd sucked on a mouthful of pennies and spit them out. I stuck a stick of passion fruit gum in my mouth.

Then I made a mental note that passion fruit was not a good mix with copper.

Mark kept a straight face, never letting his act waver. I took a few slow breaths to rein in most of my anger. In the meantime, I removed an inch-long thread from inside my dad's handkerchief and kept it hidden in my hand. When I was sure I wouldn't punch Mark—or kick him, bash his face in with my Foods book, set him on fire, or otherwise give away that I knew what a slime he was—I looked at him.

He pulled at the collar of his T-shirt. "I would have visited, but her parents said she wasn't allowed anyone."

"They're keeping it to only family and a couple friends."

He nodded.

"You have something in your hair." I reached up and plunked a few strands from the back of his head.

"Ouch!" He leaned away from me and rubbed the sore spot.

"Sorry," I lied and wiggled my thumb and index finger over the floor, pretending to be getting his hair off my hand. What I managed to nab from him was pressed between my palm and two fingers. I feigned embarrassment. "My nail must have caught. You have a piece of thread in your hair." I reached up with my other hand and ran a few strands of hair through my fingers—no yanking this time. I then showed him the thread I'd brought from home.

When he wasn't looking, I wrapped the hair I'd nabbed in the handkerchief.

The absolute worst class to be in was History, the room Kaylee had lost it in.

Paige got to class after me. She stopped at my desk and asked, "Is Kaylee still jumping on desks?"

Emma, who was standing next to her with her arms wrapped around her books, snickered. "I wish I'd gotten that on film." She laughed harder as she pushed Paige toward their seats behind me.

"Nice." I hung my purse over the back of my chair and faced the blackboard, hoping Paige would continue with her usual tradition of pretending I didn't exist. Unfortunately, it seemed like the only time Paige didn't ignore me was when I wanted her to.

She tapped my shoulder, which left me no choice but to turn in my seat and face her. "What?"

"I was only kidding."

"Oh, please. Like you suddenly care about Kaylee or me."

"I don't have anything against Kaylee."

Which pretty much confirmed she did have something against *me*, but I was so past caring.

"How's she doing?" Paige asked, more civilly this time.

"We're all concerned," Emma said. She rested her elbows on her desk and leaned toward me. "Really. Have the doctors been able to help her?"

Several of our classmates watched us, waiting to hear about it. I sighed. "She's about the same."

Sarah sat in front of me and rested a hand on my arm. She looked around us. "I'm sure Madison has been asked about Kaylee all morning. Let's give her a break." When the others went back to pulling books and pens out of their backpacks and talking amongst themselves, she whispered, "Was last night about Kaylee? Is she better?"

Sarah was one of Kaylee's oldest friends too, and the concern etched across her face made it impossible for me to let her believe Kaylee hadn't gotten any better.

I leaned even closer to her. "Yes, but don't say anything. Not yet."

Sarah nodded, and in a normal voice, said, "Tell Kaylee to get better and that I said hi and we miss her and not to worry about the festival."

No problem on the last item. I hadn't given it a moment's thought since the last week.

Sarah went on. "I talked to Mrs. Sheppard, and she'll have her classes bake a mix of chocolate chip, oatmeal raisin, and sugar cookies. I'm going to tape up fliers in the halls at lunch asking for volunteers to bring other baked goods or work the booths. Mark and Ben said we're all set on the decorations."

I nodded.

Mrs. Parris started the day's lesson, and I did my best not to stare at the clock. That was pretty much what I did for the rest of the day: tried not to notice how very slowly the minute hand on every single clock at school ticked forward. When it was finally over, in my rush to get to the student parking lot, I tripped down the stairs and would have been kissing the floor if I hadn't landed in someone's arms.

Chapter 13

The Visitor

I tried to maintain some sort of dignity and get my feet under myself so that I could see on whom I'd just fallen, but that was easier said than done. My purse strap had ended up under the sneaker of my yet-to-be-seen savior, and my backpack twisted oddly around my arm.

"Are you okay?" asked a familiar voice.

He helped me regain my balance. His deep blue eyes met mine.

"Kevin!" My arms were around his neck before he had a chance to respond. "Why didn't you call?"

He laughed and hugged me back. When we let go, I took a step away. The last six months had been good to him. He'd grown: I'd have bet he was six feet now, and he'd lost the roundness in his cheeks, which contoured his face in all the right places. His hair was still a disheveled mass of russet brown. His smile reached his eyes.

"I called a couple weeks ago, on Saturday. Chase said you were out with friends."

That would have been the night of the party, the night I'd met Isaac. I hadn't heard from Kevin in a few weeks, and he decides to call me the night I meet someone else. I didn't miss the irony in that.

"When I didn't hear back from you," he continued, "I decided to come to Gloucester and surprise you."

I shook my head. "Chase forgot to tell me."

We stood there a moment. Kevin was right in front of me, close enough that I could have put my arm around his waist, and even though we weren't going out anymore, I couldn't get myself to tell him I was dating someone else—not after he'd come all this way to see me. Meanwhile, Isaac was waiting for me at his house. I was so screwed.

"Do you still hang out with Kaylee and Josh?" he asked.

"Um, yeah."

Damn, this wasn't fair. Two weeks earlier, I would have been thrilled to death to see Kevin. I would have been talking his ear off. This day, well, it left me confused. I liked Kevin. He had been my first real boyfriend, yet seeing him after all this time didn't make my heart race like when I saw Isaac. I really, really liked Isaac. Maybe it was because our relationship was new. Maybe he had bewitched me with his powers. I didn't know, but I wanted time to figure that out. Besides, we had pressing business to take care of. We had to bind Mark before he realized Kaylee was missing. Before he realized we were onto him.

"Kevin, I really wish you would have called. I have somewhere I'm supposed to be."

He kept his eyes on his shoes. "Can I give you a ride?"

I looked toward the exit. "Josh is waiting for me."

"Oh." Kevin rocked back and forth, heel to toe. "I'll walk you to the parking lot."

"That'd be great." We headed toward the double doors to the parking lot. The silence between us seemed louder than a roused-up crowd at a basketball game. It drove me crazy, so I asked, "Will you be in town for a while? Maybe we can get together another day?"

Kevin's mood seemed to perk up. "For the week. I'm at my grandparents' house."

He grabbed my backpack, fished out a crumpled piece of paper from its depths, and held it up. "Need this?"

It was a worksheet I'd completed last month for History. "No."

"Great." He found a pen next and scribbled across the back of the paper before tearing it in half. "My new cell phone number. Call me when you get home."

He stuck the pen back in my backpack and handed me the number. "Don't lose it."

"I won't."

Josh was leaning against his car when we approached.

"Dude." Josh gave Kevin one of his playful slugs in the shoulder that he reserved for his good friends. Kevin smiled and slugged back. "I didn't know you were in town." Then, as if Josh had just realized I was standing here, he added an uncomfortable, "Oh."

"Yeah, isn't it great?" I giggled nervously. "He wanted to surprise me."

"Yeah. Great," Josh repeated, his eyes wide.

"Am I missing something?" Kevin tensed and looked from Josh to me. "Are you guys dating now?"

Josh choked out a "What?"

I had to pick my jaw up off the asphalt. "Of course not! He's dating my best friend."

"Well, you guys are acting awfully strange." Kevin shoved his hands into the pockets of his jacket.

"It's been a strange couple of days," Josh admitted. He then explained, "Kaylee's been sick."

"I'm sorry." Kevin's shoulders relaxed. "Is it serious?"

"Doctors haven't been able to say," Josh replied. "Her parents aren't allowing many visitors. We're heading over to see her."

"I'm sorry Kevin, really," I said, resting a hand on his arm. "Your timing's just bad."

Boy was it bad — two-weeks-late bad. There was a time I would have told Kevin anything, and I felt horrible not telling him the truth now. But how could I? The truth included Isaac. How would I word that? *A lot has changed since you left. I discovered I have magical powers. Josh does too. Kaylee was cursed, but Josh managed to break the curse by destroying a necklace. Now we're putting together a spell of our own to bind the jerk that did this. Oh, and by the way, the person who did this likes me, and I have a new boyfriend, who has powers too.*

You just didn't have conversations like that. Men in blue coats would come take you away in a white jacket with extra-long sleeves, and I had it on good authority there was a vacancy on the fifth floor at the hospital.

"You around awhile?" Josh asked. "It'd be nice to catch up."

Kevin nodded. "I'm at my grandparents'. Madison has my new number."

I held it up as proof.

"Do you need a ride?" Josh took his keys from his pocket. "I could drop you off before we go to see Kaylee."

"No." Kevin tilted his head toward the other side of the parking lot. "I have my grandma's car."

"I'll call you," I promised. And I would. Not because my powers made my word unbreakable, but because I wanted to know how he'd been and what life in Minnesota was like. I gave him a hug, minus a kiss—which was weird considering our history—and got in Josh's car. Josh said his goodbyes and got in next to me.

"That was awkward," Josh commented.

I groaned. "He must think I'm a jerk."

"He couldn't have picked a worse time to visit. We can't tell him about the powers or what happened to Kaylee."

My head fell back against the seat. "I know that."

"Sooo…" Josh let the word drag on while he started the car. "You and Isaac are dating, right? I mean you guys seemed to really hit it off, and The Grill was a date, wasn't it?"

"Yes," I moaned. Why couldn't life be easy? Why couldn't it leave old doors closed after new ones opened?

Josh ignored the pained expression on my face and continued, "And now Kevin's back, and you promised to call him."

"Josh. Stop. Please. Kevin and I had a lot of great times. I can't tell him to get lost. To answer the question you're not asking, yes, I like Isaac." An understatement, really—I was falling hopelessly in love with him, but I didn't need Josh relaying that to Isaac. "I'd like to spend more time with Isaac once we get this situation with Mark under control. I will call Kevin because I told him I would and because he came all this way to see me. I'm screwed, okay? I don't want to hurt Kevin, and I don't want to lose Isaac. Ugh! My head's spinning just thinking about it."

Josh studied me. I crossed my arms over my chest and frowned.

"O-kaay," he said. I wished he'd started driving already. "We'll talk about something else. Did you get what you were supposed to?"

I held up my purse with the handkerchief and Mark's hair tucked inside. "How about you?"

Josh pulled a not-so-white sock from the pocket of his jacket. "Nabbed it while he was in the shower after Gym. You should have heard him when he went to get dressed. He was still swearing when I slipped out of the locker room."

I was anxious to get back to Isaac's. Josh put the car in reverse, made it about a foot out of the parking space, and slammed on the brakes. I looked behind us in time to see a yellow hatchback speed past. Then, when we were a couple of blocks from the school, a guy in a blue minivan ran a red light at the exact moment we were going through the intersection. It was like the van had come out of nowhere. Josh threw his right hand up, and his power streaked past me. The van suddenly moved in slow motion. I could have reached out and plucked the Toyota logo off its grill; we were that close. A series of brakes screeching and car horns blaring rang out behind us as I tried to get my fingers to unlock themselves from around the door handle.

I looked over at Josh in amazement. His hands clenched the steering wheel as he took several slow, deep breaths. We should have been dead or at least in critical condition, like Kaylee should have been last week. The day her car had acted up, if Josh hadn't been following her home, the semi-truck would have turned her MINI Cooper into a pile of mangled metal with her inside. I would have thanked him for saving her and us if he didn't look like he needed a few minutes to let what had just happened sink in.

Josh's full attention remained on driving, which left my mind to wander back to Kevin. It was good to see him, even for just a few minutes, and knowing he came here to see me made me feel like a loser for not dropping everything to spend the afternoon with him. But I couldn't, not until we took care of Mark. I figured I'd make it up to Kevin. Maybe invite him over for dinner; Chase and Dad would love to see him. And with Kevin only being here a week, there was no reason for me to mention Isaac.

I had the entire dinner planned—right down to the chopped nuts and whipped cream for the hot fudge sundaes—before I realized I'd been so lost in thought I hadn't paid any attention to where Josh was driving, so it took me by surprise when he stopped the car in the middle of nowhere. We were on a dirt road. Off in the distance, surrounded by untouched countryside, an abandoned barn leaned against the horizon. One glance at the clock told me I'd managed to zone out for close to twenty minutes.

"Why are we here?" I didn't like the feel of the place. It was desolate, and the air was wrong. Chilled. Not your normal autumn chill, but a deep-down-in-your-soul chill. Maybe only those who have embraced the powers would feel it. I wished I couldn't.

"Isaac texted. We need dirt from a crossroad." Josh grabbed some paper out of the glove compartment and went to open his door.

I grabbed his arm. "Don't you feel that? It's not safe."

"I feel it. It's safe enough. Just don't go burying a box of personal items and asking for a favor." His tone was as serious as a priest's at a funeral.

I nodded, remembering an old myth—maybe there was some truth to it—about burying personal items in the middle of a crossroad and making a deal with the devil in return for your soul, to be collected at a later date by the hound dogs of hell.

Josh used the heel of his shoe to loosen the dirt, and then he scraped it onto the paper with his school ID. I scanned the country-side, looking for the eyes I could feel watching us. The one minute we were there was the longest sixty seconds of my life. I didn't feel safe until we turned into Isaac's driveway and passed under the red and gold web of maple branches extending from his yard.

Isaac's mom answered the door. She had a dishtowel in her hand.

"Hi, Mrs. Addington," Josh said. "Is Isaac home?"

"He's in his room." She stepped aside to let us in. "Go on down."

"Thanks," I said.

Josh and I made it to the top of the basement stairs and stopped. An inky void, blacker than the darkest night, loomed before us. The air smelled musty like an old crawlspace and seemed to moan and groan. I didn't want to go down there, which turned out to be the same feeling the basement had about us. I could have sworn I heard a low guttural growl say, *Go away.*

Josh went to step down on the first step, but paused and brought his foot back up to the hallway. He held his arm out to the side. "Ladies first."

I looked into the darkness. "No way."

"Josh, Madison." Isaac's voice drifted up through the void. "Come on down."

An amber glow reached up toward us. Vanilla and spice replaced the rank smell. The candles in the nooks came alive all at once, light-ing the stairway. I let Josh go first; this way, if the candles went out,

I'd be closer to the first floor. My nerves were on edge. I made it a few steps, tripped, and slammed into Josh's back with all my weight. He grabbed one of the nooks in the wall to keep from falling.

"Sorry," I said, more embarrassed than anything else.

"It's okay." Josh helped me steady myself and asked, "Are you okay?"

"Yeah." And to get the attention off my clumsiness, I asked Isaac, "What was that darkness all about?"

"I added an unwelcome ward," Isaac explained. "I have to invite you down before you're able to see what the basement really looks like. Once you're invited, you always see through the spell."

"Didn't your mom ask why you'd need that?" Josh inquired.

"Kaylee hid in my bathroom while I asked my mom if she could bring me some aspirin, which essentially invited her down here. I'll come up with a way to invite my dad when he gets home. Did you get everything?"

Josh held up the sock and folded piece of paper. I took the handkerchief from my purse.

Kaylee sat on a pillow in the center of the room. She had a half-full sixteen-ounce bottle of soda, needle, thread, and several small bowls filled with various things I didn't recognize arranged in front of her. Isaac handed me a ceramic plate, container of salt, and a small dagger-like knife. He handed Josh a length of rope, a white votive candle, and a bottle of water.

"Unravel a few pieces of rope," Isaac instructed. "We'll need them for the poppet."

"Poppet?" I asked. The knife slipped from my hand and fell to the floor, point-down and a mere hair's width from my boot. I quickly picked it up.

Isaac raised an eyebrow.

Kaylee grabbed a couple more pillows from the bed and tossed them on the floor so there was one for each of us. "It's the doll for our binding spell."

I had a pang of jealousy that Kaylee had gotten to spend the day with Isaac. She probably knew more about magic than I did. I wanted my best friend to be informed, but while she'd spent the day learning about spells and poppets with my boyfriend, I'd gotten to take a pop quiz in history, endure an endless parade of classmates asking me if Kaylee was okay, and sit next to the slime ball who'd caused this mess in the first place. My hands became sweaty, and this time the knife *and* the plate and salt slipped and fell onto the floor. The plate shattered into a gazillion small pieces.

"I'm sorry." I dropped to my knees, pushing my purse behind me, and started to pick up the pieces.

"It's okay." Isaac moved his hand as if waving a thought aside. His powers brushed past me, sweeping the pieces into a neat pile. He used a dustpan to pick them up. "Is that what you wore to school?"

I looked down at my faded jeans and T-shirt. He was not going to tell me there was a dress code for preparing the doll. If there was, then Kaylee was underdressed too.

"Yeah," I replied cautiously.

"You didn't take any more jewelry from Mark, did you?"

"Of course not."

"Check your pockets."

"What?"

"Just check them."

I did—empty with the exception of Kevin's number. I quickly stuffed it back in my pocket. "Is there a reason you're—"

The rest of my sentence never made it past my lips. Isaac slipped my purse off my shoulder and tossed it to Josh.

Before I could ask what he was doing, Isaac had swept me off my feet, tossed me onto the end of the bed—nothing romantic about it—and proceeded to yank off my right boot. "I would have taken them off upstairs if your mom had asked me to," I said. The unexplained pat-down was starting to annoy me.

Isaac, however, either didn't notice or didn't care. I debated which it was as he turned my boot upside down and shook. He reached inside it next, groping around the toe. I'm not sure what he expected to find. He did the same with the left one.

"Here it is." Josh held up a small brown sachet that he'd pulled out of my purse. He untied the strap holding it closed. "Red pepper, black yarn, bird talon, and hair."

"A hex bag," Isaac said. "It explains the sudden streak of bad luck."

Isaac only knew the half of it. I couldn't believe it: the near-miss car accidents, me falling down the stairs, dropping the knife—all the work of a spell.

"He tried to curse me again? That jerk!"

The talon was stained with blood as if it had been freshly ripped from the bird and placed in the hex bag. I remembered the crow Chase found at the park. How many birds had died for their body parts?

I stuffed my feet back in my boots. "So he killed an innocent bird to make that thing?"

"There are a lot of spells that require a talon from a raven or a black bird. Most of them are for dark magic," Isaac said absently.

Josh created fire in his hand, burning the contents of the hex bag in his blue flames. "Come on. Let's do this before he makes another one of these things."

Isaac handed me another plate. We took a seat on the pillows.

"I want to cast a summoning spell first," Isaac said. "Madison, put the plate on the floor in front of us and give Kaylee the salt."

I did.

"A summoning spell is a way for a coven to know if one of its members is in trouble," Isaac said. "It will connect our wills, and if we need help, we can call each other without a phone."

He then explained the steps to the spell. We sat cross-legged on the pillows, hands palm-up on our knees, eyes focused on the plate. Kaylee began to build the circle.

"By the power of earth." Kaylee poured a large pile of salt onto the plate.

All eyes turned to me, my cue to perform my step of the spell.

"By the power of air." I drew a cross in the salt with the knife and placed the candle on top of it, twisting it from side to side to make sure it was stable.

"By the power of water." Josh poured water around the edge of the plate, leaving the salt in the center like an island surrounded by a shallow pond.

"By the power of fire." Isaac waved his hand over the candle, pushing out a small amount of power and lighting it.

I could hear our circle close around us with a snap.

"Kaylee and I made these today." Isaac handed each of us a hemp bracelet. He placed his on the plate and told us to do the same.

We did. Isaac then pricked the tip of his finger with a pin and gave the pin to Josh, who did the same and passed it to Kaylee. I got it last. I stabbed my finger fast, getting the sting over with quickly, and watched as a bead of blood formed.

Isaac held his finger over the plate. "Swift as the wind, in times of need, let my cry be heard." He used his thumb to force more blood out of the pinprick and let it fall in the salt. We each did the same.

Kaylee and I looked at a sheet of paper on the floor between us. It contained the words to the spell. We then nodded to the guys. Together, the four of us said, "By the powers of three times three, so we will it, so mote it be."

The flame grew brighter, then returned to its original glow. The salt had absorbed the water, and the fire — filled with Isaac's, Josh's, and my magic — had dried our bracelets. When the candle flickered out, the spell was cast, and we were to keep our bracelets on at all times. Josh slid the plate to the side as we moved on to our next spell.

There was no way our sock poppet could be mistaken for a child's doll. We stuffed it with dirt from the crossroad, sulfur, a spider web, Mark's hair, shredded newspaper, and a few other items Isaac had ready. An unraveled piece of hemp rope separated its head and limbs from the body. Its arms were uneven, its torso too short, and its legs — which Kaylee had sewed after carefully cutting the top of the sock — were too long. If we penciled in a mouth and beady little eyes, it would have looked frickin' creepy.

Isaac believed Mark would know within seconds that someone was binding him. We needed to cast the spell quickly.

Isaac twisted black ribbon around the poppet's legs as he spoke the words to the spell, stopping halfway up its legs and handing the poppet and ribbon to Josh. Josh twisted the ribbon further up the poppet and repeated the spell, then gave it to Kaylee, who did the same and gave it to me. When I finished, the poppet's head was wrapped. I gave it back to Isaac, who said the spell one more time as he wrapped the ribbon back down its body.

"What's next?" I asked.

"We'll bury it," Isaac said and wrapped the handkerchief around it. "In a graveyard would be best, but under the corkscrew willow out back should work too. We better make sure Mark can't bind us first."

The spell to protect us was easier to cast than the spell to bind someone else. We already had the dirt from a crossroad and hair from the person we wanted to protect ourselves from. Add ash, salt, and spit, wrap in a cloth, tie closed with hemp rope, say a quick spell, and instant protection. We didn't even have to get a shovel to bury it.

The trickiest part of the day came when it was time to leave. Kaylee couldn't stay missing forever, and with Mark's powers bound, she was safe. She had to go home. One look at her, and her parents were going to know she hadn't spent the last twenty-four hours wandering aimlessly around Gloucester. She was showered, her hair and make-up were done, she was wearing the clothes I'd given her, and it was obvious she wasn't starving.

"Can't you cast a spell to make her parents forget the last few days?" I asked — more like groaned and pouted.

"No." Isaac tied my hemp bracelet to my wrist and pushed me toward the stairs. "You can do this."

I didn't want to face Mr. and Mrs. Bishop, but I'd been elected to go with Kaylee for support. "How about turning back time?"

"You can't relive the past," Josh called over his shoulder as he followed Kaylee up the stairs. "Let's just get this over with."

I didn't miss Josh's choice of words: *You can't relive the past.* Nor did I miss the look Isaac gave Josh after he'd said it. I gave the subject some quick consideration. I'd have been willing to bet that while you can't relive the past, it isn't impossible to visit it. Just my gut feeling; I knew Isaac would never confirm it, so I didn't ask.

Isaac heaved a sigh. "I told you, time moves in one direction, forward. Besides, if we could turn back the clock — which we can't — but if we could, the poppet wouldn't be made because we wouldn't know it needed to be made."

Isaac picked me up and placed me on the bottom step.

I quickly wrapped my arms around his waist. "Couldn't we hang out for a while? Pop some popcorn? Watch a movie?" With me standing on the first stair, I could look directly into his dreamy brown eyes. "With all this curse stuff going on the last few days, we really haven't spent much time together."

Isaac kissed my upper lip then nibbled on my lower one before the corner of his mouth pulled upward into a knowing smirk. "You're stalling."

"No. I'm trying to spend a little time with a pretty cool guy."

He bellowed out a laugh. "Is that so?"

"Definitely."

"You coming?" Josh called back down the stairs.

Isaac gave me a quick peck on my lips. "Just cast the calming spell I taught you."

Easy for him to say; all he had left to do was bury the poppet.

"Fine." I spun on my toes and marched reluctantly up the stairs after Josh and Kaylee.

Josh dropped Kaylee and me off in front of her house and sped away.

Coward. Not that I blamed him; Kaylee and I wished we were still in the car too.

We walked nervously up to the front door. Kaylee fidgeted with her keys as she looked at me, her eyes wide with worry. I dried my sweaty hands on my jeans and tried to relax. Not only did I have to face Kaylee's parents, I had to face my dad. While simply telling my dad that Kaylee was home was tempting, I knew Kaylee's parents would eventually call him. I knew it was better to tell the truth, or our version of it, right away. I could hear my dad now: *You're grounded until you turn eighteen!*

I uttered the words to the first half of the calming spell Isaac had taught me while Kaylee unlocked the door. Her parents bolted out of the kitchen as we stepped into the foyer. Her mom's hand flew to her mouth as she gasped. Her dad turned as white as the walls. Tears streaked their faces. I nonchalantly held my hand in front of me and mumbled the rest of the spell, pushing my powers out in all directions. Her parents' shoulders relaxed, and their tears stopped. Even I could feel the effects of the spell. I let out a sigh of relief.

I admitted to sneaking Kaylee out of the hospital, swearing I'd only done it because she'd begged me to. Kaylee explained that the medications the doctors had her on had made her hallucinate, and each time she'd started to feel better, it had been time for another dose. If it weren't for how totally sane Kaylee was as she said this, we probably wouldn't have been able to convince her parents. The calming spell helped as well.

"Where have you been all this time?" her father asked. His tone was much more placid than the vein popping out of his forehead would have made you think possible.

"I was afraid you'd just take me back to the hospital." Kaylee glanced over at me. "So I talked Madison into letting me stay at her house."

"Her father would have known if you were there," Mrs. Bishop said. "He would have called us."

"He didn't know," I replied. "I snuck her into the house when he was at work, and she hid in my room until she felt better."

Our story provided an explanation for how Kaylee had been able to shower, why she was wearing my clothes, and why she wasn't starving. We also offered a theory as to what had happened at school, which included someone dropping some type of drug into Kaylee's mocha.

You can bet I cast the calming spell before I said anything to my dad too. I'm sure he noticed the holes in my story, but the spell made him unwilling to argue. I dismissed myself as soon as I could, afraid if I kept rambling he'd break free of the spell and I'd be in big trouble.

I spent the rest of the evening trying to catch up on my reading for English.

That didn't go well. By no fault of the author, I was snoring before I reached the end of chapter one. Considering I should have been halfway through the book by now, I was so screwed when it came to passing English this semester.

Chapter 14
Guilt

Kaylee's parents drove her to school the next day. They wanted to have a talk with Principal Douglas to let him know Kaylee had been drugged. No doubt it would launch an investigation, but we'd deal with that later.

I got a ride from Isaac.

"How'd it go?" he asked when I got in the Jeep.

"I would have been grounded for the rest of my life if it weren't for the calming spell." I exhaled, blowing my bangs out of my eyes, and shuddered at the thought of only being allowed out of the house to go to school. "My dad looked as if he wanted to yell, but only managed to squawk out a *Do you know what you and Kaylee put everyone through?* and *I'm very disappointed in you.* Kaylee's parents just seemed relieved to have her home. I hope they didn't wake up this morning and realize they were way too relaxed about the whole situation."

Isaac rested his hand on mine and squeezed. The warmth of his powers wrapped itself around my hand, my arm, and then my entire body. It was an awesome feeling.

"What's done is done. Latte?" he asked.

"Yes, and I'll grab Kaylee one too. I bet she'll need it."

In an effort to ease Kaylee's return to school, I spoke to Mr. Chapin before class to let him know our version of what had happened. She arrived twenty minutes after the bell. Mr. Chapin stopped his discussion long enough to welcome her back. All eyes followed Kaylee as she made her way to her desk. I handed her the lukewarm mocha.

Thanks, she mouthed, ignoring everyone else.

I could barely concentrate on the lesson. Kaylee looked well, not at all like a person who'd spent the morning being chewed out by her parents. I'd hoped for a few minutes to talk to her, but the day's lesson centered on a debate over the differences between the writing styles of past and present authors. I tore a piece of paper from my notebook and scribbled a note to Kaylee on it instead:

How'd it go?

I folded it in half and passed it to Kaylee when Mr. Chapin had his back to us. Kaylee took a minute to write her reply and handed the scrap of paper back to me:

Okay. Principal Douglas is calling the police.
He wants a full investigation.
You might be called down to his office.

I nodded.

"Are you going to be okay?" I asked Kaylee after class.

The first couple of days back to school were going to be the worst. A lot of people had seen Kaylee hopping up and down on her desk, screaming for help. Even more had heard about it.

Kaylee rubbed the metal cross Josh had given her. "I'll be okay. See you in History."

I was more than anxious to get to Foods. I had to know if Mark would show his face in school now that we were onto him. I wouldn't if I were as evil as him. Then again, he had shown no signs of remorse so far. Would getting caught even bother him? I had my answer soon enough.

"Madison," Mark called to me when I entered the classroom.

He'd saved me a seat, as usual. If there'd been another open stool anywhere in the room, I would have sat on it. I sighed at my luck and headed toward his table. It did occur to me that his friendliness might be a trick. He might have figured out I was one of the people who'd bound him from harming others. What if he confronted me? What if he was waiting with another hex bag or a spell?

I brushed that thought aside. We bound him. Nothing he could do now could hurt me. Besides, I wasn't afraid of him.

Not much, anyway.

"Hi," Mark said as I plopped down on the stool.

I was careful to keep my backpack away from him. "Hi."

"Is it true? Is Kaylee back?" He looked truly excited at the news. So excited, I wondered if he'd put a glamour on himself.

"Yeah, she's back." I pretended to be interested in my Foods book, hoping Mark would take the hint that I didn't want to talk.

"That's great," he said. "So, what did the doctors come up with?"

Oh! I wanted to punch him right in his freckled nose. I turned my head and looked into his beady, mud-colored eyes. "They believe someone dropped something into her mocha. Then she had an allergic reaction to the medication she was on."

"I knew they'd figure something out." Mark tapped his pencil on the table as he talked. "I'm glad she's back," he whispered before turning his attention to our teacher.

I had no idea how to take Mark's comment. On one hand, he seemed to actually care. On the other, why would he be glad Kaylee was back if he wasn't planning something else? I decided he had to be gauging my reaction, trying to figure out if I'd had anything to do with binding him. That's when a terrifying thought occurred to me. Maybe our binding spell hadn't worked. Maybe he was smug because we had no idea we'd failed.

No. I refused to let my imagination get the best of me this time. Isaac was sure about the poppet and the spell. If he believed in it, then I did too. That didn't stop me from wondering, though, if Mark had realized he'd been bound. Isaac could have been wrong about Mark feeling the effects of the spell as we'd cast it. Mark might not know his powers were useless until the next time he tried to use them.

"Try all you want," I mumbled under my breath. "It won't work."

"Did you say something?" Mark asked.

"Just talking to myself."

I spent third period in the principal's office, telling our story to him and a couple of officers, one of them being my dad's friend, Joe Zimmerman. The younger officer with a buzz cut quizzed me over and over and over. I tried not to fidget as I answered his questions but kept rubbing my hands on my jeans. When he asked me why I was so nervous, I asked him if he was going to arrest me for helping Kaylee sneak out of the hospital. To my relief, he answered no. No one pressed charges. Kaylee's parents were just happy to have her home and healthy. And the hospital didn't want to be sued for misdiagnosing Kaylee, for not noticing the drugs they'd prescribed had made her worse, and then letting her walk out the front door unnoticed. My actions seemed heroic, really.

The interrogation ended when the bell rang. Kaylee and I reached History at the same time.

"I'm so glad to see you back," Mrs. Parris gushed when Kaylee entered fourth period. She dropped her voice to a whisper. "Principal Douglas told me what happened. Don't you worry about a thing; the police will find who did this."

Kaylee thanked her. I bit my tongue before I could reply *Wanna bet?* We took our seats.

Sarah greeted Kaylee with a hug. "I'm *so* glad you're okay."

"Thanks," Kaylee said.

"Is it true?" Sarah whispered. "That someone drugged you?"

Kaylee half nodded, and I said, "Yeah."

Sarah gave Kaylee another hug. "The festival's this Friday. Are you up to coming?"

I'd completely forgotten about the festival. Kaylee looked at me, excitement hiding just under her carefully arranged expression. Leave it to Sarah to know exactly what to say to cheer Kaylee up. It was nice to see her excited.

"We'll be there," I replied.

Kaylee's smile lit up her face. "What's left to do?"

"We're pretty much ready," Sarah said. "Mr. Hoffman delivered the cornstalks and bales of hay. He brought a few people with him, and they're setting up a maze now. Mark and Ben recruited a bunch of guys to help set up the props and booths. Only things left are some last-minute decorations and to set up the bake sale booths. We can't do that until Friday, so we could use your help then."

"Sure," Kaylee said.

"Great. Friday's a half-day. We can walk to Mrs. Sheppard's room after class. We'll grab the cookies—" Sarah broke off when she saw Paige.

"Sarah, Madison," Paige said as she took her seat behind me. "Kaylee, you're looking good."

"Thanks." Kaylee eyed her, no doubt wondering why Paige suddenly cared.

Emma slid into the seat behind Kaylee. "We heard someone drugged you."

"I'd rather not talk about it," Kaylee said, looking a little tired of the whole subject.

Emma shrugged and took her History book out of her backpack. "I'm not eating or drinking anything that's been out of my sight ever again."

"The important thing is you're better," Paige said. "And back in time for the festival. You'll be there, right?"

"We'll be there," I said.

"Great," Paige said to Kaylee, even though I was the one who'd answered. "Will Josh and Isaac be there?"

Kaylee narrowed her eyes. "I'm sure Josh will. I can't speak for Isaac. Maybe Madison knows."

It bothered me that Paige asked about Isaac. It was like a slap in the face. She might as well have said, *I haven't given up; he will dump you for me.* I had news for her, though—if Isaac did come to the festival, it wouldn't be to see her. She needed to stop chasing him; he wasn't interested. I would have pointed this out if I didn't know that Paige would then work even harder to get his attention. I fought not to let my emotions show.

"I'll ask him when he drives me home this afternoon," I said.

"Don't worry about it," Paige said in a sugar-laced tone. "I'm sure I'll see him at some point today."

Mrs. Parris told everyone to stop talking before I could reply, which may have been to my advantage because I was about to lose my temper and tell Paige off.

The end of the day couldn't come quickly enough. I lost track of how many people had asked me about Kaylee. Most of them would be keeping a close eye on their food and beverages.

It was a relief when the last bell of the school day rang. Seeing Isaac and Paige deep in conversation near the double doors to the parking lot, however, stirred up quite the opposite emotion. Emma stood a few feet away from Paige. Isaac appeared to listen attentively, totally interested in what Paige was saying. He even laughed and didn't slap her hand away when she'd handed him a sheet of paper.

It was hard to explain, but I wanted Isaac to despise her as much as I did. For as long as I'd known Paige, she had to have whatever I did. She used to shop at the same stores as me. Buy the same clothes. Hang out with the same people. Crush on the same guys. Now, she obviously wasn't stopping at pining from a distance. Ugh! I just wished she'd go away.

It bugged me that Isaac talked to her. He shouldn't stand there smiling. With the way Paige kept showing up, he had to know she liked him. I seethed in my anger, and the taste of copper stuck to my tongue. I needed to get out of there, away from both of them.

As soon as I had that thought, Isaac's gaze met mine. Maybe he could read minds after all. Now that he knew I was there, I couldn't run the other way. I inhaled deeply, letting the air out of my lungs in a slow ten-count in an effort to control my emotions. Isaac would taste my anger. Paige might too. I forced myself to walk past a bored-looking Emma and join them.

Isaac greeted me with one of his crooked smiles that always made me feel special. Paige frowned. I felt better.

"Hi," I said, but not before I gave Paige the evil glare.

Isaac regarded me quizzically.

Paige quickly composed herself. I think her tone was supposed to be sweet, but it had an acid bite to it. "I was just asking Isaac if he was going to the festival."

"Didn't trust me to ask him?" I replied.

Isaac grabbed my backpack and said, "I'll talk to Madison about the festival."

"Sounds good." Paige's sugary tone didn't match her scowl.

I smiled, knowing I'd won this little battle. She joined Emma, and they left school.

Isaac bent down and gently brushed his lips to mine. "How was your day?"

With a greeting like that, I couldn't stay upset.

"Long," I admitted.

"I saw Kaylee." He held the door open. "She and Josh just left. She's holding up pretty well."

"It's nice to have her back." I stepped through the first set of doors leading to the parking lot. The blue eyes that bore into me stopped me dead in my tracks. *Not this*, I thought. Not now.

"Kevin," I whispered.

Isaac stopped next to me. I wanted to disappear.

Kevin clenched his teeth. "You never called. I stopped by your house this morning, but your dad said you'd already left for school." Kevin moved his cold stare from me to Isaac.

The bitter taste of orange peels filled my mouth. I looked at Isaac, wondering if it was his jealousy I tasted, even though he had nothing to be jealous of. Kevin was just here to visit old friends.

Okay, not even I believed that, but it was the only thing that kept my legs from giving out.

"I'm sorry I didn't call. It's just been crazy these past few days."

Isaac took a step away from me. "I'll wait for you by the Jeep."

I wanted to grab Isaac before he could walk away, and I wanted to drop to my knees and beg Kevin to forgive me. Unable to do either, I studied a scuffmark on the floor and nodded. I counted to three, trying to keep the tears building in my eyes from spilling over. When I finally looked up, Kevin's deep blue eyes blazed down at me.

"Kevin, I'm sorry. I should have told you about Isaac when I saw you yesterday, but with everything going on with Kaylee and you surprising me, I didn't know how. I just met him a couple weeks ago. Honest."

I would have preferred that Kevin yell at me. Instead, he let the silence between us grow until I wanted to scream. I couldn't take it.

"Please. Kevin." I reached for him, but he took a step back just like Isaac had. "Say something."

"I didn't expect you to never date again." He shoved his hands into his jeans pockets. "But I didn't know how much it would bother me to see you with someone else."

Kevin's understanding didn't make me feel any better.

Not being a couple didn't mean we'd stopped caring about each other. We'd ended things on good terms. Kept in touch. I couldn't blame him for thinking that one day we'd get back together. If I were to be honest with myself, I'd have admitted that I had been thinking the same thing—until I'd met Isaac.

"I wanted to talk to you," he went on. "There's no one at home I can talk to about this. I thought you might understand."

"You can talk to me about anything." I rested my hand on the sleeve of his jacket. He didn't swat it away; that was good. He looked so lost. "What is it? Did something happen back home? Are your mom and dad okay? Did you get in trouble at school? You didn't get a girl pregnant, did you?"

"God, no!" Kevin closed his eyes and ran a hand through his hair. "My parents are fine. Dad likes his new job, and Mom's made a couple friends at the health club."

"Then what is it?" I knew it had to be catastrophic. Anything smaller and he would have just called.

Kevin opened his eyes. "It may have been a mistake coming here. Don't worry about me. Really. Life's great. I even made the basketball team."

"That's great."

"Yeah." Kevin turned away from me.

"Kevin, what is it?" I grabbed his arm. "Please. Don't leave like this. What did you want to talk about?"

He looked over his shoulder at me. "It was nothing. You have someone waiting for you." And he left.

I stood between the glass doors for a few minutes. People streamed past me on their way to life outside of school.

I should have gotten an award for sabotaging my own happiness. I had pushed Kevin away, something I would never intentionally do, and I may have given Isaac enough reason to rethink our relationship. Sure, we were in a coven together, but that didn't mean he still had to date me. I forced down the lump of guilt and confusion that had formed in my throat and headed outside to where Isaac had parked that morning—if he'd waited for me. I wouldn't have blamed him if he'd left.

I found him leaning on the back bumper. Without a word, he pushed off the Jeep, walked to the passenger door, and opened it. Just as silently, I got in.

He didn't head to his house; instead, we were speeding down Washington Street. A mix of songs from his iPod filled the otherwise silent car. Isaac had one hand on the steering wheel and the other clasped around the stick shift as he accelerated to pass a car. I had to say something. I knew that. But where to start and how to get my mouth to form the words was a problem.

"He's just a friend," I mumbled. I didn't even know if he heard me over the music.

We were approaching a curve when a semi-truck traveling in the opposite direction crossed over the double yellow lines. Isaac swerved, missing the front bumper of the truck just before an ear-piercing *BOOM* cut through the sound of screeching tires. Burning rubber threatened to choke me as the Jeep careened sideways. I screamed and braced my hands on the roof, pushing my powers out of me, willing the soft top above our heads and the metal around us to hold as the Jeep spun out of control. Isaac's powers pulsed around me.

It all happened quickly. We slid through the smoke from the tires. The sound of the semi truck's brakes locking up drowned out our music. The truck struck the rear driver's side of our Jeep and passed through us as if it were a hologram. I saw the worn black treads in its tire and the chrome hubcap, then the rusted rim, brake drum, and caliper in a weird sort of 3D way as we continued through the shocks and suspension bar, through belts and fans and other moving parts of the engine that I never, ever in my life wanted to see like that again.

Once through the truck, we passed through the guardrail in the same weird way. The Jeep tilted sideways. Isaac's powers pushed out harder around us, coagulating the air in the Jeep and providing a barrier that held me to my seat. The Jeep rolled. I screamed again.

Then we were still, the Jeep right side up. I had to tell myself to lower my arms. We were safe. Isaac turned down the radio.

From where we sat at the base of the embankment, I could see the semi had stopped half a mile up the road, intact. The driver leaned out the window and scanned the area we'd just been in, no doubt looking for the battered remains of our Jeep that wasn't there. He didn't look past the guardrail to where we were. Why would he?

The guardrail remained solid. Undamaged. He closed his door when the car we'd passed earlier drove by and continued on its journey.

I looked at Isaac, not bothering to close my mouth. For the second time in less than two days, I should have been dead. Our bodies should have been mangled in a wreck of metal and rubber.

Isaac wiped sweat from his forehead and looked above then around us. Everything inside the Jeep was the same as it had been a couple of minutes ago. Our backpacks were still in the backseat. The windshield was unbroken. The metal around us was whole.

"Nice use of your powers," he said.

I wished I could say I knew exactly what I'd done a moment before we sailed through the truck, but the truth was instinct took over. Fear of becoming road kill had me praying I could turn a soft-top Jeep into a tank. While I know I hadn't physically turned the Wrangler into anything, I had made it more durable than it would have been on its own, and Isaac had layered his powers on top of mine, preventing us from being flung around the front seats like ragdolls. Between me pushing out my powers out to will the Jeep to hold together and Isaac pushing out his to keep us from becoming a statistic, we'd managed to save ourselves.

"Ditto," I managed to reply.

We got out on shaky legs. The body of the Jeep was exactly as it had been when we'd left school, other than the dent in the driver's side rear quarter panel. The front driver's side tire was also blown. Isaac bent down and placed his hand on it. I caught a taste of his powers as the rubber melted back together and the tire inflated. Something fell from the wheel well, and Isaac picked it up. He then walked to the back of the Jeep and rested his hand on the dent, willing his powers into the metal, which pushed outward with a groan and a crunch.

"Good as new," he said.

I ran my hand over the smooth surface. He could make a killing if he opened a body shop.

"Josh's tires *were* flat," I said in awe.

Isaac's lips tugged upward into a modest half smile. That night at The Grill, I knew I had seen both tires on the Mustang as flat as deflated balloons. No wonder Kaylee hadn't been able to tell they were driving on the small spare—they wouldn't have been. Josh and

Isaac would have fixed the flat tires on the Mustang the same way Isaac had just fixed the Jeep's.

Isaac held out his hand, revealing a small hex bag.

"I thought binding Mark was supposed to keep him from being able to make those things."

"It should." Blue flames erupted in Isaac's hand, suspending the hex bag inches above his palm and turning it to ash. "He could have made it before we cast the spell."

I got back in the Jeep, mumbling, "You should have let me smack him while I had the chance."

Isaac drove off-road until we found a place to get back on Washington Street. The uncomfortable silence returned.

A few minutes later, he pulled into the fifteen-minute parking at Annisquam Lighthouse. This was it, my chance to let Isaac know Kevin and I were just friends. I rested my hand on Isaac's arm before he could get out.

"I—" A lot of words were supposed to follow that, but they caught in my throat.

Isaac removed his arm from under my hand. "We can talk on the tower."

"Are you going to push me off?" I joked.

Isaac snorted and shook his head. "Come on."

The seagulls above seemed to snicker at me with their calls, as if to say I'd f-ed up royally. Even the *swoosh* of the waves crashing into the rocks sounded like it was mocking me.

Though the smell of the sea filled my lungs, the calm serenity of being on the balcony of the lighthouse was almost suffocating. Isaac took a seat overlooking the harbor. The height didn't bother me as much as before. Maybe that was because, no matter how guilty I felt at that moment, I trusted Isaac to keep me safe. I sat a couple of feet from him, leaning my forehead on the spindles of the black iron railing, and watched the waves swarm the rocks below. I had to make Isaac understand.

"Kevin and I are just friends," I said without looking at him. "I mean, we used to date, but he moved away."

Smooth. I might as well have said that the only reason Kevin and I had broken up was because we now lived in separate states.

Which was true, but that didn't mean we would get back together now that he was back in town. Nor did it mean we'd be hooking up for a quick fling. I had to get my thoughts in order.

I could feel Isaac's eyes on me. It was weird, but I could always feel it when he watched me. Like an invisible line somehow connected us. I rambled on, letting my emotions tumble out.

"I won't lie to you. Kevin and I used to be close, and I still care about him, but it's different now. It has been for a long time. I didn't know he was coming. He surprised me. Some surprise, huh?" I forced a smile and continued to watch the waves. "With everything going on with Kaylee, I haven't had time to talk to him. And now—" I swallowed. "I won't blame you if you hate me."

If Isaac was waiting for a chance to jump in and tell me he didn't care who I'd dated before we'd met, that pause was it. The sun blazed down, making me feel like I was under a spotlight. A yellowthroat bird landed on the railing and glared, its black eyes judging me. There was nothing else I could say. If Isaac decided we should be friends and not a couple, I'd have to accept that.

Isaac moved closer and wrapped his arms around me, dissolving my trepidation. A tear escaped the corner of my eye as the warmth of his powers embraced me.

"I don't hate you," Isaac breathed the words into my hair. "And I know about Kevin."

I looked at him. "How?"

"Josh."

I wiped at the tears that ran freely now. I'm not sure what I did to deserve Kaylee and Josh, but I swore with each breath that I breathed that I would always be grateful that they were in my life, picking up the pieces before I knew they need picking up. Filling in the words I couldn't seem to say when I should say them.

Isaac explained, "Josh called me last night. He mentioned an old friend was in town and that you used to date him. He said something about knowing you well enough to know you'll avoid the subject if at all possible and that I shouldn't worry. Was he right?"

"Yeah." I rested my head on his shoulder. "He got it right."

"I don't want you to be afraid to talk to me."

"I know."

"Even if you think I might not like what you're going to say."

"Okay."

But saying that was easier than following through with it. I'd never been good at confronting uncomfortable situations, and I doubted I was going to be able to snap my fingers and change who I was. Unless there was a spell that could increase a person's confidence. If there was, I'd have bet Isaac would disapprove.

He slid out from behind me, taking my hand and pulling me onto his lap so that I was straddling him.

"I'm serious," he said.

I bit my bottom lip, debating if I should echo my previous responses or promise I'd be more open. Only, with my powers, that vow would be binding, and I wasn't quite ready to commit like that.

"Madison," he tickled my waist, making me squeal. "It's not a hard request."

"Okay, okay." I giggled and squirmed, trying to grab his hands so that he'd stop. "I know I can talk to you."

"Good."

We were both laughing by the time he relented.

My hands rested on his broad chest. My fingers traced their way up to his shoulders then over the muscles in his arms. He wet his lips; I wondered if he realized he'd done it. His hands held my hips, as if frozen there. When I leaned in, he cupped my cheeks.

Isaac's kisses tasted sweet, like chocolate-covered cherries and just like the candy, never lasted long enough. I scooted closer, if that was even possible, and threaded my fingers through his hair, pulling his mouth back to mine.

But this time, his kisses were no more than a series of polite pecks. Then, without notice, he quickly shifted, lifting me off his lap and setting me gently on the landing next to him.

He was still holding back. Still questioning something. Maybe our kiss had just confirmed for him what I didn't want to be true: that the excitement of the last week had messed with our heads and it was only a matter of another day or a week before we'd both wake up and realize we were wrong for each other.

"Sorry," I muttered.

"I'm not," he replied.

I eyed him quizzically and knew right then I should tell him how much he meant to me. He needed to understand that, and then I could better understand how much I meant to *him*. But when I opened my mouth, the words didn't come.

Isaac stood and offered me a hand. I looked up at him and noticed the glint of doubt in his eyes and how rigid his body was. It all but confirmed that, even as I let him pull me up to my feet, I was setting myself up to fall.

Chapter 15

In the Shadows

That evening, I dug the jeans I had on the day before out of the hamper and pulled the slip of paper Kevin had given me from the back pocket. I plopped down on my bed and dialed the number. I had mixed emotions about the call going to voicemail. Part of me worried that he might be avoiding my call, yet another part of me was relieved to have a little more time before I'd have to talk to him.

I sighed. "Kevin, it's Madison. Give me a call when you get this message."

I tossed the phone on the floor, grabbed my copy of *Death of a Salesman* out of my backpack, and fell back onto my mattress with my head toward the foot of the bed and my feet resting against the wall. I needed to get my mind off being such a jerk to Kevin. I should have just told him about Isaac when I'd first seen him. I could have spared him the shock of seeing us together.

I'd reached the end of the chapter before I realized I didn't remember much of what I'd read. I jotted down short answers to the questions on the worksheet and vowed to put more effort into the next one.

I tried Kevin again. Still no answer.

The next couple days were a blur. The halls at school were a buzz of excitement over the festival. Besides the maze and bake sale, we had a kissing booth and dunking tank. The faculty would be manning grills, cooking hotdogs and corn on the cob. The festival was the only thing Sarah talked about, and it drove me nuts.

Since news had made it around school that someone had slipped drugs into Kaylee's mocha, people were keeping a close eye on their food and beverages. It was probably a good habit to be in anyway, so our little white lie might have been good for everyone.

I scraped by with a sixty-two percent on the pop quiz in English. Add that to my homework grade, and I was failing. Mr. Chapin gave me until Monday to turn in my missing assignments. He added a not-so-subtle hint that I needed Bs or higher on everything to pull my grade up to a C, which was so not going to happen.

Mark was being his normal, friendly self, as if he still hadn't noticed he'd been bound. It was almost as unnerving as finding Paige talking to Isaac in the halls. I swear she was stalking him. She found more excuses to touch him too: a tap of her hand on his shoulder as she laughed at something he said. Brushing against him as if the halls weren't wide enough to fit a full-size pick-up truck, let alone a hundred-pound bitch. And she'd smile this angelic-devil sort of smile that I would have loved to wipe off her face with the bottom of my shoe. I was finding it harder and harder not to let her see she was getting to me.

Thursday afternoon, Kaylee and I took Chase to the park with my dad. Chase told me I wasn't any fun. How could I be? Paige was never going to give up on Isaac, and the way Isaac kept his guard up when we were together, I was sure he was close to giving up on us, and Mark was being too nice — I couldn't shake the feeling something big was about to happen.

Even with all this going on, I knew damn well I should have been locked in my bedroom, working on my English homework. Problem was, I couldn't keep my mind from wandering while I read the book. Within minutes, my bedroom seemed to close in on me, ready to squash me like a spider under heavy boots.

To top it all off, Kevin wouldn't return my calls.

"Read through my notes," Kaylee had said when we got home from the park. "It will catch you up to chapter fourteen."

My head dangled over the side of my bed as I stared at her curvy writing, trying to figure out when she'd had time to read the darn book. Not that I was complaining. Thanks to Kaylee, I would be able to complete three worksheets and the two short essays before class on Friday. I'd be lucky to pull off Cs on the essays but could get Bs on the worksheets. That would bring my grade up to a solid D.

I groaned. What was the point?

I threw the notes on my bed and headed for the door. I needed to get out of there. I made it to the top of the stairs before I spun on my heels and marched back to my room to grab the book, Kaylee's notes, and what I needed to complete the worksheets. I wasn't totally sure why I felt compelled to grab these items; I planned on walking until my legs gave out.

I couldn't figure out how things had become so screwed up. When did life get so complicated? I really missed the simple days of just last year.

I walked several blocks and had yet to come up with an answer. The sun barely peeked over the town when I found myself at the black iron gates of the cemetery. The air was still, and the little sunlight left made the shadows of the tombstones reach out toward me. The voices of those long-buried whispered in the back of my mind. Knowing about the powers made me realize I wasn't imagining them. I should have been petrified to set foot in there. I should have run the other way.

But I didn't. My legs brought me to the cemetery because I needed the comfort I could only get from being near my mom.

She'd died giving birth to Chase. At first, I'd been angry, and I'd hated my brother for taking Mom from me. It had taken me several months to admit to myself it hadn't been his fault and several years to realize sometimes the people you love can't be saved.

I walked the long way to her grave. After brushing the leaves away from her headstone, I took a seat. I somehow knew the shadows that slithered over the ground and the whispers that tried to lure their victims into the night couldn't touch me when I was within her reach.

I pulled Kaylee's notes from between the pages of the book, could barely make out her curvy handwriting in the dim evening light, and put them away. I really didn't want to read anyway. I lay down in the grass next to my mom's grave, using the book as a pillow, and stared at the sherbet-colored sunset. Gossamer clouds floated across a near-full moon as I drifted to sleep.

I didn't know what time it was when I woke, freezing my ass off. It was the voices that had roused me — the hushed whispers of two beings who shouldn't have been there and didn't want to be.

"Over here," I called.

A white beam of light reached through the darkness to find me. Kaylee and Sarah walked closely together. Kaylee's eyes kept scanning the graveyard nervously.

"I wish you'd find somewhere else to go when you're upset," Kaylee said as she took a seat on the grass next to me. She stood the flashlight on its end in front of us so that the light fanned upward. "This place gives me the creeps."

Sarah handed me a jacket. "Put this on before you freeze to death." I gladly took the ski jacket. She sat down and went on, "As soon as Kaylee called looking for you, we knew where you were."

The breeze brushed past us, bringing with it an oddly sweet scent — like cherry popsicles.

Kaylee rested a hand on my arm. "You okay?"

"Yeah. I just needed to get out of the house." I shrugged. "This is where I ended up."

"Want to talk about it?" Sarah asked.

I had to be careful what I said in front of Sarah. She didn't know about the powers, and I didn't want to put her in the middle of that. How wonderful it must be to believe that everything is fine, to believe the police could protect you and your loved ones, and to feel like life was going on as it always did. I knew better. There were powers in the world the police could do nothing about. Powers that, if in the wrong hands, could harm people and *had* harmed people.

I couldn't say any of this to Sarah. Powers weren't my only problem.

Sarah rested a hand on my knee. "They'll find who drugged Kaylee. You shouldn't worry about it."

Kaylee let out a high-pitched laugh then covered her mouth with her hand.

"I'm not worried about that," I said. At least not in the way Sarah thought. I sighed. "It's guy problems."

"Guy problems?" Sarah repeated. "Didn't I see you with the new guy?"

"Isaac," I said. "His name's Isaac. Kevin saw us together too."

Sarah's eyes grew wide. "Kevin's back in town?"

I nodded. "And Mark asked me out."

"He what?" Kaylee blurted. Disapproval and disgust warred for first place in her expression. I guess I'd neglected to mention that little detail to her.

"It was before," I mumbled. I studied a patch of clover as if it were the most interesting thing I'd ever seen. The whole necklace drama kept coming back to bite me.

"Before what?" Sarah asked.

I glanced up at Kaylee. "Before he gave me the necklace."

Kaylee's jaw fell to her chest. "You told me he wanted to get rid of it. That you were just holding it for him."

"I was." I knew now it was stupid to have taken the damn thing. "I'm sorry." Not just for conveniently leaving out an important part of the story but for putting her in danger.

Kaylee shook her head. "Madison, you are so naïve sometimes."

"Let me get this straight," Sarah said. "Mark asked you out on a date. You declined. Yet he gave you a necklace, which you took even though you said no to going out with him. Soon after, you're dating the new guy Isaac, and out of the blue Kevin shows up and sees you two together."

"Well." It sounded even worse hearing her sum it up like that. I bit my bottom lip. "I ran into Kevin a few days ago, so I knew he was in town."

"And you didn't mention Isaac to him?" Sarah asked. I got the impression she wanted to say more, but she snapped her lips together instead. After a long pause, she said, "Okay. Start at the beginning."

So I did. I told her about everything but, of course, the witchcraft. When I finished, I covered my face with my hands. "I've made such a mess of things. I wish I could hide from everyone."

Sarah twisted her hair into a knot. She used my pencil to hold it in place at the back of her head. "The first thing you need to do is set things straight with Mark. You have to give him the necklace back and tell him you value his friendship and don't feel right having it."

"She can't," Kaylee said.

Sarah looked at the metal cross around Kaylee's neck. "You can't keep it."

Kaylee covered her necklace with her hand. "This one is from Josh. I don't have the one Mark gave Madison. I—I lost it."

More like had it ripped off her neck and crushed to break an evil curse, then stuffed in a poppet and buried in Isaac's backyard, but Sarah didn't need the details.

"Then Madison has to offer to replace it," Sarah said. "She can't string Mark along. It's not right."

"I didn't string him along," I said into my hands, my voice muffled. "I told him we were just friends." My fingers slid to my temples. "Besides, he knows I gave it to Kaylee, and I don't think saying sorry is going to help. It may only make him madder, and I'm sort of afraid he might be planning something big to get back at me."

Kaylee's eyes grew wide in recognition of my none-too-subtle hint. Her voice shook when she spoke. "Make him madder? Planning something big?"

I hated to worry Kaylee, but she needed to be careful around him. "I'm not so sure everything is over, if you know what I mean."

Kaylee didn't have to tell me she knew what I meant. Even in the dark, I could see all the color drain from her face.

Sarah leaned forward so that her elbows were on her knees. "I think you're being paranoid."

My reply came out as a crazed laugh.

"Then you need to apologize," Sarah insisted. "Tell Mark you're sorry and you hope you can be friends."

I nodded. There was no way for Sarah to understand just how bad things with Mark were, and since I couldn't provide specifics without spilling my secret, I didn't want to continue to talk about him.

Sarah took my silence as concurrence. "Then you have to pick who you want to date and tell either Kevin or Isaac it's over."

"Kevin and I *are* over," I replied immediately. "We have been for a long time, remember?"

"He must still have feelings for you if he came back to visit," Sarah said. "And you must still have feelings for him if you're beating yourself up because he saw you with Isaac."

"No." I shook my head. "I mean, yes, I still care about Kevin, but he came back because he wanted to talk and didn't have anyone at home he could confide in."

Sarah couldn't be right. Kevin couldn't have come all this way because he wanted us to get back together. The whole long-distance thing would never work out, unless he planned on moving in with his grandparents. That couldn't be why he came back.

Kaylee brought my attention back to the conversation. "Josh talked to Kevin. They hung out the other night."

I grabbed her hand. "Did he tell Josh what he wanted to talk about?"

Kaylee shook her head. "I don't know. Josh hasn't said anything."

"Just call Kevin," Sarah said. "You two were close, you can work this out."

I moaned. "He won't return my calls."

Kaylee said, "Try him again." At the same time Sarah asked, "Are you sure you and Kevin are over?"

Kaylee and I looked at Sarah. She continued, "Seriously. You're driving yourself crazy thinking about him. Maybe things between the two of you aren't as over as you thought they were. Maybe, just maybe, your heart's trying to tell you that breaking up was a mistake."

I shook my head. "That can't be it."

This time when the breeze brushed past us it was tainted with the sharp taste of metal. It made me all too aware we weren't alone, and it wasn't the spirits of those buried there watching us. When a quick scan of the cemetery came up empty, I grabbed Kaylee's and Sarah's arms and pulled them to their feet.

Sarah rested her hand on my shoulder. "Madison, you can't have both. You need to choose."

"I know." But I couldn't choose between Kevin and Isaac. I needed them both. And I wouldn't choose that second, not with an unknown audience. "Let's get out of here."

We walked at a fast clip to the gates. I told myself to keep my eyes forward, not to let on that I could feel the eyes that watched us. I looked back as we stepped onto the sidewalk. Tombstones reached up like crooked teeth, laughing at me, daring me to come back.

I didn't.

I called Kevin when I got home and wasn't the least bit surprised when I got his voicemail. I left another message.

I read through Kaylee's English notes and completed the worksheets I needed to turn in as I mulled over what Sarah had said. She was right—I needed to straighten out my messed up love life before things became worse. That meant I'd have to talk to Mark and make him understand we'd never be more than friends. Maybe then he'd leave me alone. I'd also have to figure out exactly what Isaac and I shared; even though he'd told me our powers had nothing to do with our feelings, I needed proof.

Either way, I didn't know what to do about Kevin. Sarah had me remembering how well we'd fit together and how I used to think we'd always be a couple. She even had me thinking about how lost I'd been when he had first moved. I could step right back into our relationship and be happy, but was that what I wanted? I vowed to figure it out the next day before the festival.

It was after one in the morning when I switched my bedroom light off.

Chapter 16

Knowing

Morning came too quickly. I hit the snooze button on my alarm clock twice before I stumbled out of bed and into the bathroom. I took a cool shower, hoping to shock myself awake. The cold water didn't work nearly as well as my dad banging on the bathroom door, telling me to hurry up.

When I opened the door, he glanced at his watch like I didn't know how majorly late I was running.

"You're not dressed?"

My pink fuzzy robe pretty much answered for me, so I waited for him to either move out of my way or tell me why he'd knocked in the first place. I didn't have to wait long. "Isaac's out front."

I squeezed past him. "Thanks."

It was the day I vowed to straighten out my problems. Mark was the easy one; I didn't have an emotional bond with him. Isaac I'd figure out as soon as I talked to him. It was Kevin I worried about. Ever since I met Isaac and until last night, I hadn't questioned whether I still had feelings for Kevin. Somewhere between tossing and turning while trying to get to sleep and the alarm startling me awake, I had to remind myself that we were friends and I liked it that way.

I nodded to myself. Of course I did.

In my room, I grabbed the first thing I saw—a pair of jeans and a blue hooded thermal top—and threw them on. I was still shoving my homework into my backpack as I jogged down the stairs.

"I'll see you later," I yelled to my dad before rushing out of the house. I didn't wait for a reply.

Isaac put the Jeep into gear as I climbed into the passenger seat.

"Sorry I'm late." I tossed my backpack in the back seat and buckled up.

"No problem."

Isaac looked exceptionally handsome that morning. He wore a black sweater that hugged the muscles in his shoulders and chest, making him look as if he were made of stone. His face was fair in comparison to his dark spiked hair. When he looked at me, it was with eyes that warmed my soul.

I kept telling myself now was the time to talk to him. I twisted the strap of my purse into a knot around my fingers as I worked up the nerve to broach the subject. We were a block from school when I finally found my voice and asked him to pull over.

He eased the Jeep onto the shoulder of the road, parked, and turned in his seat to face me. "What is it?"

"You told me you blocked most of your powers so I wouldn't be able to feel them," I blurted before I changed my mind and said nothing. "At least until I discovered my own."

"Yeah," he replied cautiously and freed my fingers from the purse strap. "I didn't want to shock you every time we touched."

"How do you do that? Is it something I can do?"

Isaac's brow furrowed, but he didn't ask me what was up with all the questions. Instead, he said, "I take a moment to center myself and gather my thoughts. From there, I pull my magic deeper inside of me." He paused. "Have you ever been so excited or angry about something that you have to stop yourself and take a minute to breathe, to collect yourself so others don't notice or you don't do something you'll regret?"

Sure. Keeping my magic a secret had me doing that more and more. I nodded.

"It's sort of like that," he said. "It might take a little practice, but you should be able to do it too."

"Can you block your powers completely? So I can't feel them at all?"

Isaac nodded and watched me, his expression unreadable.

I closed my eyes and prayed. "Can you do it now?"

He brushed my cheek with the back of his hand. There was no jolt of power or the tingling sensation that often accompanied his touch. Even with Isaac right in front of me, I felt alone. I fought to keep from trembling. I suddenly wasn't sure I wanted to go through with my test. I did my best to clear my mind, which wasn't easy with all my thoughts screaming at me.

I touched his hand. "How am I doing?"

Isaac gave a weak little smile. "Not too bad."

"I want to try something." I leaned over the stick shift and stopped just before our lips met. There was no scent of the vanilla or spearmint. Isaac's breath brushed my lips as he watched me with curious eyes. I don't know what he saw. Probably fear. Confusion. His fingers touched my cheek softly and traveled down my jaw-line to my lips. No powers, just warmth and caring. My heart did an unsteady leap in my chest when he closed the distance between us and kissed me. A tear of relief escaped the corner of my eye. Even without Isaac's powers dancing over my skin, without my powers fully there, I was crazy about him.

The question remained, did he share my feelings?

He pulled away. "What's this all about? Did something happen?"

"I'm so confused. You know?" I wiped at the tear and looked down at my hands. Damn, I didn't want to cry. There was so much I didn't want to say. Yet my mouth, having that inconvenient habit of speaking when I *didn't* want to, ran off on its own.

"I needed to know if our powers were making me feel the way I do when I'm with you."

"And?"

I shook my head. Do I tell him I'm undeniably and without a doubt falling in love with him? Would he run the other way, thinking I'm needy and obsessive? *Baby steps*, I reminded myself. I had the answer to one of my problems.

"It's not our powers," I said.

"And that upsets you?" he asked, clearly confused.

"Yes. No. I mean—I don't know how you feel about me, and… it's just we seem to have a good time together, and then I see you talking to Paige, and I know she likes you—" I bit my bottom lip and kept my eyes on my hands. I couldn't do this. I was too afraid

I'd ruin whatever it was we did have to discuss my lingering doubts. "Never mind. We should get to class."

I pulled my sleeves over my palms and gripped the cuffs like a child squeezing a security blanket, hoping Isaac would stop watching me and speed off to school. But he didn't drive.

"First of all," he began in a low, heartfelt tone. "Paige keeps cornering me at school because she wants me to join her coven. She felt my magic at the party when she brushed up against me, and she's been hounding me ever since." Isaac lifted my chin so that I had to look at him. "That's it."

I didn't trust my voice, so I twitched a shoulder in reply.

Isaac continued, "I know whatever you and I share is not because of our powers. I told you that before, and I wouldn't lie to you. I've never felt this way about anyone else. You complicate things for me. If I were smart, I'd stay away from you." He said the last sentence more to himself than me. With a shrug, he added, "But I've never been known to do what I should."

I was glad to hear that last part. I had mixed feelings about the rest. It was great to know he'd never deceive me and that I was special to him. But if that were true, why would he say he should stay away from me? I couldn't imagine how I made things difficult for him.

"Complicate things how?" I asked.

Isaac's eyes, while still caring and gentle, held a new edge to them. "For one thing, I have to be careful not to let our powers collide. It's not always that easy."

"You do a pretty good job." If I didn't know better, I wouldn't be able to tell he had any.

"I'm always conscious of them, keeping them pulled in when we're close, but when—" Isaac pursed his lips as he seemed to choose his words. "There are times it's not that easy, and you have little control over yours."

"I don't understand," I admitted. "If I'm not trying to use them, why do I need to control them?"

Isaac traced my lips with his thumb before he ran his fingers through my hair, twisting them around its length at the back of my head. His gaze scalded. I sucked in a breath, waiting to see what he'd do next. He leaned closer, his mouth inches from my ear. "That drives me crazy."

It was hard to think straight with him whispering in my ear. I had to try a couple times before I could ask, "What does?"

"The way your breath catches."

Oh, he could hear that. My cheeks warmed with embarrassment, but he couldn't see them, not with his lips against my neck.

He continued in his silken voice, "My powers awaken, and I have to try harder to control them. Part of me doesn't want to, because then I can't hear your heart race. Are you still holding your powers in?"

I'd stopped holding them in the second his hand had traveled to the back of my head. I closed my eyes, did my best to ignore his lips as they traced their way from my jaw to my chin, and pulled my powers in. I think. My thoughts were a bit preoccupied.

Isaac's lips moved to mine, and he kissed me more passionately than he ever had. His tongue brushed mine and retreated behind his lips, which moved over mine more urgently. The kiss lasted longer than any of our others, until a sharp sting made me recoil. It traveled from my mouth all the way to my toes.

"Ow!"

A smug smile stretched across Isaac's face. "That's one complication."

I had an entirely new reason to learn how to control my emotions and magic. I could still feel the bite of our powers colliding on my tongue.

"What's the other thing?" I asked. It couldn't be as bad as the first.

Isaac let go of my hair and leaned back. The muscles in his jaw tensed.

Okay, maybe the other thing was worse. I waited.

"Before I met you, I knew without a doubt I was in control. I wouldn't use negative emotions to fuel my magic. But now that I've seen what a curse can do…" Isaac raked his fingers through his hair. "I've been questioning the composure I thought I had. If push came to shove, I'm not going to be able to press pause and sort through my feelings before using my powers. I'm beginning to realize I'd do whatever it took to keep someone I care about safe — expose what I am, harness my anger, let my darker side take over. That's one promise I know I can make without regret."

"You — you can't," I stammered, knowing very well his promise bound him to his words. "You'd be giving away part of your soul."

He shrugged. "I can't help how I feel, and you are one of the people I care about. You have my promise, I'll do — "

"No!" I covered his lips with my fingers. "Don't bind yourself to something like that. I don't want you losing your soul because of me."

I bit my bottom lip. Isaac's powers were impressive. They were stronger than Josh's and mine combined. Powerful enough to allow us to pass through a semi truck as if we were ghosts. Fluid enough to wrap around me, making me feel secure, without needing to touch me. I didn't want to see what he could do if he embraced his darker side.

"Promise me you won't use negative emotions to fuel your powers," I begged.

Isaac studied me a moment. I held his gaze, trying not to fidget. Then he reached over the center console, placing a finger under my chin as he leaned in and tenderly kissed my lips, without his powers present. My heart still twirled with excitement. An audible moan slipped from my throat. God, I wanted to get lost in his kiss.

Afterward, he ran his tongue over his lips as if wanting one last taste of that kiss and replied, "No," to my earlier question. I was about to protest when he then asked, "What about you? Just what are your feelings toward me?" I must have hesitated because he laughed, light and warm, yet there was a bitter edge to it. "I just told you I'd embrace the dark to protect you, and you still can't open up to me?"

I knew I should have just told him I loved him, but those three words kept getting caught in my throat. When I did speak, my reply came out in a whisper. "I really like you and the thought of losing you scares me."

Isaac leaned down, letting our lips meet once more. His powers wrapped me in their embrace.

"I'll accept that, for now." He rested his forehead on mine and asked, "Is there anything else bothering you?"

I didn't want to ruin the moment by mentioning Mark, and I couldn't tell him I'd briefly had second thoughts about Kevin. I settled for shaking my head no.

Isaac put the Jeep in gear.

We arrived at school more than twenty minutes late.

Mr. Chapin frowned when I entered English. He didn't care that I had stayed up late to work on his homework assignments. You'd think after all my hard work completing the worksheets, he would be a little grateful. I had read the book — well, Kaylee's notes — and exerted a lot of energy to answer the questions. Instead of giving a thank-you, Mr. Chapin glanced over the first sheet, frowned, and told me to take my seat. The bell rang a few minutes later.

Dealing with Mark was next on my list. I planned on marching up to him and asking what his problem was. I would put him on the spot and make him realize he needed to leave my friends and me alone. When I got to Foods, though, Mark wasn't there. My kitchen's oatmeal raisin cookies were cooling on the rack before I'd accepted the fact he wasn't going to show up.

By fourth period History, I was ready for the end of the day, which would come with the bell for those involved in setting up the last-minute decorations and booths for the Harvest Festival.

"Did you talk to him?" Sarah asked when I got to my desk.

"Which *him?*" I asked as I sat down.

She mouthed *Mark.*

Kaylee, who had arrived to class before me, turned in her seat and waited for my answer.

"No," I whispered. "He wasn't in class, but that reminds me. Kaylee, can you have Josh ask Kevin to please return my call?" I wasn't sure what to say to him, but I figured the words would come to me once I had him on the phone.

"Kevin?" Paige asked. I hadn't seen her take the seat behind me. "Is he in town?"

There was no way I was going to give Paige any information about Kevin. I knew if he and I really were to remain friends, I shouldn't care whom he went out with, but that didn't mean I was okay with Paige slithering her way into his life.

"That's none of your business," I said.

"Does Isaac know?" Paige asked. "It is *his* business if you're dating other people at the same time you're dating him. Isn't it?"

Great. All I needed in my messed up love life was more of Paige's interference.

"I'm not dating Kevin," I snapped.

Kaylee let out a loud huff and asked Paige, "Why are you always so concerned with what Madison's doing?"

Paige glared at her, eyes narrowed and mouth forming a thin line.

Kaylee continued, "Admit it, you're jealous of her. You've always been jealous of her because she always comes out one step ahead of you."

My mouth fell open at Kaylee's candidness.

"Watch yourself," Paige warned.

"Are you threatening her?" I asked. Paige was going to have to go through me to get to Kaylee.

Emma walked by me toward her desk. She stopped and whispered something to Paige, who nodded and pulled out her History book instead of answering me.

I couldn't believe she was letting our argument go, and I wanted to know what Emma had said to her. What if Paige planned to tell Isaac that I was dating Kevin? Would he believe her over me? My stomach cramped as if they'd punched me in the gut.

We managed to ignore each other for the rest of class, although I wouldn't have been surprised if Paige and Emma were making faces at Kaylee and me behind our backs.

After class, Kaylee and I went with Sarah to Mrs. Sheppard's classroom while Paige went to the back of the school to help set up the dunking booth.

"Did you at least get a chance to talk to Isaac?" Kaylee asked as we walked.

"Yeah, that's why I was late for English."

Kaylee grabbed my arm. "You guys are still together, aren't you?"

Sarah stopped walking and huddled close to us.

"Yes." A flutter of excitement traveled through me now that I knew he wanted our relationship to continue as much as I did. And, well, I got a sneak peek at what I had to look forward to once I learned to tame my emotions. When it came to Isaac, life was good. I could finally see that with clarity now.

"Did you tell him you don't like how chummy he is with Paige?" Sarah asked.

"Not in so many words," I replied and started walking again. "But she did come up, and he said Paige is the one who keeps cornering him." I looked at Kaylee when I said the next part. "She wants him to join her circle of friends."

Kaylee mouthed the word *Oh* then said, "That sounds like something she'd do. How long has she, you know?"

"Since the party at the beach," I replied, knowing she meant how long had Paige known about Isaac's powers.

We stopped at my locker to toss our backpacks in.

"What about Kevin?" Sarah asked.

"I love Kevin," I admitted. "But things have changed since he moved. It's not the same feeling I have for Isaac. I still want to talk to him, though. I don't want him going back to Minnesota with the last thing between us being that awkward day at school."

Mrs. Sheppard had several white boxes filled with cookies waiting for us. We each grabbed a stack and headed to the football field. Refreshments were being set up at the booths closest to the school. Smoke rose in billowing clouds from two large grills. The sweet scent of melted butter mixed with the charred scent of grilled hotdogs. We set the boxes on one of the long tables across from them. Another table had brownies and cupcakes. A sheet of white paper dangled from the front of the booths, listing the prices of each item. The rest of the booths were scattered behind us. Ben was setting up a small square table at the entrance of the maze. Mark's back was to us as he fastened a sign to the cornstalks behind the table.

Sarah followed my gaze. "If you want to talk to Mark, Kaylee and I will set up the booth."

I didn't want to make a scene. I shook my head. "Now's not the best time."

The sight of Mark had Kaylee biting the inside of her cheek. "What if he tries something?" she whispered to me when Sarah went to grab a permanent marker and tape off of the table next to us.

"He's not going to try something with everyone here." At least I didn't think he would.

Kaylee nodded.

Sarah came back, holding the marker and an empty dispenser. "Can one of you run back into school and grab some tape?"

I had the eerie feeling of being watched, like I'd had the night before at the cemetery. I looked up in time to see Mark look away. A shiver ran down the length of my spine.

"I'll go," I volunteered before Kaylee could. It had to be safer for her to be in a crowd of people.

Chapter 17

Kevin

Mrs. Sheppard wasn't in her classroom when I got there. I grabbed the tape from her desk, turned to leave, and froze.

Kevin stood in the doorway, twisting a hat in his hands. The muscles in his arms flexed from the simple movement. Basketball had fine-tuned his body, making him lean and toned. He watched me through wisps of russet brown hair. He looked good. So good that I even had to ask myself if I was sure I didn't want to be with him again. Which I was, but for a brief moment I allowed myself to silently admit that I was still attracted to him.

He offered a smile. "I saw you head back to the school. I was hoping we could talk."

Kevin's timing was almost as bad as it had been the other day when I ran into him on the stairs. I glanced at the tape I was holding and ignored my inner voice that nagged me to hurry back to the festival.

"I, uh, yeah. You didn't return any of my calls."

"Sorry about that. I had a lot of thinking to do."

We both took a few steps closer.

"Kevin, I am sorry I didn't tell you about Isaac," I said again. "I didn't want to hurt you. You know that, don't you?"

"I know." His lips didn't quite make it into a smile.

He looked so sad and lost. I wanted to close the gap between us and hold him tight, as if that could take away whatever it was that bothered him.

"What is it?" I asked, "What couldn't you talk to anyone else about?"

Kevin stepped further into the classroom and leaned against one of the tables. "Actually, I talked to Josh."

All sorts of things went through my mind. Were the people at his new school making his life miserable? What if Kevin was sick? What if he was dying? The possibilities were endless.

"You're scaring me," I said when he still didn't offer any information.

He patted the top of the table. My legs carried me, a bit shakily, closer to him.

"It would be easier for me to show you." Kevin rested the tips of his fingers on my bare arm and sent a startling jolt into me. In all the time Kevin and I had dated, *that* had never happened. His fingers glided over my arm in a figure eight, and though it left my skin tingling, it wasn't in a way that made my heart sing.

"When? How?" I stammered.

"A few weeks ago, just before I last called you, and I don't know how. I didn't really understand what it was. I wanted to talk to someone, and I knew you and I could always talk about anything. Then I saw you with that other guy, and my confusion and anxiety turned to something else, and I just wanted to explode. I called the only other person I trust enough with this. Josh told me about his powers, and about you recently finding *yours*."

I put my hand on his, to see if maybe the earlier shock had been static electricity, and yanked my hand back when the contact with his skin sent another sting of power through me.

"But how come our powers are colliding now?" I asked. "You and I dated, and we weren't shocking each other every time we held hands."

"Josh believes it's because neither one of us had embraced our powers. They would have been dormant, hidden deep inside us."

"Do your parents have them?"

Kevin shook his head. "This doesn't come from my mom's side, my step-dad wouldn't count, and I don't know much about my birth father."

"How did you find out about yours?"

"It's been sort of showing itself in spurts." He shoved his hands into his jean pockets. "The first time was during a basketball game. I got into a pushing match with one of the players on the other team.

The coach sent me to the locker room to cool off. I was pissed. The other guy started it, and he didn't get kicked out of the game. I punched a locker. Left a nice-sized dent. I knew if the coach saw it I'd be off the team. I didn't know what I was doing. I just rested my hand over the dent thinking I shouldn't have done it. Next thing I knew, the metal had pushed its way back out.

"After that, I started to experiment," he continued. "I tried breaking a plate and resting my hand on the broken pieces to see if I could fix it."

"Did you?" I couldn't imagine what it must have been like for Kevin to wake up one day being able to do magic. He must have thought he was losing his mind.

"No. But I did keep trying different things. Eventually, I figured out how to summon something small off my dresser or a table, like a pen or my keys. I searched the Internet for any information on what was happening to me. One search led to another, and before I knew it, I was reading articles on witchcraft, which led back to Essex County."

Kevin raised his hand, and I pulled in my powers to block the shock when he touched my cheek. His hand lingered for only a moment before he let it fall to his side. "Josh said you went seeking yours. That you embraced them fully and have used them."

I nodded. "I was looking for a way to help Kaylee. My search took me from schizophrenia to witchcraft. As hard as it was to believe magic was real, I knew Kaylee wasn't crazy, that there was something else causing her to be sick."

Kevin nodded. "I'm sorry about Kaylee. Josh said she's better."

"Yeah." I looked into Kevin's endless blue eyes. "Are you going to embrace your powers?"

Kevin gripped the edge of the table. "That wouldn't be good for me."

"Why?"

Kevin was the type of person who'd tell a cashier she'd given him too much change or talk to the ugly girl at the party just so she wasn't sitting alone. I couldn't imagine what harm could come from him embracing his powers. With Josh's and my help, he'd learn how to control them.

"You don't understand," Kevin began, and then stopped when someone knocked on the open door.

Isaac looked from me to Kevin. The air filled with the bitter taste of orange rinds and steel. Several burners on the stoves lit on their own. Kevin and I pushed off the table and faced Isaac, who turned off the burners with a wave of his hand.

"Sarah sent me to find you," Isaac said, without acknowledging the magic that had just taken place. "She needs the tape."

"Right." I looked apologetically at Kevin. "You coming?"

The muscles in Kevin's jaw tensed. "I'll catch up with you later."

"You sure?" I looked from Kevin to Isaac, then back to Kevin, wishing there was a way for us all to be friends. I knew that wouldn't happen.

Kevin gripped the table tighter, causing his knuckles to turn white. "You go."

Talk about awkward situations. I wanted to finish my conversation with Kevin but knew he'd never discuss his powers with Isaac—who he didn't know and I don't think wanted to know—there.

I rested my hand on Kevin's sleeve so I wouldn't shock either of us. "Promise me you won't leave before we get a chance to talk."

Kevin took a deep breath, which he held for a long moment. We ignored the bag of microwave popcorn that popped where it was on the counter—I was sure it was Kevin's untamed powers that caused it because Isaac would never lose control like that. When Kevin exhaled, he nodded to my earlier question.

Isaac and I walked down the hall. I wasn't sure how long he'd been watching Kevin and me. But by his stiff shoulders and lack of conversation, I got the feeling it had been a while.

"Thanks for coming to find me," I said, hoping to ease the tension between us.

Isaac had his hands in the pockets of his jacket. I could hear him jingling something, maybe his keys or change. He looked straight ahead, his mouth set in a thin line. When we reached to edge of the football field, I grabbed his arm to stop him. I went up on my tiptoes and kissed him. His response was polite. Robotic even. Like when you let a relative you barely know kiss your cheek hello.

"Kevin's going through a hard time," I said. "He needs people he can talk to."

"You can talk to whomever you want," Isaac replied in a steely tone.

"Kevin and I are just friends." I wanted to feel Isaac's powers wrap around me, comforting me and telling me everything was fine. That didn't happen. "Say something," I begged.

"You didn't see how you looked at him." Isaac started walking. "Sarah's waiting."

I had to force my legs to start moving. My relationship with Isaac had just taken a step forward that morning only to take a gigantic leap backward that afternoon.

Sarah and Kaylee had the cookies in neat rows on the table when we got there. A small tan cash box sat between the chairs. Sarah held a sheet of paper listing the prices. I handed her the tape.

"I'm going to find Josh," Isaac said.

I nodded and watched him walk away.

Kaylee pretended to fix the skirt around the table. She whispered, "Are you okay?"

Afraid my voice would crack or I'd break down and cry if I spoke, I nodded my reply, which indicated *yes* but really meant *NO*. Kaylee eyed me, so I forced a smile.

"I'm fine."

I saw Kevin walking the long way around the field toward Mark and Ben, who were manning the table near the entrance of the maze. Mr. Chapin—dressed in shorts and a polo shirt—climbed onto the bench in the dunking tank. Paige shut the door as the last bell of the half-day rang, releasing a flood of students who drifted toward the festival. Emma walked past the refreshments and took a seat on the table where Paige was collecting money from a couple of freshmen.

Sarah, Kaylee, and I sat at the bake sale booth. It didn't take long for things to get busy. When Josh arrived to see how we were doing, I pulled him aside.

"Where's Isaac?" I asked.

"Don't know. I haven't seen him since Gym."

"He saw me talking to Kevin and—" I tried to keep the desperation from my voice, but just thinking about the cold and indifferent look Isaac had given me made me want to curl up in a ball and cry. "Can you find him for me? Ask him to come and talk to me? Please."

Josh nodded, handed me some money in exchange for three cookies, and walked toward the school.

We sold more than half the cookies, and Josh still wasn't back. Nor did Isaac show up. With most people enjoying the activities, sales at our booth slowed drastically. Kaylee took a break and headed to the bathroom. Sarah got up to check how the rest of the booths were doing. That left me to wait for Natalie to relieve me.

I kept scanning the crowd, looking for Isaac. We'd driven together, and while I knew I could get a ride home from Kaylee and Josh, I just couldn't believe Isaac would leave without telling me. It wasn't like he'd walked in on Kevin and me making out. We were talking. No different than all the times he's talked to Paige. I kept expecting him to show up wearing that crooked smile of his, asking when I'd be free.

When that didn't happen, I thought about tracking him down and begging him to talk. But then, maybe he needed time to think. He'd realize he had nothing to worry about. Wouldn't he?

"Sorry I'm late," Natalie said, breaking into my reverie. She had her friend Lauren with her. "We got lost in the maze."

"No problem." I pushed myself up out of the chair.

I decided that I would let fate take over. If I was meant to talk to Isaac that afternoon, then I'd bump into him. I wandered around the festival. Everyone else was having a great time, laughing and joking with friends. It only made me more miserable. My legs carried me to the maze, and I was thankful that Mark wasn't there. I really wasn't in the mood to talk to him. I gave Ben a dollar, my admission to the labyrinth of cornstalks, and walked through the entrance.

The maze was a lot like my life: a series of paths that led to choices, turns that often led me astray, and dead ends that forced me to rethink where I'd just been. No matter how hard I tried, I couldn't find the exit or my happiness. I'd get close, but then there'd be one more choice to make, one more obstacle to get past, one more wall of cornstalks blocking the way.

There were a few other students wandering around the narrow paths. I hadn't realized just how big the maze was, or maybe I'd kept walking in circles, but after a while it became claustrophobic. I wanted out. My heart raced as I started to pay attention to every turn I took. Before I found the exit, I ran into Mark and Emma.

Mark's eyes lit up when he saw me. I would say that I'd imagined it, but Emma's face burned an odd shade of scarlet as she scowled at me.

"Hi, Madison," Mark said with way too much enthusiasm considering Emma was standing right in front of him.

Emma crossed her arms over her chest. "Don't have enough guys chasing after you, you had to come looking for Mark?"

"I was just walking…I wasn't looking…What?" I asked, totally confused.

She fixed me with an obstinate stare. After the looks I'd gotten from Kevin and Isaac, hers seemed almost friendly.

I chose to ignore her. "I didn't realize how big the maze was. I was trying to find the exit."

"Around this way." Mark pointed behind him.

"Thanks." I nodded and walked past them. When I got back to the bake sale booth, Kaylee was still gone, so I headed toward the school to find her. I checked the first floor bathroom, which was packed with several girls, none of them Kaylee.

I headed toward my locker next—thinking Kaylee might have stopped there to grab something from her purse—and ran into Kevin and Paige. They looked at me. I'm not sure what emotion they saw on my face, but Paige's mouth twitched upward into a smile. Kevin's gaze didn't meet mine.

Out of all the girls in Minnesota and Gloucester combined, would Kevin really go out with Paige? He had to know she would date him simply because he was once mine. He had to know how much it would upset me. Maybe that was the point.

I quickly composed myself and tried to act natural. "Have you seen Kaylee?"

Kevin shook his head.

Paige pointed down the hall. "She was looking for paper towels."

I wanted to grab Kevin by the arm and ask him what he was doing, but I didn't want Paige to see she was getting to me.

"Thanks," I said and walked by them as if I couldn't care less that I'd found them huddled together in a deserted hallway.

My pulse pounded in my ears as I forced myself not to run. I slipped into the first classroom I saw, which ended up being Mrs. Parris's. It was empty. I leaned against the wall, my breaths coming in short bursts. I had to pull myself together. If Isaac saw me so upset over Kevin talking to Paige, I'd lose him forever.

I slid down the wall until I was crouching and, with my hands over my head, tried to steady my breathing. Kevin was allowed to date whomever he wanted, I reminded myself, even if it was Paige. It wasn't that Kevin was talking to another girl that upset me, though; it was that he was talking to my archenemy. I was so preoccupied reasoning with myself that I didn't hear the classroom door open.

Chapter 18

Sometimes There's No Saving Yourself

"Well, well, well. What do we have here?" Emma stared down at me through the parts in her blond hair, one hand on her hip. She had the brass black widow that Mark used to carry with his keys dangling from her belt loop.

They must be back together. If she weren't such a bitch, I would have warned her not to trust him.

I looked up long enough to tell her to go away. I was too busy wallowing in my own self-pity to deal with her. I could handle Kevin dating anyone except Paige. He had to know that.

"What's wrong?" she taunted. "Afraid Mark won't take you to that movie?"

"What?" How the heck did she know Mark had asked me to the movies? I stood back up, my back still against the wall. "There's nothing going on between him and me."

"Really?" Her hand flew to her hip. "Then why did he give you my necklace?"

Not the frickin' necklace again. "I was holding it for him. That's all."

"I bet you were." Emma clucked her tongue against the roof of her mouth.

"In case you haven't noticed, I'm seeing someone," I spat. "So, unless you have another reason for being here, why don't you find someone else to annoy?"

"I have a reason to be here." Emma walked over to the teacher's desk, running her hand along the top as she moved toward the drawers. She opened each in turn, searching without touching.

"Look, you have nothing to worry about. Mark and I are just friends." I grimaced again. We weren't even that. "He's all yours."

"Problem is, he won't go back out with me, and I think it's because of you."

I became very aware of the fact we were the only two people in the room, probably the only two people in this part of the school. There was a glint of evil carefully hidden in the look she threw my way. A faint stench, one I couldn't quite place, slithered through the classroom. It was like a neon sign screaming, *DERANGED WITCH IN ROOM*. And then it hit me that Mark might be part of a coven, and if he were, Emma and Paige would be logical members. I knew one thing: I didn't want to be alone in a room with any of them.

"Well," I said as I pushed myself away from the wall, "you have nothing to worry about. You and Mark make a cute couple."

I reached for the door handle at the same time the lock clicked in place.

"And you're nothing but a nuisance to my friend, Paige," Emma said, picking up the tin pencil holder on Mrs. Parris's desk. She examined a letter opener and then put everything back down. "Did you know she had the biggest crush on Kevin, but he asked you out and not her?"

At the time, I hadn't known that. Kevin had asked me out during our freshman year, and it hadn't been until I'd seen how distant Paige had become since then that I'd guessed she liked him. It wasn't like I'd stolen him from her.

"Then we saw Isaac at the party. I'd just finished convincing Paige to go over and talk to him, and you showed up."

I shook my head in disbelief. "You're talking as if I purposely set out to ruin Paige's dating life. You do realize she and I were friends before she started hanging out with you?"

"That was before she realized just how much you were holding her back, before I gave her the power to do something about it."

"You what?"

Suddenly, Paige's and Emma's behavior made sense. When Kaylee and I had been friends with Paige, she'd been shy and sort of awkward in her own skin. I hadn't seen her much over this past summer, but she'd come back to school confident, dressing totally differently and best friends with Emma. Damn, I should have connected Emma to Mark and Paige sooner. The only thing I wasn't sure about now was if Mark or Emma had put the curse on the necklace.

I stared across the classroom into her dark eyes and saw nothing but hate. I breathed in and choked on a scent so vile it made me cringe. It took me a moment to place what it reminded me of, and when I figured it out I nearly stumbled sideways. Sulfur. The same odor the guys had smelled after the beach party. It burned the fine hairs in my nostrils. My heart pounded in my chest, and I had to tell myself not to panic. I had to get out of the classroom. I had to find Josh and Isaac.

"Open the door, Emma," I ordered.

"No." Emma studied her nails with calculated boredom. "The way I see it, if you were gone, then both Paige and I could be happy."

I pulled at the door. It didn't budge. "You're crazy!"

That realization didn't help me remain calm. It didn't give me the feeling that Emma just wanted to talk and mark her territory, that being Mark himself.

Emma waved her hand in a jerky motion from left to right, sending one of the students' desks skidding across the floor toward me. I threw my arm up in a blocking stance, as if she were throwing a punch, and pushed power away from me. Its force collided with the desk with a bang and ricocheted it away.

"I see you finally embraced your powers," Emma said. "This could be fun." I didn't like the gleam in her eyes, and *fun* was the last word I'd use to describe what we were having. "Let's see just how much you've learned."

Emma thrust her hands forward as if pushing something out of the way. I was slammed against the wall and lifted to the ceiling by the force of her power. I clutched at my stomach where her spell held me pinned. Emma took the scissors out of Mrs. Parris's desk and twirled them around in her hand. I fought harder to get free. I needed help.

"Isaac, Josh," I half whispered, half sobbed — hoping our summoning spell would work.

In my head, I heard Kaylee's panicked voice calling Josh's and my name in reply.

Emma threw the scissors like a dart. They soared toward me, and I screamed as the point of the scissors sank into the wall next to my ear.

"We can do this the easy way or the hard way." Emma sat in Mrs. Parris's chair and passed the stapler from one hand to the other as she spoke. "I was planning on killing you, but that would be a waste of your magic. I mean, really, if you were to drop dead right now, what would happen to all your powers?"

I figured they would die with me but was too stunned by Emma's behavior and the turn of events to ask. I tried wiggling to free myself.

"You're lucky I've seen how effective a curse can be, and there are a couple spells I'd love to try out. They won't hurt much. There's full-blown crazy where you'll think you can fly just like Dumbo, or I've been reading up on one that puts different voices in your head. You know, imaginary friends only you can hear." Her eyes widened. "Maybe you'll think you're the next messiah or something like that." She laughed. "Or would you prefer to be just far enough gone that people call you 'special' and send you to a special school? I can make that one look like an accident, like you hit your head and knocked something up there loose. You pick."

She acted as if she'd just asked me something as simple as which movie I would like to go see later that night.

I could taste my own fear, like rotten strawberries. With my left hand still gripping my stomach, I held my right hand in front of me and focused on my power, forcing it to travel down my arm and into my hand. I pushed it out to my fingertips and into a ball of energy that streaked toward Emma. She ducked, releasing me at the same time. I fell to the floor and scrambled to my feet. Emma was nowhere to be seen.

Her mocking laughter came from behind the teacher's desk. "Not bad. Did you know that negative emotions make your spell stronger? That embracing the darkness within you can open up doors to your powers that you never knew existed?"

"And corrupt your soul in the process." I tried the door again. Still locked.

"You have to taste the power it gives you to understand. It's amazing. So incredible, you want more and more of it." Emma stood back up. "Did you know there's more to be had, if you're not afraid to take it? I wasn't afraid. I can share my powers and not even miss the little

I give away. Paige was eager to become someone else. Someone who could walk through the halls of school with her head held high. Someone who wasn't afraid to approach guys. I gave her power and showed her how to use it to turn herself into the person she wanted to be."

"There was nothing wrong with the old Paige." I looked around me for anything I could use against Emma, a book to throw at her or a chair to slam down over her head. Problem was, not much in the classroom was going to help me fight against a vamped-up psycho with her kind of power.

"The old Paige wouldn't have had the guts to walk up to a guy and ask him out," Emma went on. "You know, Isaac would have fallen in love with her if he hadn't had the ability to block her charm." Emma smirked. "He gave himself away that night at the shore."

"Maybe Isaac wasn't interested in having his mind played with." I gave some serious consideration to throwing fire at her, but with the door locked and the type of luck I seemed to be having lately, I was afraid I'd end up burning myself alive in the process. "People should be able to choose who they want to spend time with."

Emma shrugged. "Says you. Paige is happier now. She's more fun to be with too. Slashing the tires on Josh's Mustang was her idea. We were supposed to have dinner that night at The Grill, but when Paige saw you with Isaac, she didn't want to stay."

I hadn't even known they'd been there. I'd have to start paying better attention to my surroundings. That is, if I made it out of this classroom alive and with my sanity.

"So you slashed Josh's tires? What sense does that make?" I asked, hoping to keep her talking until I figured out what to do.

Emma walked around to the front of the desk. "We didn't know what Isaac drove, and we figured since you were there with Josh and Kaylee, we'd still be interrupting your date. Hexing the necklace Mark gave you was Paige's idea. She got it from the spell I have on my little friend." Emma patted the black widow lovingly. "My spider knows when it's in the hands of another girl. She causes paranoia and a string of bad luck. Anyway, Paige thought it would be funny if the next girl Mark gave the necklace to threw up all over him. I decided the curse should be more potent. The longer the necklace was worn, the stronger the curse became. That should have been you in the hospital fighting demons. You know that, don't you?" Emma smirked. "Does she still see them?"

"You bitch." I charged her, making it a few feet before she socked me with a blast of power that pushed me right back to the wall, a few inches from the door. This time she locked my arms to my side.

"The hex bag on Isaac's Jeep was all me," she said calmly. "I do wish I could have seen what happened when his tire blew."

The memory of sliding through the motor of the semi-truck gave me an involuntary shudder. "You almost killed us."

I struggled to free my arms. Someone shook the door, trying to open it.

"Madison! Are you in there?" It was the loveliest voice I'd ever heard.

"Isaac!" I pushed what power I could from me and freed my arms, or maybe Isaac's presence had distracted Emma and she lost focus on her spell. She raised her hand, sending a spell at the door that caused it to momentarily glow an eerie orange around the edges, sealing it.

"Move away from the door!" he yelled.

I struggled harder, but it was no use. Emma's spell held me pinned to the wall. "I can't!"

Isaac swore, then rammed into the door. It didn't give. He did it a couple more times before the doorframe groaned under the impact. When the door flew open, it swung toward me. I held my hand up just in time to save my face. Isaac's powers reached out and wrapped around me. As I became completely enveloped in them, Emma's spell broke, and I slumped to the floor. Isaac shot a narrow-eyed glace at Emma, his powers sending her tumbling over the teacher's desk. Kevin and Paige stood in the doorway.

Paige looked less smug than she had in the hall. Her eyes traveled from me to the scissors stuck in the wall. Kevin stood rigid as he watched Isaac help me to my feet. I threw my arms around Isaac's neck and hid my face in his shoulder.

The bitterness I'd tasted at school when Isaac and Kevin had first seen each other and again at the graveyard when I'd talked to Sarah and Kaylee caught in my throat, and I gagged. I glanced at Kevin. Something dark stirred in his eyes as he watched Isaac holding me.

"Kevin?" I wasn't even sure the word made it out of my mouth. I grabbed at my throat.

The deep blue eyes that bore down on me weren't the blue eyes of my Kevin. They belonged to someone who had little control of his emotions and his powers.

Isaac looked from me to Kevin. Emma laughed and leaned against the desk to watch.

"Can't—breathe." Even as I fell into Isaac, I couldn't take my eyes off Kevin. Isaac guided me to the floor.

The room filled with anger and hatred and jealousy and fear. My fear, and not for myself but for what Kevin and Isaac would do to each other. I knew in my heart Kevin wouldn't intentionally hurt me. He just couldn't. And Isaac, he had made it very clear that he would embrace the dark to protect me. I had no doubt he'd meant it. The stale air in the room turned icy.

It was selfish on my part, but I didn't want to lose either of them. I'd rather die, which didn't seem too far off. My lungs burned for the oxygen that wasn't making it past my throat. Isaac covered my mouth with his and blew air and power into me. I savored it. The heat threatening to burn a hole through my lungs softened enough for me to take another breath on my own. As soon as Isaac moved away from me, though, the glory of breathing—something I'd always taken for granted—vanished. The burning returned to my lungs, and I struggled again for air.

Isaac stood in front of me, his powers no longer the scent of spearmint and vanilla that was him. I tried to scream for them to stop, but my throat closed around the words. Paige tugged at Kevin, trying to pull him out of the classroom. With a sweep of his hand, Kevin sent Paige flying across the room. She landed near the chalkboard.

"Do something!" Paige yelled.

Emma sat on the edge of Mrs. Parris's desk. She had a ringside seat for the fight that seemed inevitable.

"A few more minutes and they'll have taken care of our little problem for us," Emma cooed. "Our hands will be clean of her blood."

Oh hell, that didn't sound good. I slipped into unconsciousness with those words swirling in my head.

I couldn't have been out long. I woke with Isaac over me again, his warm lips covering mine, blowing air and power into me. I wanted to say thanks and tell him not to be angry with Kevin. Instead, I sucked in air like a drowning person rising to the surface.

"You're killing her!" Isaac yelled. He barely raised his hand when he stood, which threw Kevin across the room and crashed him into the window before he came to a stop. The glass groaned as a crack emerged and raced like lightning over the smooth surface of the window to the metal frame that held it in place.

I grabbed the leg of Isaac's jeans, trying to hold him back. I didn't want them fighting over me. I didn't want them *killing* each other over me. I could barely speak; my voice came out in a hoarse whisper. "Isaac, please. He doesn't know what he's doing. One of you has to stay in control."

Isaac shook his leg free and moved out of my reach.

"Isaac!" I screamed, his name coming out in a dull, scratchy hiss instead of with the volume and intensity I'd tried for.

"Do something," Paige begged Emma, "before they kill each other."

"No." Emma's voice was cool, collected. Uncaring.

With Kevin on the other side of the room, still getting to his feet, I could breathe. Well, *gag*, really. The air reeked of power—strong and pungent. Kevin's bitter jealousy and Isaac's rage mixed with Paige's sudden remorse and Emma's sweet joy. It tasted oddly delectable as it eased the burning in my lungs and the pain in my throat. I swayed as I pushed myself to my feet. I kept one hand on the wall until the room stopped spinning.

I had to gather my emotions before Isaac and Kevin fought power against power. I didn't want to be the reason Isaac embraced the dark and tainted his soul. He was good and kind and deserved to stay that way. Spearmint and vanilla. And Kevin only needed training, to learn to use his powers without negative emotions. All he had come here for was friendship and help, and all I had managed to do was push him away and cause him more pain than he deserved.

I staggered forward, grabbing the first desk I stumbled into for support. I glanced at Emma in time to see her lift her hand. My arm raised automatically, my forearm in front of me in a perfect blocking stance. Desks and chairs skidded across the floor as her powers rushed past me. I managed to create an invisible shield that kept anything from hitting me. Isaac and Kevin battled nearby, but I didn't dare take my eyes off Emma. Paige stood a few feet away, tears streaking her face. *She should be scared*, I thought, trapped in a room with four witches: two pissed-off, one crazy, and one desperate.

I didn't have time to gather my powers. I simply pushed, sending an uncontrolled amount of magic gushing forward. It hit Emma and Paige with vigor and sent them flying into the blackboard. Emma hit her head, knocking her out. Paige appeared too scared to move.

I inhaled deeply and moved forward one desk at a time. Kevin stood facing Isaac, one hand on the back of his neck, his eyes unfocused. Isaac's back was to me. He stood with his feet shoulder-width apart and his palms in front of him. With a thrust of his hands, power rippled forward.

Kevin doubled over as Isaac's spell hit him in his stomach. He stood quickly, sending his own powers out toward Isaac, who in turn was thrown into the teacher's desk.

"Please," I begged, my voice stronger than before. "Don't do this."

Isaac and Kevin both unleashed a spell—their powers collided in an explosion of red.

I moved closer to Isaac. His beautiful brown eyes were black. Kevin faced him, his features twisted in fury.

"Don't do this!" I screamed. Tears ran freely down my face. I was losing everything. Isaac. Kevin. If they destroyed each other, they'd destroy me.

Their powers crackled around me, stinging my skin with its energy. Neither of them noticed me. I didn't even know if they remembered I was there. They were beyond reasoning with, but I had to try.

I grabbed Isaac's raised arm. "Listen to me!"

He shrugged me off easily.

I lunged for Kevin next. He stepped to his side, moving before I could throw my arms around him to keep him from striking Isaac again. My knee hit the heater along the wall of the classroom. Isaac advanced on Kevin.

I had to get their attention. I had to make them hear me.

"Stop it!" I screamed as I ran between them, my arms out to my side, one hand on each of their chests. Power surged into me, and I shook viciously.

Have you ever accidentally stuck a screwdriver into an electrical outlet? The shock caused by the voltage traveling through the screwdriver into your hand causes your fingers to lock in place. Your body trembles, and at first you can't move. The jolt short-circuits your brain for a brief moment before you are able to react. I can only imagine that standing in water while you did this would make the whole ordeal that much worse. The water would act like a conductor and keep feeding electricity back into you.

Having my hands on Isaac and Kevin while their powers ran through them uncontrolled was sort of like that, only ten times worse.

I could feel their emotions.

Betrayal, confusion, and jealousy emanated from Kevin, but his emotions went deeper than just him and me. They compounded into loneliness, feeling like an outsider in the town he'd grown up in. He hadn't asked for these powers, and he didn't want them.

There was a tinge of jealousy in Isaac too, but more than that, he was angry and scared. As scared of losing me as I was of losing him. But wrath and determination fed his powers, and I had no doubt he would be the one who walked away from this fight. His powers exceeded Kevin's, and he'd yet to unleash the full force of his strength.

I wish I could say, in that moment standing between the people I loved, that I saw hope — a bright light that assured me things would be okay. Sometimes, you just know that isn't true. Sometimes, you end up hurting the ones you love. You can't save them or yourself.

Things went crimson — a beautiful shade of red that quickly changed to the color of dried blood, then turned black.

In the blackness, there was nothing.

Not even peace.

Chapter 19

Death

In the dark, there is only more darkness. It's like swimming in a pool of oil. Not exactly what I'd thought the journey to heaven would look like. I'd pictured it as more scenic. Those I passed seemed distressed. I would have told them not to worry, that everyone says heaven is a wonderful place, if only I could talk.

"You're not doing it right!" someone yelled. I couldn't see where the voice came from.

"It's not like healing a bone! Just blow!" another person shot back.

Air rushed past me. I could almost taste it: warm and oddly like the rind of an orange. Was heaven one big orchard complete with delicate blossoms, or was that just the part of heaven where I was headed? I wasn't that big of an orange juice drinker. Maybe I could transfer to somewhere with fields and fields of coffee beans.

That would be truly heavenly.

"Please no. Please no, Please no." The chant was soft. The voice quiet and familiar. I didn't know why it was so sad.

I was shoved forward through the blackness. It hit me I might not be in heaven.

It was my fault I'd gone down instead of up. I had copied Kaylee's homework one too many times to be on the "good" list. That had to be why I wasn't in the bright lights of paradise. I'd never pass the golden gates. But would cheating on a couple assignments really earn me a one-way ticket to hell? My skin didn't feel like it was on fire. Maybe I was in purgatory. Maybe there was still hope for me.

Someone else called from the distance. "I'm not sure if I'm doing this right."

"I'm a little busy," was the rebuttal. This voice was near to me, strained.

"How is she?" the distant voice asked.

I still couldn't see anything. Air rushed at me again. My mouth must have been opened. I should close it.

"Damn it, breathe!" demanded the nearby voice.

I knew this voice. It belonged to the person who made me whole. The person who had embraced the dark to defend me. Oh God, he'd died too.

"Let me do that," that first voice said.

"You've never healed. Just blow!" snapped the nearby voice.

This time when the air filled my mouth, I coughed it back out. Through my narrowed eyes, I saw Isaac and Kevin leaning over me.

Kaylee came into view, her face stained with tears.

Apparently, seeing Isaac and Kevin alive was enough for my conscience, because I passed out again. I woke sometime later in my bedroom. Kaylee was lying on the bed next to me, asleep, my hand in hers.

I offered a little squeeze, which ended up being a slight wiggle of my fingers. My body felt rubbery. Kaylee opened her eyes and looked at me expectantly.

"Hi." I tried a smile, not sure if my lips had the strength to pull upward.

"Hi." Relief consumed the one word. Kaylee brushed hair away from my face. "Thank God, you're okay."

"What happened?"

I remembered facing Emma, pushing my powers out and sending her crashing into the chalkboard. I remembered Isaac and Kevin about to duel until only one was left standing. I remembered both of their lovely faces looking down at me afterward, before things had gone black.

"You tried to break up the fight between Isaac and Kevin," Kaylee replied.

Oh yeah, I had done that. I grimaced at the memory of that much power flowing into me.

"They feel awful," Kaylee went on. "Both of them were here. Your dad shooed them out last night."

"My dad?" I tried to sit up. I made it to my elbows before I collapsed back onto the bed. "I'm surprised he didn't rush me to the hospital."

Kaylee sat up and faced me. "He would have. One look at you passed out in Isaac's arms and he ran for his keys. Isaac had to quickly pass you to Kevin, which he didn't look happy about. He rested a hand on your dad's shoulder, mumbled something, and then told your dad you were just tired. You needed sleep."

"I was afraid they were going to fight until someone was dead." My words came out in a whisper.

Kaylee squeezed my hand. "They would have, if you hadn't gotten in the way."

"Then I'm glad I did."

I had so many questions, but my eyes betrayed me and closed.

It was Kaylee tracing circles on my arm that woke me the next time. Light filtered into my bedroom window.

"What time is it?" I asked.

Kaylee looked toward the dresser where my alarm clock was. "Almost eight. Isaac should be here soon. I thought you might want to freshen up."

My mouth tasted as if I'd been sucking on steel and cotton at the same time. I pushed myself up, glad my muscles weren't as lethargic as they'd been in the middle of the night. "Be right back."

My trip to the bathroom brought a slew of questions to mind. I quickly brushed my teeth, splashed water on my face, and raced a brush through my hair.

Kaylee was sitting cross-legged on the bed when I got back to my room.

I grabbed my pillow and placed it in my lap as I sat down. "Where'd you go yesterday? When you didn't come back from the bathroom, I looked everywhere for you. What happened?"

"Emma." Kaylee frowned. "She cornered me when I was leaving the girls' bathroom. One minute I was telling her to get lost and walking away, and the next I was locked in the janitor's closet with my arms tied behind my back and tape over my mouth. Josh thinks she tried to bewitch me, but her spell wouldn't have worked because I'm wearing his necklace." Kaylee rubbed the back of her head. "I think she clobbered me with the fire extinguisher. It left a lump."

I was overwhelmed with relief that Emma hadn't wanted Kaylee dead.

"It was awful," Kaylee added. "I couldn't call for help. I just kept repeating Josh's and your name in my head."

That explained why Josh hadn't come to the classroom with Isaac. He would have gone to find Kaylee.

"Emma had a spell on the door," Kaylee continued. "Josh couldn't unlock it and was afraid if he blasted it open with his powers he'd hurt me. He ended up finding something he could use to pry it open."

"That's going to cause another investigation at school." Damage to school property wasn't taken lightly.

Kaylee shook her head. "He fixed it before we went to find you and Isaac."

I nodded. "I know why Emma hates me. She said she wanted me out of the way—that I interfered with her and Paige's happiness. Her reasoning was warped and frighteningly unsound, but it was there. Why did she hate you?"

Kaylee's nose crinkled. She grabbed the metal cross around her neck. "I was getting in her way when it came to getting back at you. She really hates you."

I gave her a look that said, *You think?*

She continued. "She might have done worse to me if she knew to take the necklace off."

There was a knock on the door. I told whomever it was to come in.

"Hi." Kevin's blue eyes met mine. He shoved his hands in his pockets and looked from me to Kaylee.

"Well." Kaylee stood. "I need a toothbrush and a shower." She leaned down to kiss the top of my head. "Call me later."

Kaylee rubbed Kevin's arm on the way out of my bedroom. Kevin took a few steps closer.

"I'm really sorry about yesterday." He groaned as he rolled his eyes. "That's so lame. Sorry I nearly *choked* you to death. I don't know what happened. I saw Isaac helping you to your feet. A few months ago that would have been me. Then you were so relieved to see him. I could feel it."

I cringed, knowing how much that must have stung him.

"I couldn't think straight after that." Kevin forced a smile. "Funny part is, I'm such a hypocrite."

"What?"

Kevin moved closer, taking a seat on the end of my bed. "I've been seeing someone too." Kevin diverted his eyes, suddenly finding the lint on my comforter fascinating. "I feel like an ass, having such a strong reaction to you dating. I wasn't going to tell you about Megan either. I didn't want to ruin our friendship."

I was actually happy for him, knowing he had someone at home, and relieved to hear our friendship meant as much to him as it did to me.

"It's just that I came back to Gloucester because I wanted to tell you about my powers. You should have seen the begging I had to do to get my parents to let me miss school, but I was going to burst if I didn't tell someone. I wanted to see your expression and to know if you've heard of anything like this. When I saw you with Isaac, though, something inside of me snapped." Kevin looked back up at me. "I was mad at myself, not you. Then I spoke to Josh. Not only did he know about the powers, he had them. And the things he knew…" Kevin let out a low whistle. "We spent most of the night talking about them. That and what had happened to Kaylee. As he told the story, I could *feel* his grief and worry, then his relief and anger."

I nodded. The image of Kaylee strapped to the hospital bed, afraid of demons, is something I would never forget. "You should have seen her, scared to move. We got to her just in time."

A comfortable silence followed as Kevin and I got lost in our thoughts.

After a moment, Kevin offered a half smile. "Do you think we're all drawn to each other?"

That was a very big possibility. Josh and I had always been friends; even before he'd started dating Kaylee, we used to hang out. I'd looked up to him as a sister would a brother for as long as I could remember. Then there was how Kevin and I had clicked, knew exactly what the other was feeling without words. And obviously Isaac had pulled me to him. He'd had my attention the first time I'd seen him.

"I do," Kevin said before I could reply. "I think that's why Josh and I are the best of friends. Why you and I fit so well together. After what I did at school, I'll understand if you want me to leave and never call you again."

"Don't be stupid." The words were out of my mouth before I had time to arrange my thoughts into something nice. I hit him playfully with the pillow I'd been squeezing. "Of course I want to be friends. Best friends."

He snatched my weapon from me. "Kaylee's your best friend."

"I can have two," I said defiantly. It occurred to me that Kevin wouldn't have support back in Minneapolis. Not the kind he needed. "Can you stay another week? Josh and I can help you learn to use your powers."

"I don't want them," he said, his voice flat and final.

"But you've already embraced them." Isaac had been clear about that point. He hadn't told me about my powers because once I knew, I'd have little choice but to embrace them. "You can't go back." Another point Isaac had made very clear. Time travels in one direction; you can't go back in time and erase the things you don't want to happen.

Kevin's expression was solemn and pained. "Madison, you don't understand, I can't control them."

"You could if you had some training." I refrained from telling him Isaac had taught me to control mine and planned on providing additional training once things with Mark—well, Emma—settled down.

Kevin shook his head. "You have no idea how unbelievably incredible it feels to have that much power coursing through you. To know with a little more anger, a little more jealousy, it could get that much better. I've never been seduced by something so strong. Once that feeling starts, I don't want it to stop. I couldn't stop myself even when I saw what I was doing to you. I would have killed you if Isaac wasn't there." He gave a fleeting smile. "I guess I owe him."

He didn't look at all happy to owe Isaac anything.

"I don't want these powers," he repeated. "They scare the shit out of me. I'm afraid of what I might do. Next time, there won't be anyone there to stop me."

Kevin's pain rolled off of him to me. I ached with him. "Do you mean it? You don't want them?"

He nodded.

"Then promise me you won't use them until you're ready and properly trained."

Kevin snorted. "Like I'll be able to keep that promise." Yet something in my expression made him sit a little straighter. "I'm sorry Madison, but when it happens, I don't have any rational thoughts. I'm not going to stop to say, 'Hey, I promised Madison I wouldn't use my powers.' I couldn't even stop myself from trying to kill you."

That was definitely something he was going to keep throwing out there. "I knew you weren't doing it on purpose."

The look in Kevin's eyes made me recoil. "That doesn't make what I did any better."

Josh must not have told him. "Kevin, knowing about your powers, using them, means that you have embraced them, whether you want them or not. That makes your promise binding."

I told Kevin what had happened when I'd promised not to use my powers until I was shown how. I told him about the sting that had followed when I'd almost broken that promise, and how my spell had fizzled and failed.

"If you mean it," I said, "if you don't want the burden of these powers, then promise me you won't use them until you're ready and properly trained, or unless your life depends on it." After what I had just been through, I felt he had to have a get-out-of-your-promise-free clause. "If you change your mind, if you feel you are ready to embrace them again, then you have Josh and me to help you. You have *my* promise on that."

Silence blanketed the room as Kevin considered what I was saying. He leaned forward and kissed my cheek. "I promise."

When he stood to leave, it was as if a part of me was leaving with him. "Do you have to go?"

"Yeah, my flight's in a couple of hours. I really should have been on my way to the airport, but I promised you I wouldn't leave until we talked." Kevin raised a hand in a half-wave. He made it to the door before he turned to face me one last time. "I kept that promise because I wanted to. Not because I felt compelled to. I'll call you when I get home."

I lay back down and closed my eyes when I heard Kevin's car door slam shut.

"That was a brave thing you did."

I opened one eye to find Isaac leaning on the doorframe. He looked exceptionally sexy standing there. His hair, which was usually spiked, was tousled as if he'd run a towel over it after his morning shower and nothing more. He wore a loose-fitted, long-sleeved shirt and black jeans.

"You heard?" I asked.

"Sorry," he said, obviously feigning remorse. "I couldn't help myself."

The spell Isaac had cast over my father must have been a strong one. So far he'd let two boys upstairs before I was dressed. Part of me wanted to be mad at Isaac for eavesdropping on my conversation with Kevin, but another part of me knew I would have done the same thing if Isaac were in his bedroom with an ex-girlfriend.

"Do you think he'll be okay?" I asked.

Isaac came and sat down on the bed next to me. "Yeah. He'll be fine."

I wasn't so sure discussing Kevin with Isaac was the best idea. I knew what I'd seen coming from them when we'd been connected. If their emotions had flowed into me along with their powers, my emotions would have flowed into them. I loved them both. Not something easily explained to the guy you're hoping to get to know better.

I changed the subject instead.

"How did Emma become so strong?"

"She made a deal for a taste of power. My guess is she made it with a demon, so her problems have just begun. Whatever she was given, it wasn't enough. She wanted more. Like Kevin said, dark magic is seductive. Emma went looking for more, and she found it in the lady who used to own my house."

"Mrs. Lawson?"

"It makes sense, doesn't it, that power ran through the veins of the family who built the house. Just look at my room."

Like Isaac had said, he couldn't have designed his room better if he'd tried. "It's the perfect place to practice magic," I said.

Isaac nodded. "My parents were sold on the house as soon as they saw it. Mrs. Lawson's magic was good; we could feel that much. Her health declined quickly, didn't it?"

"Yeah." I remember my dad being surprised at how quickly her mind had gone.

"That happens when your powers are slowly siphoned from you."

I cocked my head to the side. "People can siphon powers from each other?"

And here I thought having powers would make a person close to invincible.

"It's not a good thing, but I'll get to that. After Josh robbed Emma of the powers she had —"

"He what?" I blurted. "Isn't that bad? I mean, Emma was bad, why would he want her powers?"

Isaac held up a hand as if to say, *Calm down.* "He did a spell that takes what isn't rightfully hers. Her powers didn't flow into him, though. The spell isn't like the one she used on Mrs. Lawson. Once I knew you were okay and Emma could no longer cast any spells, I asked her a few questions."

"And she answered them?" You can bet your last dollar that if someone had asked me about something I shouldn't have been doing, I would have lied my ass off.

"I used a little persuasion."

"Oh." I wished I could have seen Emma's expression when she'd woken up to find that her powers were gone and someone had put her under a spell. I bet it wiped the smug smile she'd had the last time I'd seen her right off her face.

"Emma realized she was killing Mrs. Lawson, she saw how her health was deteriorating, but she didn't care. Each time she took a little more of Mrs. Lawson's powers, the stronger she felt. The final phase of the spell required a sacrifice. Remember the rabbit we found the night we met?"

"The dead one?" I asked, but it really wasn't a question. I'll never forget the sight of that poor animal lying in a pool of its own blood.

"Yeah, Emma went just about as dark as you can go. Not only did she make the deal, she stole powers from another witch, killed, and cast with the intent to harm others."

One of the articles I had read when I'd first suspected Kaylee might have been cursed talked about the responsibility that came with the gift of magic. It talked about how a witch's actions were what made her good or evil. At the time, it had seemed more like common sense than anything else. The whole *Do unto others as you'd have done unto yourself* thing. I hadn't stopped to consider just how ruthless people can be.

"I still don't understand why taking Mrs. Lawson's powers killed her."

"Mrs. Lawson was a natural witch; her powers came from within her, and they were connected to her life force. She wouldn't have been able to survive without them."

"And you think Emma knew she was killing her?" I asked. I already knew the answer, given that I'd witnessed how ruthless Emma had become, yet it still shocked me.

"She admitted it when I questioned her."

"And the doctors wouldn't have known what was happening to Mrs. Lawson." What an awful way to die. "Is Emma dead, now that Josh took her powers?"

Isaac shook his head. "She was working on borrowed powers, so taking them from her won't kill her."

"So she just gets to walk away, even after murdering Mrs. Lawson and trying to kill me?" I'm not normally an eye-for-an-eye-type person, but that was totally unfair.

"She's getting what's coming to her," Isaac said. "She woke up while Josh was draining her powers. She tried to fight him, but I'd bound her before he started. She couldn't move." I'd been bound by Isaac before; when he didn't want you to move, you didn't move. "But her struggling to hang onto her powers while Josh was casting the spell caused something inside of her to snap. It turned the spells she cast back on her threefold. All the mean things she did to others are coming back on her."

I pictured Kaylee screaming for me to get the spiders that hadn't been there off of her and how terrified she'd been of demons that hadn't existed. Emma had killed Mrs. Lawson, and who knows what else she did. She was in for a rough time if her spells were going to come back three times as badly as the ones she'd cast on others. I couldn't bring myself to feel sorry for her.

"We dropped Emma off at the hospital's front entrance before we brought you home."

I pictured Emma propped against the door to the hospital, a sign taped to her chest that read, *Psycho Bitch*. It almost made me laugh.

"What about Paige?"

"She was less resistant. After seeing what Emma was capable of, she didn't want to have any powers. She wanted to go back to being who she was before she became friends with Emma."

I was less angry with Paige, mainly because I'd been able to sense her remorse and fear back in the classroom. The things she had done were harmless pranks, not life-threatening acts of evil.

"What if she tells someone? Won't we be in danger of being exposed?"

A sly smile pulled the corner of Isaac's lips up. "You're underestimating my powers. She's bound not to speak of it."

"I've been wondering, how did you become so strong?"

Sure, his parents had been teaching him spells since he'd been small, but so had Josh's, and Josh could only do a fraction of the spells Isaac had already mastered. And maybe having two parents with magic coursing through their veins gave a person an edge over others, an instant power boost, but Isaac's abilities were off-the-chart superb. He'd healed the bones in my wrist when I'd fallen off the stepstool and kept me from dying at the school. He'd ghosted us through a semi and beamed me from one spot in my room to another.

His hand went to his chest, touching the charm he wore on a silver chain. The one his grandfather had given him. "He had cancer, and treatments were only making him sicker. One day, he stopped going and moved in with us. Doctors gave him six months, but he lived with us for six years."

"Did he teach you how to heal?"

Isaac shook his head. "Healing takes years to master. He did teach me things like how to teleport an object from one place to another and how to fix a flat."

I smiled, thinking I wouldn't mind learning either of those tricks myself. "If your grandfather could heal, why didn't he heal himself?"

"He couldn't. I'm not sure if the cancer was spread too far or if he just didn't know how."

I nodded, waiting for Isaac to go on.

"One day he woke up and knew he didn't have long. He said he could feel his life force draining from him. He didn't want my last memory of him to be him lying on his deathbed waiting to take his last breath. He willed his powers to me."

I did my best not to let my eyebrows shoot upward or my mouth drop open in shock, but I was pretty sure Isaac heard my sudden intake of air. "He gave you his powers?"

"Yeah." For the first time ever, Isaac actually looked like a small boy caught with his hand in the cookie jar before dinner. "He said he couldn't stand the thought of his powers dying with him. He passed away the next day, and my parents were stuck with a twelve-year-old who could do spells they'd never dreamed of."

"Were they mad?"

"Not really." He paused. "Though I think they would have appreciated a heads-up. Time to prepare."

"You mean time to make sure you promised not to misuse you newfound powers."

"Exactly." His brown eyes met mine. "I've never told anyone that before."

"Mum's the word." I made the gesture of locking my lips with an invisible key. How Isaac's powers had grown to be what they were was really none of my business, and keeping his secret was the least I could do after all he'd done for me.

Emma and Paige were taken care of. They'd never hurt another person with curses or hex bags. That left one person unaccounted for.

"What about Mark?"

"He has no idea what Emma was, or what we are. His actions have all been sincere."

"Really? I would have guessed he was one of the elements in Emma's coven."

Isaac shook his head. "The other corners were Natalie and Lauren. But Paige told us they didn't want anything to do with Emma or her coven after Kaylee became sick. They felt responsible for what happened to her and gave up the powers Emma had gifted them that same day. They're not going to mention it to anyone."

They should feel responsible—and guilty—at the very least.

Then I remembered the look on Natalie's face when Kaylee had been crouched on top of her desk screaming, and the apology that made more sense now than it had when she'd said it. It was Emma who had made the curse on the necklace more potent. Maybe their guilt was punishment enough.

I wracked my brain for another question, anything to delay the conversation that was sure to come once we'd finished talking about everyone else. I came up empty. The silence between us was not a comforting, pleasant silence. My hands shook knowing I would have to broach the subject sooner rather than later.

"Isaac," I began. "About yesterday. I don't—" Ugh. I sucked at putting my feelings into words. I took a slow breath and told myself I could do this.

He didn't wait for me to gather my thoughts. His shoulders slumped forward. "I'm sorry for what I did. You have no idea how sorry. I knew Kevin wasn't in control. I could taste it. I shouldn't have let myself become so upset, but it's like I told you, I would have done whatever it took to keep you safe. At the time, safe meant taking Kevin down."

I bit my bottom lip to keep from saying, *Oh my God*, out loud as I realized how truly lucky Kevin was to be alive. "You can't do that," was all I managed to say.

He laughed, loud and dark. "Could have, and probably would have if you hadn't jumped between us." His velvet brown eyes met mine. "You shouldn't have done that. We almost killed you."

"But you didn't."

"Your heart stopped."

"Oh." That would explain the nothingness. "But it started again," I said as if we were talking about his Jeep and not one of the most important muscles in my body.

He snorted. "After several minutes of CPR and several jolts of power. Madison, for a moment there, you weren't responding. You were dead."

I wasn't quite sure what to say. I settled on gratitude. "Thanks—for saving me."

My response earned another dark laugh from him. When he stopped, there was no trace of humor in his beautiful face. "I'll understand if you don't want to see me again. Just say the word and I'll go."

I wanted to know what was with everyone that morning. For the second time that day, someone I cared about was offering to walk out of my life. Did they really believe I needed them less then than

I had the day before? Hadn't my actions been proof enough that I needed them both alive and in my life? My temper fueled my response.

"Why do you think I hurled myself between you and Kevin?" I snapped. "It wasn't because I wanted to know what an electrical conductor felt like."

"No." Isaac lowered his gaze. "Is that really how you feel?"

"You're going to have to be a little more specific than that," I said. "I was sort of being fried at the time." I held my breath and waited for his reply, knowing full well what he was referring to.

I forced myself not to look away when his eyes met mine with fierce determination. I hoped that determination was to get the words out and not anger.

"Love for Kevin."

I winced and fought to keep my expression neutral.

He continued, "You feared you had already lost his friendship and would lose even more if he continued to battle his powers against mine."

So far, he was right on target. "He's a friend. I care about him."

"You have similar feelings for me." I didn't miss how he left out the *L* word.

Isaac watched me expectantly. I needed to put what I felt in my heart out in the open and trust that things would fall into place. I needed to tell him just how important he was to me, that I loved him.

"After what you've seen, do you have to ask? I've only known you a short time, and yet my feelings for you go all the way to my core. You make me whole." I let out a nervous laugh and continued to babble on. "I didn't even know I was missing a large piece of myself, and the thought of losing you scares the crap out of me. It twists my insides into knots. You had to feel how much I need you and that my biggest fear is losing you. You had to, because I felt that same thing from you."

"Need." The word rolled off his tongue with contempt. I flinched at how it sounded. Cold. Necessary. Not at all warm like the word I hadn't said. "You feel whole because you've embraced your powers, not because you met me. And as nice as it is to be *needed*, you can learn more about your powers without me." He stood. "Our relationship had its obstacles anyway." Isaac looked through me as he spoke. "Kevin was lucky you stepped between us. He's alive today because you did. It's better for everyone if my—" He paused, clearly searching for the right words. "If my emotions aren't complicated like that."

"What? Wait!" My breath came quickly. Panicked. Even knowing my fear of losing him, he was dumping me. "Please don't do this."

I wasn't sure if the obstacles Isaac referred to were our powers colliding if we didn't suppress them or Kevin. But I did know what would happen if his emotions were *complicated.*

"Then promise me you won't embrace the dark. Promise me, and then you can't," I begged. I could feel a hole ripping open in my chest knowing he was about to walk out of my life.

"Madison, I can't make that promise," he replied dryly.

"Can't or won't?" I whispered.

"Won't." Isaac's gaze grew fierce. Adamant. "The promise I made before stands. If we are apart, I won't be tempted."

His words played back in my mind: *I'd do whatever it took to keep someone I care about safe—expose what I am, harness my anger, let my darker side take over.*

"I don't want you giving away your soul for me. Ever. No matter what the reason. Not even a little piece."

"I think it's best if I'm not tempted," he repeated. "Don't you? You say you feel the same for me as I do for you, but I don't think that's true. *Need?*" He said the last word as if it were toxic. He leaned down and kissed my forehead. "It's better we don't complicate each other's lives. It'd be too much work."

The sound of my heart breaking echoed in my ears.

"Isaac," I choked out. He stiffened, hands balled at his side, and his eyes closed as if he couldn't stand to look at me. "Don't do this, please. It'll kill me if you leave."

Isaac turned away from me without opening his eyes.

"Please, Isaac." I'd let my heart guide me when it came to him, yet I couldn't say three little words out loud.

It took three tries to get the words out; they kept catching in the back of my throat. He was at the door when they finally made it to my lips.

"I love you." I wasn't sure I'd spoken loudly enough to be heard.

Isaac stopped, his back still to me.

"I love you," I said louder.

His shoulders relaxed a little. "Don't say it because you think that's what I want to hear."

How could I have been so stupid? I'd spent so much time worrying that he didn't feel the same way about me that I'd never stopped to consider he would need to be reassured of my feelings as much as I needed to be of his. He'd all but said the words to me before, and my replies had always fallen short. Now that I'd said them, it was easy to spill my heart to him. I got up and stood behind him.

"I'm saying it because it's true. I love you, and I was so afraid these feelings I have for you were a product of our magic or even the thrill of being in a new relationship, but now I know it's more than that. It scares the crap out of me, feeling this strongly for someone I barely know. It scares the crap out of me knowing just how hollow I'd be inside if you weren't in my life." I rested my hand on his arm. "It's not the powers that make me whole, it's you. I've been so afraid to even admit it to myself. But I do. I love you."

Isaac turned to face me. Whatever he saw on my face caused his eyes to soften and his jaw to relax. He wrapped his arms around my waist and pulled me closer. He spoke into my hair. "I love you too. I needed to hear you say it. If I'm going to risk being shocked when we kiss or giving in to the dark to be with you, I need to know it's for the right reason."

"I do." I craned my neck so that I could see him without having to step back. "Forever, but you have to promise me you *won't* give into the dark."

His lips brushed mine. "No. I will promise you I won't use my powers to hurt someone you love if I can avoid it, if I have any other option available to me, but I will not promise to stand by and do nothing if you are in trouble. The promise I made to you yesterday stands."

I would have to be careful never to need that kind of protection, then, because I knew arguing wouldn't get me anywhere. His tone had shown no sign of yielding.

"That's enough, for now," I whispered.

His powers wrapped around me like the wings of an angel. It was a feeling I never wanted to be without.

Chapter 20

Life Goes On

Kevin called me that night, as promised. He was glad he'd visited, relieved to be able to talk to others about the powers he had and happy to know they couldn't bubble over anymore. I think one day he will decide he wants to embrace them. When that time comes, he'll be back to learn how to control them.

I didn't mention this out loud. Instead, I kept the conversation to what he'd been up to for the last few weeks. He told me about basketball and Megan, his girlfriend. She sounds nice. I'm truly excited that things are going so well for him.

Ever since the festival, school has seemed downright boring. Emma has been admitted to the hospital and is in for an extended stay behind the solid white door on the fifth floor. We figure her time there depends on just how much evil she's done. I'm willing to bet it will be a long, long time. To be safe, in case she gets out one day and makes another deal in exchange for powers, we dug up the poppet and made a new one that included a few strands of Emma's hair and a piece of the shirt she'd been wearing.

The events from the day of the festival have seemed to humble Paige. Her appearance hasn't changed, but like I said before, black suits her. She's even kept some of the confidence she'd gained while having the powers—only without the smug attitude that had made me want to yank her hair out. She apologized to Kaylee and me, saying she'd never meant for it to go as far as it had. She seemed to want to mention other things, but didn't. We forgave her because that's what friends do, although we have no intentions of hanging out with her or anything like that. Paige had ruined any chance of that happening when she'd stuck by Emma's side.

Mark didn't know about the powers or what had really happened to Kaylee and then later in the classroom. And his crush on me faded after he asked Sarah out and she said yes. Not that I'm complaining. Having a not-so-secret admirer is definitely more trouble than it's worth, and I can tell by the silly grin that takes over Sarah's face whenever his name comes up that she really likes him.

Josh and Isaac gave a small amount of their powers to Kaylee, just enough to allow her to protect herself should she ever need to. I wanted to give her some of mine too, and I wasn't the least bit happy when I was told I'm not strong enough. Boys, always thinking they're the stronger sex. I would do it anyway, if I knew how.

I don't, which suits Isaac just fine.

Mr. Chapin had a weak moment and gave me two generous Bs on the essays I'd handed in on Monday. With the homework I had turned in last week, it pulled my grade up to a seventy-one percent, a small miracle I am grateful for.

As for Isaac and me, we're taking the time to get to know each other. A bit backwards considering we're in love.

Friday, I met him in front of the double glass doors to the parking lot.

"Want to go for a drive?" he asked.

We had spent every afternoon of the week at his house, studying and practicing magic. A drive sounded nice. We ended up at the lighthouse.

"Life seems a little slower without the threat of evil classmates and curses," I commented as we climbed the winding stairs to the top.

"Don't tell me you miss that?"

"Not really."

We stepped onto the landing. Wispy white clouds brushed a powder blue sky. The breeze was light, pulling my long hair away from my face. The sunlight sparkled off the water like a sea of silver and white confetti.

Isaac took my hands in his, lacing our fingers together, and backed me up until I was pinned against the windows. His mouth tugged upward into the sly grin of a fox.

"Want to try again?"

The air between us sizzled with our magic, mingling vanilla and spearmint with chocolate and strawberries, dancing with excitement. It heightened my senses so much I could just make out the steady beat of his heart. It was the polar opposite of mine, which broke into a sprint the moment the heel of my sneaker bumped the solid wall. I was sure he could hear it. His grin stretched to a smile.

"Sure," I replied, doing my best to pretend it was no big deal. Something we did all the time with no effort at all. Like normal couples. Only, we weren't so normal.

"You need to concentrate."

"I know." And I was focusing on every bit of him, from how the sunlight revealed golden highlights in his dark hair to how his thumb drew small circles on the back of my hand.

He stepped even closer, so that there was nothing but the fabric of our clothes separating us. I tried not to think about how his chiseled chest would feel if he lost the shirt or how my thigh had ended up between his. My fingers curled tighter around his hand.

"I think we could start a fire with the amount of energy circling us," he commented. "You're going to have to do better than that."

"It's not just my powers I smell," I pointed out.

"Okay." And just like that, the scent of vanilla and spearmint vanished. He nibbled my ear. "Your turn."

He wasn't playing fair. He never had, and I secretly loved that he didn't. I closed my eyes and focused on unpleasant things, like how much homework I had to do when I got home and how I was behind on my chores. I tried, I really did, but my mind was too busy wondering where his mouth would end up next. Right then he was skimming my collarbone.

"You're not helping," I muttered.

He made one last pass over my neck, up to my ear, before releasing my hands. He placed his against the windows on either side of me.

"Sorry." His eyes met mine. No longer smoldering. More playful. "Take your time."

He didn't look the least bit sorry, and not having him touching me did not make it any easier to gain control of my racing heart, nor did it stifle the elated tingling that coursed through me. His gaze dropped to my lips.

"You know, this would be a whole lot easier if you wouldn't do that," I said.

"What?"

He knew damn well what. "How am I supposed to concentrate with you looking at me like that?"

"I can't look at you now?"

"Of course you can look at me, just not like *that*." I waved my hand up and down to indicate everything about him, from his sultry gaze to his close proximity.

Isaac laughed. "Madison, you're over-thinking this. Take a deep breath." He waited for me to follow his instructions. "Pull your magic in, and then let out the breath."

I did.

His fingers tilted my face upward. His mouth found mine, kissing me softly at first. Then he slid his hand to the back of my head while the other moved to the small of my back. Mine were resting on his hips. His tongue brushed mine, ever so lightly. I rose to the balls of my feet, enjoying the moment, which lasted longer than our last kiss.

Then it happened. A hint of power licked my fingertips. I tucked it behind my subconscious. He pulled me closer. My insides warmed right behind my belly button a moment before my power burst free, shooting through every part of my body. The spark of it colliding with Isaac's carefully concealed power was bright enough to see through closed eyelids. We jerked apart.

"Sorry," I whimpered.

He bit his lips between his teeth and held up a hand, indicating he needed a moment. My tongue felt as if I'd pressed it to a nine-volt battery. Several seconds passed.

"You did better than the last few times." He smiled at me, but I could tell his mouth still stung too.

I gave him a *You're just trying to make me feel better* look.

He snaked an arm around my waist and pulled me close again. "No. Really. I bet if we'd timed it, we made it twenty-three seconds, and the jolt only rattled half my teeth this time."

I whacked him in the arm. "Not funny, Isaac!"

I tried to push away. He tightened his hold on me. "I have an idea. One that should keep us from frying each other's brains in an attempt to get a kiss."

I stopped struggling. "And what might that be?"

We'd practiced for a week, and it hadn't gotten any easier.

He kissed me, a quick peck. "I've been thinking." He kissed me again. Briefly. His lips on mine barely a second.

"Go on," I coaxed, dying to know this idea of his.

"We've been going about this whole closeness thing all wrong." He lips met mine again and were gone.

"We are?" I cocked my head to the side, intrigued. "Do tell."

He kissed me. Another peck, really. "We're over-thinking the whole process."

"You've said that already."

"No." Another peck. "I said *you* were over-thinking before." His lips brushed mine. "I'm willing to admit that we both are."

"How honorable of you." My tone was serious, but I couldn't hide my smile.

Another fleeting kiss.

"Have I told you you're an excellent kisser?" he asked.

This time when he kissed me, his tongue skimmed mine. My reply, which would have been no because he hadn't told me that before, came out as more of a moan.

"So I figured—" another peck "—if we don't worry about the long seductive kisses and go for the quick passion, we might stand a chance."

"I like that." I wrapped my arms around his neck. Kissed him. "And I think—" another quick kiss "—it might just work."

Embraced in Isaac's wings, I decided that change wasn't such a bad thing. It actually gave flight to a whole new world I couldn't wait to explore.

Acknowledgments

I am very grateful for the following people:

Colleen Keough Wagner, my amazing editor, whose insight, expertise and direction were essential in molding this book.

Omnific for this opportunity and to Kayla Watson, Kathy Teel, and the publishing team for all they did to help launch Embrace.

My wonderful family. Dad and Mom for believing in me and for never once telling me to get my head out of the clouds when I was growing up. Vince for being the spark in my inspiration and for letting me bounce ideas off of you at all hours of the day and night; I would have never made it this far without you. Kyle, Cory, William and Ethan because, without you, my life just wouldn't be the same and because I know there were times I didn't cook so I could write and you never once complained. And to Pam for your invaluable support and advice.

My talented critique groups who always pushed me to write the best story I could and never settled for less. Kym Brunner, Katie Sparks, Sarah Barthel, Trina Sotira, Lisa Bierman, Pippa Bayliss, Michelle Sussman, and my Schaumburg group who are too many to list. Finally, my writing coach, Esther Hershenhorn, whose guidance and wisdom helped me improve my craft.

Thank you from the bottom of my heart.

About the Author

Cherie believes there's a little magic in everyone. She also believes in following her dreams and never giving up. Her books are proof of that.

Besides writing, Cherie enjoys spending time with family and friends, reading, the great outdoors, and she loves a challenge. While she has had many great experiences, what she finds most satisfying is seeing her children and stories grow into their own exciting and distinct entities.

Cherie lives in Illinois with her family. This is her second book for young adults. To learn more about Cherie and her novels, visit CherieColyer.com.

‹———›Erotic Romance‹———›

Becoming sage by Kasi Alexander
Saving sunni by Kasi & Reggie Alexander
The Winemaker's Dinner: Appetizers & Entrée by Dr. Ivan Rusilko &
Everly Drummond
The Winemaker's Dinner: Dessert by Dr. Ivan Rusilko

‹———›Paranormal Romance‹———›

The Light Series: Seers of Light, Whisper of Light, and Circle of Light
by Jennifer DeLucy
The Hanaford Park Series: Eve of Samhain & *Pleasures Untold* by Lisa Sanchez
Immortal Awakening by KC Randall
Crushed Seraphim and *Bittersweet Seraphim* by Debra Anastasia
The Guardian's Wild Child by Feather Stone
Grave Refrain by Sarah M. Glover
Divinity by Patricia Leever
Blood Vine and *Blood Entangled* by Amber Belldene
Divine Temptation by Nicki Elson

‹———›Historical Romance‹———›

Cat O' Nine Tails by Patricia Leever
Burning Embers by Hannah Fielding
Good Ground by Tracy Winegar

‹———›Romantic Suspense‹———›

Whirlwind by Robin DeJarnett
The CONduct Series: With Good Behavior & *Bad Behavior* by Jennifer Lane
Indivisible by Jessica McQuinn
Between the Lies by Alison Oburia

‹———›Anthologies‹———›

A Valentine Anthology including short stories by Alice Clayton,
Jennifer DeLucy, Nicki Elson, Jessica McQuinn, Victoria Michaels,
and Alison Oburia